ABSOLUTE
silence

Copyright © 2021 Jill Ramsower

Print Edition ISBN: 9781734417258

Cover Model: Billy Eldridge
Photographer: Chris Davis
Edited by Editing4Indies

❀ Created with Vellum

ABSOLUTE SILENCE

JILL RAMSOWER

CHAPTER 1
Camilla

M y fingers self-consciously tugged at the hem of my dress. I'd agonized for hours over what to wear. What exactly was appropriate attire at a sex club? Showing up in a slutty dress seemed a bit cliché—I didn't exactly need to advertise what I was after—but I didn't want to be too casual. The Lion's Den was the most exclusive club in New York. I'd done my research.

It was a members-only, highly secretive club hosting ticketed events and nightly entertainment for those able to pay the hundreds of thousands to join. If I liked what I saw tonight, I would pay the hefty price and join the inner circle of its members.

Wardrobe planning for such an occasion was challenging, to say the least. In the end, I figured I couldn't go wrong with an LBD. The little black dress was a classic for a reason. My chosen LBD, however, was suddenly feeling microscopic. Maybe it was the subzero January temps, but I was starting to suspect my ass was hanging out the back. Did it matter? For all I knew, everyone stripped naked as soon as they walked in the place.

My stomach dipped as though it contained a swerving bait ball of fish.

This was either going to be the best day of my life or an unforgettable disaster—it could go either way. My guess was as good as anyone's. I could have walked away, but the unknowns would have haunted me forever. Living a lie simply wasn't an option.

I'd agonized over my decision for months. Debated and analyzed. Waffled and wavered in an unending horror show of indecisiveness. That wasn't like me. I was normally logical and grounded, making decisions with the cool detachment of a sharpshooter picking off a target. However, I eventually realized I had to take the risk if I ever wanted to move forward. I'd been staring at this fork in the road for long enough, attempting to divine where each path led, but the only way to know was to follow the bumpy, rocky trail to its end. Enough stalling.

I took one last look at the austere façade housing the club that would change my life forever. I couldn't fathom an outcome where my life wasn't profoundly affected by what I'd find inside. Either I'd embark on a new form of self-expression and embrace my sexuality, or I'd discover that my intuition had been wrong, and I'd need to reassess what I was looking for in life. The innocuous three-story dark-stone building nestled discreetly in the middle of Manhattan was a compass that would illuminate the direction my life would take next. For some, it was just a club. For me, it was so much more. Even the golden lion emblazoned on the crest over the door eyed me in warning. Do not enter if you are not ready.

Well, Mr. McJudgy Lionface, I'm ready.

I took in a lungful of the crisp evening air and pulled open the heavy metal door. No pictures from within the club were posted online, so I'd had no idea what to expect. Opulence? Vulgarity? Would they utilize the sleek lines of contemporary décor to aid in sanitization? For the cost of membership, I expected exemplary hygiene regardless of the aesthetic design.

The front entry encompassed a modest space that felt surprisingly comfortable. Soft lighting from a series of wall sconces gave a feeling of warmth. An elegant rug eased the harshness of the stately marble floors in a plush seating area across from a modest hostess station. Low ceilings crafted an intimate setting rife with understated elegance.

A wave of reassurance helped calm my erratic heartbeat. A small part of me had worried I'd find one giant hedonistic orgy when I walked inside. I blamed television for my overactive imagination. This place was classy. Respectable. At least, that was my initial impression. I'd not seen the main club yet, but the reception area alone was enough to put me more at ease.

I smiled at the woman rounding the desk to greet me. She wore a floor-length black gown with her hair expertly pinned atop her head, a gracious smile polishing the ensemble.

"Welcome. You must be Camilla. I'm Beth. We spoke on the phone." She shook my hand and led me to a leather armchair. "I'm so glad you've decided to join us this evening. If you'd like to have a seat, I'll get Dante to show you around. He's the owner and prefers to greet all new members personally. Would you like a water or champagne before I grab him?"

"I'm fine, thank you." Alcohol would only tighten the knot in my stomach.

"I'll only be a moment." The kind older woman was even more elegant than I'd given her credit for over the phone. She'd helped me through the application process, which was more extensive than I'd expected. The onboarding process required health screenings and a mandatory nondisclosure agreement before I was allowed through the door. I had to agree to confidentiality before I was even given the address.

The strict requirements were reassuring. Deciding to apply for membership had been risky, and I preferred that the other members were equally as vested in the sensitive nature of such a club. If my family ever found out ... I couldn't bear the thought. My devout Catholic mother, regardless of her own past indiscretions, would shit herself. My strict mafia father would probably lock me away until I was fifty. And my sisters? I couldn't even imagine what they'd think.

Joining the club was something I was doing for myself. I wasn't doing it with a partner or because some friend had urged me to give it a try. I didn't know a single person inside those walls, and I preferred it that way. The Lion's Den would be my dirty little secret, assuming I liked the place and finalized my membership after orientation.

After signing on the dotted line, would I participate in the evening's activities? Would I even want to be intimate when my nerves were a jumbled mess? I wasn't sure about the protocol. They might require payment to have cleared in their bank before a new member was allowed to play.

Calm down, Cam. You're getting ahead of yourself.

Right. I hadn't even seen the place yet. As if that would stop me from analyzing all the potential outcomes. I preferred to have a handle on my life at all times. I had control issues, but that was exactly why I'd sought out The Lion's Den. Because I had a feeling handing over that control to the right person would be more liberating than any meditation or self-help book could ever offer.

"Ms. Genovese, how lovely to meet you."

I surged to my feet in response to the deep voice behind me. A devastatingly handsome man in a tux crossed the room to my side, placing a chaste kiss on my knuckles. This was the owner?

I'd expected an older man to greet me, but there were no silver temples or wrinkles in sight. Dante couldn't have been five years older than me, which would put him at twenty-seven or twenty-eight—surprisingly young to own such a lucrative business.

I was intrigued but mostly relieved. I'd been worried about finding the other members attractive, but if this man was any indication, I could scratch that concern off my list.

"My name is Dante Capello, and I'd be delighted to show you around our little home away from home here at the Den." He was dashing in a fairy-tale way, as if Prince Charming had stepped straight out of a Disney movie and stumbled into a porn film. The glint in his obsidian eyes was warm and inviting. Sleek black hair swept gently back, trim on the sides in a debonaire pompadour 'do without a trace of facial hair. Straight white teeth with a perfect smile enchanted while the slight indentation in his chin endeared him as a trustworthy friend. He was the perfect specimen to allure and reassure prospective new members.

"Thank you, Dante. And please, call me Camilla." Heat blossomed in my cheeks. Not surprisingly, being in a sex club cloaked every exchange in a veil of implied intimacy.

He nodded and extended his hand toward the double doors leading into the club. "Shall we?"

Here goes everything.

I smiled and followed his lead, involuntarily holding my breath as the anterior doors swept open only to reveal an elevator in an empty hallway.

"As I'm sure Beth explained when you first spoke, we hold two ideals above all else here at the Den," Dante explained as we stepped into the elevator. "First is consent. We have a zero-tolerance policy regarding lack of consent by any party. All complaints concerning violations of our consent policy are taken very seriously, and memberships can be revoked at our discretion. Second is privacy. The ground floor houses our administrative facilities while the second and third floors are for members, and we use fingerprint technology to ensure only current members enter. In addition, any mention of other members or activities within the Den is strictly forbidden beyond these walls. No descriptions. No names."

"That won't be an issue for me." My eyes lifted to his briefly before dropping back to the panel of buttons on the wall.

The elevator doors opened to a wall adorned with a Renaissance-era painting of opulent women swimming or perhaps bathing outside in the nude. While it had surely been a risqué painting in its day, it was tasteful by today's standards. Nothing else hinted at the club's existence except a sultry strain of music pulsing from beyond the hall, beckoning us further.

"The heart of the Den is just around here. If there isn't an event scheduled, members engage in group activities in this gathering room." Dante led me through one last doorway that finally revealed the subject of my single-minded obsession for nearly a year—the inner workings of a sex club—and it was everything I had imagined.

The room centered around a raised dais a foot higher than the rest of the room with a tufted bed-sized ottoman in the middle. Spotlights highlighted the center showcase while more intimate settings were created in the various seating areas surrounding the stage decked out in luxurious jewel-toned fabrics. The walls on either side of the grand room were lined with glass and mirrors. A couple of servers drifted through the room with drink trays, stopping to check with members who weren't otherwise engaged. Some were fully dressed, talking quietly on sofas in groups of two or three as if oblivious to the sensual acts of eroticism going on around them. Some blatantly watched the few bold adventurists providing the night's entertainment. Dotted here and there throughout the room were scenes of erotic pleasure being played out. A woman with her halter top dress draped down around her waist with a man lavishing her breasts with attention. A fully naked threesome with two men penetrating a woman from both ends.

I hadn't sought out the club in the interest of voyeurism, but I had to admit, watching was highly arousing. My inner muscles clenched, and warmth pulsed in my belly.

"It's still early, so things aren't in full swing yet," Dante explained. "Let me show you to our private rooms, then we'll head upstairs."

We slipped back out the door into the hallway and rounded a corner leading to a series of doors the length of the corridor.

"These rooms are leased yearly by members for an additional fee. While we do have a camera system discreetly placed in the main Den purely for security purposes, these rooms are one-hundred-percent private. A few private rooms on the third floor can be reserved for the night on a first-come, first-serve basis for no additional cost."

He used a key card to open the first door. The space resembled a large bedroom containing a bed and a chest of drawers. A large wooden BDSM cross equipped with restraints sat opposite the bed. While there were recessed lights, several lamps gave the option for a more intimate setting. All the finishes were tastefully coordinated and appeared to utilize superior quality products. The large rectangular room was capped off on the far end with a wall almost entirely filled with a murky window looking out over the Den playroom.

"The rooms can be outfitted to the member's tastes. This one is currently available as the prior occupant relinquished the lease. The best part about these rooms is they can be as interactive as the member desires." Dante pushed a button by the door, and the coating on the window slid aside to reveal a perfectly clear sheet of glass. Several sets of eyes glanced in our direction, noting the change. "You can switch between a one-way mirror or a regular window. Should you want complete privacy, the blackout curtains can be drawn." He motioned to the heavy drapes framing the window.

A one-way mirror was intriguing. The ability to watch others while I remained safely tucked away had an appeal, but I wasn't shelling out any more money than a basic membership. It had been hard enough to discreetly pull out the money from my trust fund without drawing questions from my father.

"Are these rooms sanitized regularly by the club?"

"Absolutely. The key card registers usage, and the next morning, all rooms occupied the night before are given a thorough cleaning as well as the main gathering spaces. If sanitization is of concern to you, I assure you, our hygiene standards are exemplary."

"That's good to know."

Dante smiled warmly. "If you don't have any questions or concerns, I'll show you upstairs to our specialty rooms." He escorted me back to the elevator. "May I ask how you heard about us? Perhaps you're friends with one of our members?"

"Actually, I don't know anyone here. I'd been thinking about this for a while, did some research, and decided The Lion's Den might suit my needs."

"The waitlist for single men is a mile long, but we don't get many single women joining on their own. We often see couples in open relationships or a woman drawn to join from a close friend. I appreciate that you have the confidence to seek out your own pleasure."

I huffed out a laugh. "I'm not so sure about confidence. Honestly, I've never been so terrified in my life."

Dante placed a comforting hand on my arm. "You'll be just fine, I promise. You never have to do anything you don't want to, understand? This place is for your pleasure and pleasure alone. Sometimes that involves a little pain, but only if you desire it. If anything makes you uncomfortable, you tell me immediately. Deal?"

A genuine smile lit my face.

I could do this. I could actually do this.

Dante finished my tour with a quick stop on the third floor. One room for intricate bondage activities and another for orgies, each with a specific theme. I doubted I'd spend much time up there, but then again, I never would have thought I'd join a sex club. Who knew where life would take me in a year?

"I appreciate your reassurance. You've done your job admirably," I told him as we walked back to the elevator. "I think I'm ready to sign."

"That's excellent news. We can head down to my office for the final paperwork, then you're free to explore and play or head home, whichever you prefer."

"Lead the way." My grin was a maniacal mix of excitement and hysteria. I couldn't believe I was going through with it. My palms began to sweat and itch, and my heart attempted to pound its way out of my chest. The resulting shift in blood pressure made my head fuzzy.

"Will you be participating tonight, or do you keep things strictly professional?"

Sweet Mother of God, did I really just ask him that?

I sounded like I was throwing myself at the guy, and I hadn't even signed yet. If I could have, I would have banged my head against the mirrored elevator wall. I was so anxious about signing, I'd blurted the question out of curiosity without fully considering how it would sound.

Dante smirked. "I've been known to participate on occasion." Thankfully, he left it at that, and I kept my mouth shut for fear that something else idiotic might slip out.

He showed me to his office, where I signed my name in blue

ink on a crisp membership contract with The Lion's Den. Liquid elation coursed through my veins.

"So, what will it be, Camilla? Are you heading back upstairs?" Dante peered at me with a sultry curiosity and unabashed amusement.

I lifted my chin defiantly. "I think I will if you'll show me back to the elevator."

Dante grinned, illuminating the hint of two faint dimples in his cheeks. *Lord have mercy.*

"I'll happily escort you back upstairs. If you're interested, I can introduce you to some of the members I think you might enjoy meeting."

"Thank you, I'd appreciate that." *Please God, don't let him notice how breathy I just sounded.*

"Before we go, I want you to take my card. If for any reason you need me, it's got my cell number on the back." He extended the small rectangle between his two fingers.

Questions raced through my mind. Was he coming on to me after my awkward question? Was he interested in sex, or was he just being polite? How could I tell the difference in a sex club? I had no clue, so I slipped the card inside my clutch and smiled.

When we stepped back on the elevator, anticipation flushed my cheeks and made my head spin. The maelstrom of emotions swirled together in one giant tornado of excitement. The vortex built higher and higher as the elevator rose until the doors opened and the presence of a familiar face scattered that energy to the four corners of the earth, leaving a vacuous desperation in its wake.

Filip De Luca, the vision of pure temptation in a tux, stood in the hallway opposite us. Our gazes locked the instant the doors opened. His blistering stare assaulted me with a dozen curses without saying a word.

I'd had no expectations for how the night would go but had I walked myself through hundreds, if not thousands of possibilities...

Filip hadn't existed in a single one of them.

His brother, Matteo, was my cousin's husband. He was mafia. An associate of my father's and the very worst-case scenario for me. I knew there was a chance I'd see someone I recognized, but someone so closely associated with my family was disastrous. He'd find a way to ensure I was never allowed out of my apartment again.

My leaden gut sank to the floor.

No. He can't take this from me. I won't let him.

My instinct was to submit to his authority, but I refused to allow him that power over me. If I surrendered what I wanted without a fight, that was my own damn fault. I wouldn't give up so easily. Instead, I wrapped myself in a cloak of confidence, stiffening my spine as Dante began to speak.

"Filip, how's it going this evening?" Dante reached for Filip's hand as we stepped from the elevator, oblivious of the civil war unfolding before him.

Filip flashed his teeth in a lupine grin. "I'd say it's too early to tell. I was just heading upstairs for a moment, but I see we have a new face among us." His eyes never strayed from mine, attempting to pin me in place. The doors began to close beside us, but Filip made no effort to stall the elevator he'd been waiting for. "Camilla, this is a surprise."

Dante glanced back and forth between us. "You know each other? Excellent. Camilla was just saying she didn't think she would see any familiar faces."

"Oh, we're quite familiar. In fact, we're practically family."

"I see. Well, we just finished the tour, and I was going to help her get settled, so we won't keep you." Dante motioned to lead me around Filip, but Filip had other plans.

His hand slipped into mine, clasping me firmly. "Considering our connection, I think it would only be fitting for me to show her the ropes." He finally transferred the weight of his intense stare to Dante, who turned a quizzical eye in my direction.

I would have preferred to yank my hand from Filip and insist Dante escort me inside, but I needed to confront Filip if I wanted to have any chance of keeping my membership, and I didn't want to do that in front of Dante. This was a private matter.

I flashed a smile at Dante, keeping away the grimace that tried to form. "Thank you for showing me around. I'm sure Filip can help me get acquainted so you can get back to work. I'd hate to monopolize your night."

Dante's eyes narrowed. He was more perceptive than I'd given him credit for. "Remember what I said, Camilla. You have any issues, you come to me."

"Not sure what you're implying, D," Filip warned.

"Just don't want you causing problems for our newest member." Dante's threatening tone was a stark contrast to the welcoming host he'd been moments before.

Filip stilled. "Not your business."

"Everything that happens inside these walls is my business."

"We've been friends for a long time. Have I ever stepped out of line when it comes to a woman?" Exasperation sharpened Filip's reply.

Dante shook his head in resignation before slipping into a nearby stairwell. The second he was out of sight, I pulled free of Filip's hold.

"*Let go of me,*" I hissed.

My hands shook with fury at the prospect of losing what I'd only just obtained. I wasn't sure what Filip was thinking, but I knew it wasn't good.

We squared off like two caged tigers.

A coiled energy bristled just beneath Filip's surface, pressurizing the air around us. "What's wrong, princess? If you're not here to be touched, you're in the wrong place." His hand shot back out and clasped my own before he tugged me toward the gathering room.

"What are you doing?" I whisper-yelled, not wanting to make a scene as we approached the double-door entry to the gathering room.

Filip stilled in the doorway. My eyes locked on the occupants, but I could feel Filip's stare on my heated skin.

"I'm giving you a taste of what you wanted. You joined the Den to be fucked, right?" His harsh rasp was a sensual melody to the chorus of erotic sounds all around us. The sights and sounds stroked my body, eliciting an intoxicating hum of desire across every inch of my skin.

I had no response. I was too overwhelmed with sensation.

Filip led me farther into the room at a more casual pace, weaving until he located a vacant settee. He pulled me down flush against his body with his arm around my shoulders like we were some lovestruck couple. I tried to pull away, but his vise-like hold kept me firmly in place.

"What are you doing?" I hissed just loud enough for him to hear over the pulsing music.

"What do you think, Camilla?" His free hand reached across to my exposed thigh, then slid up under the hem of my dress. My heart tripped over itself.

"Don't," I snapped quietly, squeezing my legs together. I wanted to rage at him for toying with me, but I didn't want to make a scene in this new setting where I hoped to meet people. I'd look like a psycho if I started screaming at Filip during my very first night at the club, so I kept a tight grip on my anger.

"Why not? Isn't that why you're here? Don't you want to be touched?"

"Not by you."

"I'm no different than anyone else in here." He smirked. "Unless you were hoping for more ... *feminine* company."

My irritation flared. I had to clamp my lips firmly together to keep from going banshee on him.

Filip chuckled deep from his chest. "Didn't think so."

I lunged forward, using the element of surprise to break free from him. Filip remained relaxed on the settee. When I glared down at him, blasting him with indignant fury, a merciless grin lit his face.

"Can I have a word with you in private?" I demanded through clenched teeth.

"You're in a sex club, babe. You surrendered your privacy when you walked through that front door." He was being infuriatingly difficult on purpose. Did he get off on torturing people? Was that why he was a member here?

I rolled my eyes and wove my way toward the door. I had to get away from Filip, though I wasn't sure where exactly I was going. I locked eyes with a handsome man near the entry, causing me to slow my steps. Maybe I could get myself in a room and away from Filip. I didn't know who had rooms and who didn't, but it was worth a try. I flashed an alluring smile and watched excitedly as my possible ticket to freedom joined me.

"I can't say I've seen you here before. I'm Matthew." He offered his hand, which I gladly accepted.

"Camilla. I just joined today, actually."

"Wonderful. Welcome to the Den. Would you like to grab a drink with me?" Matthew motioned toward the bar at the other end of the room.

I started to speak when an ominous presence descended from behind me.

"I'm sorry, Matt, but this one's taken." Filip placed a possessive hand over my shoulder, branding me with his touch.

I lowered my shoulder, unsuccessfully attempting to coax him off me. "No, I'm not taken, and I'd love a drink."

Matthew's eyes stayed glued on Filip as though I hadn't spoken. "Noted, but you may want to collar her if she's off-limits." He walked back to the group he'd been standing with as if he hadn't just spoken about me like Filip's pet poodle.

I grabbed Filip's hand and yanked him out of the room. "What the hell are you doing? Is this some kind of game to you?"

"No game. That's just how it is here at the Den."

"Bullshit. You're screwing with me, and you need to stop. *Now.*"

Filip leaned in, bringing our faces a breath apart and stealing the air from my lungs. "If you don't like it here, honey. *Leave.*"

CHAPTER 2
Filip

C amilla fucking Genovese was parading around the Den like a juicy steak waiting to be devoured. All thoughts of my intended destination fled my mind when she stepped from the elevator. Never in a million years would I have imagined I'd ever see any of the Genovese women inside The Lion's Den.

Rapid-fire emotions slammed into me. Surprise. Confusion. Fury. And more than a little lust, which brought on a whole shit-storm of self-deprecation. Young Camilla wasn't much over twenty, although she appeared far more mature in that black dress glued to her slim curves. Her blonde hair hung loose around her shoulders, and her warm brown eyes weren't clouded with excess makeup like so many other women. She was innocence in a garter belt, and I wanted to wrap her in a blanket and hide her away so none of the sick fucks in the club could find her.

Some of the members were relatively straitlaced, just looking for a little spice in their sex lives, but others had some pretty twisted fantasies. No fucking way would I allow her to get wrapped up in that shit. I wanted to break Dante's perfect face for simply letting her in the door. He might not have known who her family was, but one look at her picture should have said enough. She was too good to be sullied. Too pure to be tainted with depravity. The last thing she needed was some fifty-year-old pervert acting out his incest fantasies with her.

Jesus Christ. Just the thought made my muscles clench with unmitigated violence.

I had to figure out what to do and fast; there was no time to think it through. My first inclination was to give her an obnoxious helping of club life and make her run screaming. I could have ordered her to leave, but making her decide on her own not to come back would be infinitely more effective. As it turned out, I hardly had to try before she was fleeing from the club close to tears. It had been entirely too easy.

Disappointingly easy, in a way.

Once she was gone, the club suddenly seemed lifeless. Boring. Stoking her fires had been more entertainment than I'd had in ages.

I went back into the gathering room after her departure, but I couldn't escape my thoughts of Camilla. Had she gone home? Would she try to come back? Why the hell had she joined in the first place?

I needed to know more.

Thirty minutes later, I was standing outside her apartment building. Getting her address hadn't been hard, but she lived too high up for me to see anything. I considered installing cameras outside her place so I could see her come and go but decided that might be excessive. For now.

Gathering what information I could, I checked out the building's lobby and security features before going back home. On the way, I called the guy who did all my cyber work and asked him to dig up what he could on little Camilla. I'd been around her on a dozen occasions but never gave her much thought. Never dreamed she would show up at the Den. What other secrets was she hiding?

I wanted to know everything I could before I decided whether to tell her father about her escapades. I wasn't sure why I hadn't called him immediately. Aside from the fact that ratting out anyone was against my nature, I also had a selfish desire to keep this between us. It was a risk. If her father discovered what she was up to and learned that I hadn't informed him immediately, I could be in grave danger.

It wouldn't have been the first time.

Within a half hour, I was in possession of a complete dossier on Miss Camilla Genovese. She hadn't stepped one toe out of line since high school. Interesting. I definitely needed more. When I started to question myself about why it mattered, I refused to concede any answers aside from pure entertainment.

Camilla was a mystery, and I'd been bored for far too long.

CHAPTER 3
Camilla

A week before I decided to submit an application at the Den, my mother confessed that she'd been more impulsive in her youth than we'd ever dreamed. She'd gotten herself pregnant when she was a teen. My sisters and I had a half brother somewhere in the world. It had been the turning point in my endless debate, along with the fact that my father had revealed months earlier that he was a part of the mafia.

My fundamental beliefs about my parents' infallibility were shattered but in a good way. Realizing that everyone bore the mark of imperfections gave me the courage to confront my differences and seek out something I'd been secretly craving.

Finally joining the club after agonizing over the decision for so long made the threat of losing access unbearable. Emotions overwhelmed me when I realized that Filip was going to sabotage my night at the club. Without vocally prohibiting me from participating, he effectively shut me down. He planned to ruin the club for me until I was forced to concede and cease my efforts.

It was a game to him. A war of attrition.

I was furious and frustrated but vehemently refused to be a victim of his bullying. I could probably get Dante to help, but I wanted to try to handle Filip myself before admitting defeat. This was my life, and he had no right to dictate a single thing in my world. I might have left the Den for the night, but that didn't mean I was surrendering. Far from it.

Twenty-four hours later, I was back at the grand metal doors looking the lion's head crest in the face and promising myself tonight would be better. Filip couldn't possibly be at the club *every* night, could he? He wanted to wage war? He didn't know just how inspired I could be. My back was against the wall, and I wasn't afraid to fight dirty.

I fixed my dark brown wig and stepped inside with the borrowed confidence of the stranger I was impersonating for the night. I greeted Beth, pleased when it took a second for recognition to register. As long as I didn't come face-to-face with Filip, my night should be a grand success. My bright red lips spread in a wide grin.

The Saturday night activities were well underway. Expensive suits in place of tuxedos made the atmosphere slightly more casual, but it was just as lively as the night before. No matter what they wore, the members were all remarkably attractive—far more than I would have guessed. Beautiful and seductive and totally inclusive. There was no shame within these walls, only acceptance.

I made my way to the bar and ordered a drink without a sign of Filip.

"Utterly stunning," a masculine voice rumbled beside me. "You must be new. There's no way I ever would have missed such an elegant beauty. Mind if I join you?" A man with eyes the color of a cloudless winter sky smiled down at me. He was beautiful—black hair and a square jaw. Everything about him was stark and imposing and enigmatic.

"Please, do. My name's Camilla." I gestured to the seat next to mine.

He motioned the bartender for a drink and eased into the bar chair. "I'm Cal. Cal Thompson."

"It's lovely to meet you, Cal."

"Trust me, the pleasure is all mine." His voice had the most deliciously wicked tone with just the tiniest hint of an accent I couldn't place.

I blushed. "How's your weekend going?"

"Better every minute."

I couldn't help but laugh. "You're smooth, aren't you? As you pointed out, I'm new here, so I'm not sure how all this works. You'll have to forgive me."

"Are you here alone?" He slipped his fingers beneath mine on the bar, his thumb caressing the back of my hand.

"I am." My voice grew husky while the skin on the back of my neck began to tingle with awareness.

"Well, we can have a drink and get to know one another, or if you'd prefer more privacy, I have a room."

Nervous energy suddenly flapped within my chest. I liked my prospects with Cal; he wasn't the source of my cardiac arrhythmia. Something else was bothering me. Something dangerous. I felt as though someone was watching me.

"I think..." I peered over my shoulder at the room distractedly, forgetting what I was saying. "Um..." It only took a second for my eyes to lock with Filip's.

He stood just inside the doors, one hand in a pocket as though he were casually assessing the room, but his glare was anything but casual. He'd pegged me instantly. It didn't matter that I'd been across the room, my back to him, and a wig in place. He knew exactly who I was and was demanding my withdrawal with his predatory stare.

"Your room sounds perfect." I turned back to Cal, refusing to surrender.

His smile widened. He stood and helped me from my chair, keeping my hand secure in his. "This way."

I followed him as he charted our course through the room. There was no chance of Filip letting us pass, but I clung to hope with the desperation of a death row inmate saying his last prayer.

Cal pulled up short of the exit, and I knew my night was over.

"Thompson, I'm afraid there's been a misunderstanding." Filip's voice was layered with violence and restraint, the two equally potent.

The man at my side pulled me in closer, giving my hand a gentle squeeze. "And what's that, De Luca?" Cal's spoke with absolute authority. Not a hint of wariness at Filip's disgruntled confrontation.

"She's off-limits."

"Judging by the way she's clinging to me for dear life, I'd say the young woman disagrees."

Filip's jaw clenched so tight he was going to need a dentist. "It's a *family* matter, Thompson. You need to back away before we have a big problem."

Cal's chin lifted just a fraction as he inhaled deeply, then lowered his lips to my ear. "I'm sorry about this, but there are some lines I cannot cross." He pulled back with a frown, shot daggers at Filip, then left me alone with my tormentor.

I didn't meet Filip's angry gaze. I didn't have to. I could feel it boring into me with the intensity of a thousand suns. I was so furious, but I had no idea what to do about my situation. Filip would never leave me in peace—so what were my options? Ask Dante if I could back out of my contract already? Just the thought made me spitting angry.

I wasn't the only one.

Filip snagged my hand and yanked me into the hall and around the corner to one of the private rooms. He used a key card from his pocket and ushered me inside. The door crashed shut, sealing us within.

CHAPTER 4

Filip

Camilla crossed her arms defiantly over her chest. "You have no right to do this. I'm a member just like everyone else in that room."

The foolish girl should not be stoking my anger. Did she have any idea how close I already was to losing my shit completely? I hadn't intended to confront her like this, but seeing her in disguise made me realize Camilla might be more of a challenge than I'd anticipated. I had to shut it down. I had to convince her to let go of this ridiculous charade.

"No. You are not just like everyone else, and there's no way you're keeping your membership here. I'll have Dante refund your money and—"

"Don't you *dare*." Camilla's eyes sparked as she jabbed a finger in my direction.

My lips pulled back in an acidic smile. "What will you do to stop me? Tell your father?" Even as an adult, Camilla would feel the wrath of Edoardo Genovese if he discovered what his daughter was up to. He was no help to her in this situation, and she had no other leverage over me.

Her hands settled on her hips, and she cast me a smile just as biting as my own. "I'll go somewhere else. To another club where you don't have any say over who joins."

My fingers flexed and strained with the need to pound my fist against the wall. She might have looked like an angel, but Camilla had a devilish stubborn streak. "You don't have any idea what you're saying. I can't just let you into this lifestyle. Your family would kill me."

"It's none of their business."

A caustic laugh rolled from my chest. "You're barely more than a child. Of course it's their business."

"You're hardly older than me. Why should it be acceptable for you to be here but not me?"

"There's a boatload of reasons, and if you're so naïve that you can't see them, it only furthers my point." I raised a brow.

"Look, this isn't about you or my family. This is about me and what I need. Surely, if you're a member, you understand that sometimes people need a lifestyle outside the norm." She'd moved on from anger to negotiation. Good. Soon enough, we'd reach acceptance, and I could get her out of here.

"And *surely* you can understand that as a member, I am in a position to tell you that you don't need anything here. Plenty of nice young men would be happy to experiment with you in the safety of your own home."

Her lips thinned to a harsh line. "*Fuck* you, Filip. You don't know me or anything about what I need."

"I know the world we live in, and even though it's not the same as it was for older generations, being spotted here would ruin your reputation."

"But not yours? How very chauvinistic of you."

"Not me, society." I released a frustrated sigh. "I'm trying to protect you, Camilla."

"Bullshit." She shook her head. "Now that I've seen the place and confirmed that this is what I want, I'm not giving it up. I'd considered a couple of other places, so I'll just go to one of them."

I stalked toward her and crowded her back against the wall. "Every other sex club in this city is a glorified brothel. You will *not* step foot anywhere near them."

Camilla narrowed her eyes and leaned into me, not at all swayed by my commands. "Try to stop me," she hissed.

The corners of my mouth fish hooked up in a sinister grin. "I'll tell your father if I need to." The threat hung in the air like poisonous gas.

She froze, and for a split second, I thought I'd won. I should have known better. I'd seen her sisters and cousins in action. They didn't know the word surrender.

Camilla's chin lifted a fraction, and a sense of power settled over her. "You'd surrender your own involvement in the club just to keep me out?" Her words were calm, raising the hairs on the back of my neck.

"Care to explain?"

"Silly Filip. The first rule about Fight Club is, never talk about Fight Club. Dante made it perfectly clear that naming members outside of the Den was strictly forbidden. You tell my father, and I'll tell Dante."

"Maybe you didn't realize, but Dante is a longtime friend."

She shrugged. "That may be, but would he risk his precious club for you? Should word get around that a certain member was naming other members, there's bound to be outrage."

My blood pressure pounded a punishing rhythm against my skull as I processed her threat. She wasn't entirely wrong, and it pissed me the fuck off. A frustrated growl ripped from my throat as I spun away from her. I shrugged off my jacket and rolled up the sleeves of my shirt to give myself a moment to think.

The woman was maddening. Why the hell was she so determined to join the club? I could walk away from the Den and call her bluff, but I didn't think that would solve anything. She was hell-bent on joining *any* club. I wanted to believe I could stop her, but stubborn people found ways to get what they wanted. The last thing I needed, even worse than her membership at the Den, was for her to go to some other club and get hurt. If I couldn't keep her out of the life entirely, there was only one other option.

I turned back to her, jaw clenched. "If I allow you to come here, it would be under one condition."

She lifted her chin haughtily. "What?"

"The only man allowed to touch you is me."

Her lips parted in shock. The muted strains of pulsing music from outside the window accented how utterly still the room had become. My shoulders tensed in anticipation of her response. I wasn't entirely sure what I'd done, but the deviant inside me preened at the prospect of having Camilla all to myself. My sense of decency snarled with disgust. No matter what she decided, I'd be equally thrilled and devastated.

"What?" The word was nothing more than a breath. Her eyes remained wide, a perfect window to the mass of confused thoughts racing through her head.

She wasn't the only one. I'd dumbfounded myself with my proposition, but it was the only way I could see out of this mess.

"You heard me, Camilla. What's your answer?"

"But why?" She shook her head, still grappling with surprise.

I ran my fingers through my hair and turned briefly toward the mirrored wall overlooking the Den. "Because a lot of kinky shit happens here, and this way, I can keep you safe while letting you still get what you want."

"I thought you said this was the nicest place in town."

"I did, but that doesn't mean everyone inside has earned the same distinction."

"But you come here."

"*Enough*," I barked. "Do you accept my terms or not?" She'd heard the only offer I'd make, so there was no point in stalling. It was time for her to decide our fates.

Camilla's spine stiffened, but instead of arguing, she studied me clinically. "What if you can't give me what I'm looking for?"

"I've yet to have any complaints."

She scoffed, leaning her hip against the back of the chaise lounge. "How very typical of you. Every man I've been with thought the same, yet not one delivered on what he promised."

Intrigue and challenge whispered seductively to warp my intentions, attempting to justify the devious deeds lurking in my subconscious. I would not give in to their tempting lure. I would tend to Camilla to keep her safe, not to make myself the source of her damnation.

Still, a small portion of my nature would need to be unleashed in order to keep her satisfied with our bargain. It would be a good practice in restraint, or so I tried to convince myself.

I prowled to where Camilla stood, gently turning her until her thighs pressed against the back of the chaise with me behind her. Her breathing shuddered when my fingers trailed down one of her arms.

So sensitive.

So responsive.

"Tell me, Camilla. What did you come to the club to find? What is it no other man has been able to offer you?" She was taller than most of the women in her family. Close to five-six without her heels, if I had to guess. I only had to lower my head a fraction for my lips to be achingly close to her ear.

Women were sensory creatures. They needed sound and sight and emotion to go along with touch. Men were far simpler, which made it hard for many to comprehend the complex desires of the female gender. A woman didn't just want a serenade; she needed an entire fucking orchestra. That suited me just fine because I'd devoted years to the study. Fuck fantasy football and video games. My hobby was women and sex.

"Um ... that's part of the problem," Camilla explained. "I'm not exactly sure what was missing, just that I know it should be better."

I shifted to whisper into her other ear. "Care to hear my thoughts?" I pulled back just enough to grasp her hips and spin her around in one sweeping motion.

She gasped and lifted her curious eyes to mine.

"I need an answer, Camilla." I traced a single finger along her bottom lip. "If I ask you a question, I expect an answer."

"Yes, I'd like ... I want to hear your thoughts."

Pride thrummed in my veins. The feeling of earning a willful woman's surrender was like nothing else. It was only a start where Camilla was concerned, but it boded well.

"I'd say romance doesn't do it for you. You aren't here for flowers and compliments, tender caresses and gentle lovemaking. That's where the others went wrong. What does that tell me? You appreciate a more nonconventional take on pleasure. Maybe a little pain, but I think mainly, you need a man to fuck you, not make love to you." My hands reached for the bottom of her dress, slowly lifting it past her hips. "Someone to whisper vile words in your ear while they order you on your knees. Does the thought of that get you wet?" I placed my hand over her mound, pressing a single finger slightly into her opening through the soft silk of her panties.

Camilla nodded in answer, and the moisture coating my finger confirmed.

How could any other man have been incapable of stimulating such a responsive woman? It was inconceivable. Perhaps my time with her *was* necessary. It would be a shame for her to never know the pleasure of a proper fucking. Once she learned the difference, she could find what she was looking for outside the club.

The prospect of someone else taking over my role made me surprisingly agitated. I hadn't even seen her naked yet, let alone fucked her, so why the hell would I feel any sort of possessiveness over her? It had to be her age and my need to keep her safe. My sense of duty to our families. Yeah...

I stepped back and cleared the gravel from my throat. "Take off your panties. Leave everything else."

CHAPTER 5
Camilla

Was I willing to make a deal with the devil?

Filip had done nothing but bully me at the club —could I really trust him to hold up his end of a bargain? Was I willing to accept his terms, or would I fight for complete freedom at the club? The odds of my winning weren't good. I could risk it all on the off chance I found a way to silence Filip, or I could ensure some level of exploration by agreeing to be with him.

Not having free rein of the club left me with a certain degree of disappointment, but then again, I found a welcome security in our familiarity. I didn't know Filip particularly well, but his ties to my family meant I could trust him … to an extent. His life would be in danger if my family ever discovered he'd hurt me. I doubted that would be an issue, but then again, the Filip I encountered at the club was nothing like the Filip I'd met before. He was infuriating and domineering—qualities that should have been off-putting—yet I found his behavior alluring. It wasn't entirely surprising, considering my past. If gentle and sweet had stoked my fires, I never would have found myself at the Den in the first place.

I studied the man before me. Mussed hair, angular jaw, and a strong brow perched over eyes that could drill deep into the darkest places of a woman's being. He was breathtaking—irresistible, even—and he'd just ordered me to remove my panties in a way that warmed my belly more than any love note or bundle of flowers.

Deal or not, I wanted to feel the heat of Filip's intensity.

Perhaps I was making a mistake, but it was a risk worth taking.

I lifted my hands to the hem of my dress and followed his command. His ravenous stare consumed every inch of skin I revealed, stirring a flood of arousal between my legs. Filip was nothing short of magnificent. At just over six feet, he was composed of effortless power poised behind flexing muscles. His skin was the golden tone of someone who tanned under the slightest hint of the sun. He took tall, dark, and handsome to a whole other level with his impressive aura of a man with innate self-confidence. Knowing he had a host of sharp edges lurking beneath that playboy exterior made him inescapably alluring.

Filip took my hand and led me to a soft leather chair by the window. His room was set in the same arrangement as the room Dante had shown me but had an entirely different feel. Filip's room could have been nestled in a Spanish hacienda with its solid wood furniture, black iron accents, and velvety soft fabrics to warm the space. A plush cream-colored rug filled the area beneath the bed, and I could imagine it would be soft between my toes. While he didn't have a cross in his room, the enormous four-poster bed was just as imposing. The setting was rustic but elegant. An oasis away from the world.

Filip drew my attention back to him when he opened a

drawer in a tall chest and pulled out a small purple vibrator. My stomach turned when I considered how many women the toy might have touched.

"It's never been used, Camilla. I wouldn't do that to you." He must have seen the disgust creeping onto my face.

"I had no way of knowing that." *Sex club newbie, remember?* Plus, men had different standards than women, especially when it came to cleanliness. I wasn't making any assumptions.

He ignored my rebuke and eased into the chair, which was facing the room with the window behind it. With a gentle tug, he pulled me down onto his lap. "Sit sideways, one leg over the side, the other down."

I felt open. Exposed. But not overly so, considering no one was in the room to witness us.

I should have known better.

Just as I was relaxing against him, Filip slowly swiveled the chair toward the window. I stiffened as the active playroom came into view.

"Relax, Camilla," he whispered. "The mirror is in place. We can see out, but they can't see in. I assume Dante explained that?"

I nodded, not taking my eyes from the other members. The gathering had grown, and more people were now actively participating in erotic displays. It was entrancing. I didn't know where to focus my attention.

"If your heart beats any faster, I'm afraid I'll have to do CPR." His lighthearted and calming words sounded as though he were teasing me. It was enough of a departure from our earlier dynamic to draw my gaze back to him.

Hungry eyes commanded my attention and held me captive.

Filip's free hand rose and collected the dark strands of hair that lay on my chest. I hadn't removed my wig because my own blonde hair beneath was hideously pinned to my scalp. He'd have a fight on his hands if he demanded I remove the wig. He examined the tresses with a glower but remained silent as he placed them back down over my arm and away from my chest. He then slipped a finger seductively down into the cup of my bra. He took one leisurely swipe across the swell of one breast, then pried the material down, exposing my nipple above its fabric protection just inches from his lips.

My breathing hitched.

Filip's tongue slowly glided over his bottom lip. He knew how to tease. A master of anticipation. Only once I had thoroughly envisioned that tongue brushing over my own skin did he lean forward and flick my sensitive nipple. He gave me no time to recover before grazing his teeth over the hardened peak. An electric bolt of pleasure shot straight from my breast down to my core. I gulped in a shaky breath. Filip chuckled, and I could feel the warm rumble vibrate straight through me.

Picking up the vibrator, he turned it on and lifted it to my chest. My nipples pebbled painfully in anticipation of a new sensation. No one had ever played with me like this—seen my body as an erotic playground to explore. When the vibrating device made contact with my skin, I moaned at the heated zing of pleasure.

"Look at the stage," he instructed. "See the woman?"

A gorgeous redhead was naked and cuffed to a cross that must have been lowered from the ceiling. Her flawless body was curvy and feminine, soft and rounded in all the right places. Her hair was a piled heap on the top of her head, and her face was a mask of delirious pleasure.

"See her clamps?"

I noted the woman's silver nipple clamps but could hardly focus beyond that. "Yes."

"These rosy buds will be perfect for clamping." He popped the vibrator against my nipple in repetition, igniting small fires with every touch.

Filip freed my other breast, and its initial neglect somehow made the first touch of the vibrator that much more electric. My head tilted back as my chest involuntarily arched forward. I was slipping into a mindless state of need. Nothing else mattered but his touch and the pursuit of more.

He lowered the vibrator to drift slowly down my belly. "As we move forward, I'll ask you about your limits. You also have to tell me if those limits and interests change. For now, eyes on the room. I want you to think about what it would be like if all those eyes could see you. How every person in there would covet my position."

I did as he ordered, and the resulting image made my inner muscles clench with need just as the vibrator ghosted over my clit. The barest of touches was an erotic tease that stole my breath. The sensitive tissue swelled, aching for more. A moan, more wanton and primal than any sound to ever escape my lips, tore from me.

"So responsive," Filip murmured, nipping his teeth along my breast. "Is this what you want?" He eased the device against my throbbing center, and I wondered if my body might implode. Just as I started to adjust to the sensation, the vibrator swept down toward my entrance, initiating an entirely new surge of pleasure.

He dipped the device inside me just enough to use my own juices as lubrication, then directed my body through a gauntlet of pleasure. What followed was the fastest, most explosive orgasm I'd ever experienced.

I screamed an unearthly sound.

I'd never felt the slightest inclination to scream during an orgasm, but under Filip's ministrations, I had no choice. The sound clawed its way out as part of the cataclysmic unraveling of my being. I drifted on another plane as wave after wave of bliss rocketed through me. Only once my body and mind reunited did my hand fly to my mouth with the realization of what I'd done.

"No need to worry. This is the one place where screams don't draw any attention. Or, at least, not unwanted attention." He pulled out my dress and bra with a single finger to allow each breast back into its rightful place.

Was our time over? I felt satisfied, yet I was in no way ready for the night to end. "What about you?" I asked. Was I supposed to take the lead and pleasure him the way he'd done for me? Had I just screwed up everything by asking instead of just doing? I suddenly felt horribly self-conscious.

He placed his fingers lightly around my jaw, letting them slowly drift to my chin. "Not tonight," he answered absently.

Not tonight? Why?

Perhaps sensing I was on the verge of asking another question, Filip stood, lifting me to my feet and righting my dress. He brought over a bottle of water from a small mini-fridge and ordered me to drink, though it was unnecessary. My throat was so raw from screaming that I welcomed the cool relief.

When I looked over, Filip was watching me, his face unreadable. Did he regret making a deal with me? Did I do something wrong? What the hell was going through that mystifying mind of his? If I wasn't so sex drunk, maybe I could have figured out what was happening. At the very least, I could have summoned the energy to demand an explanation. Instead, I shrugged off his odd behavior to be dealt with at a later time.

"What's your number?" He pulled out his phone, and I read off the digits. "I've just sent you a text. If you need me, you get in touch. I expect you to hold up your end of our bargain in the meantime. You don't come here without me, and you certainly don't go to another club. Understood?"

"I think I can manage that," I shot back, a spark of temper resurfacing.

He cut me a look in rebuke to my sass. "I think that's been enough for your first night. It's been an eventful day, and there's plenty of time for more exploration later. I'll walk you out." He opened the door, triggering a sinking sensation inside me.

Why did our night have to be over so soon? Would he be staying once I left? Was he going to fuck another woman once I was gone?

Jesus, Cam. Are you jealous? This isn't a relationship. Being with random people is the whole point of a sex club.

Yeah, but it was hardly fair that I was limited to him while he could indulge in whomever he desired. My thoughts argued amongst themselves as he walked me to the elevator.

I felt like I was being dismissed.

Filip had brought me to his room, given me a mind-bending orgasm, and now was sending me on my way. Was this what he planned for our arrangement? To humor me in the most expedient fashion possible, then cast me away?

A wave of embarrassment crashed over me. I felt like the child who was given a toy version of the real thing to keep away a tantrum. Was my time with Filip the equivalent of a fake plastic lipstick used to keep me out of Mommy's makeup?

Heat seared up my neck, but I resisted the urge to jump to conclusions. I'd made plenty of progress for one night to go home happy. Filip had conceded substantial ground in allowing me to keep my membership. With more time, maybe he would relax and allow me even more freedom without the threat of telling my father about the club. Even more important, I'd learned that my instincts had been right. The club was exactly what I needed—I'd never come so quickly in my life. The confirmation of my suspicions both relieved but also troubled me. A part of me had desperately wanted to be normal, but it appeared that wasn't in the cards.

In my heart, I'd known I wasn't the same as those around me. Maybe that was why I chose to go blonde and stand apart from my sisters and parents. I'd wanted to be as outwardly different as

I felt on the inside. I'd told myself that no matter what had gone on in my past, I was still the one in control—I was the developer of the landscape of my life. One hour at the Den proved that was only so true.

There was an insidious desire inside me that I couldn't deny. It wouldn't be quashed or ignored.

A taste for darkness.

I found pleasure in things that others shunned. I craved deeds only performed in the shadows of society. I should have known there was no escaping it.

Once an addict, always an addict.

I needed Filip's brand of seduction like I needed my next breath. The small taste I'd been given wasn't enough. I needed more, and I would get it, one way or another.

CHAPTER 6

Filip

I put Camilla in a cab as quickly as I could and went back inside the club. I saw the questions in her eyes but had no answers for her because I was just as disoriented as she was. I needed her to leave so I could regain my bearings. Most of all, I needed a stiff drink.

The decent thing would have been to reassure her that everything was fine, but I couldn't make myself say the words. Our initial interaction would set a precedent between us for our future encounters. It wouldn't benefit either of us if she came to think of our time at the club as more than it was. I wouldn't have walked any other woman home from the club or set her up to expect my call, so Camilla should be no different. In fact, it was even more crucial that I maintained boundaries with her. I sensed a spark of possessiveness trying to ignite when I thought of her, and that was a problem. She wasn't at the club for a relationship, and I wasn't looking for that either.

Boundaries were going to be imperative.

How did I keep a woman like Camilla out of my head when she melted in my hands? For the moment, alcohol seemed the best tactic. It would also help me forget that I'd foolishly agreed to enable one of the Genovese girls to moonlight at a sex club. If anyone in her family ever found out, I was fucking toast, no matter how good my intentions.

Okay, so my intentions weren't entirely pure. No one's perfect.

I walked back to the bar on the far side of the main gathering room and ordered a scotch. The room around me pulsed and gyrated with sexual energy, but my attention was fixated elsewhere. The club might as well have been filled with blue-haired old ladies playing bingo. There wasn't much I hadn't already seen take place inside the Den, so no amount of tits and ass was going to draw my mind from Camilla.

"Did you see Camilla come in tonight? Beth said she'd changed her appearance." Dante slid onto the bar seat next to me, motioning the bartender for a drink.

"She's gone," I snapped, pissed with the reminder of what she'd done to avoid me.

"Already? That was quick."

My eyes cut sideways to my friend, who appeared blithefully unaware. "Do you have any idea who she is?" I growled.

Dante sobered. "Actually, I do."

"What the hell were you thinking when you let her in here?" I wasn't sure the alcohol had sufficiently saturated my veins for this conversation. I was already tense, and Dante's belligerence wasn't going to help.

"That's her choice. If she wants to go up against her family, it's her decision. She's an adult."

"Barely," I muttered before downing the rest of my drink.

"You give her shit about being here?" His voice was edged in warning, drawing my gaze back to him. His black eyes assaulted me with accusation. It was easy for him to hold the high ground; he wasn't the one who'd be tossed in the Hudson if Camilla got hurt. His lack of respect for the situation pissed me off even more.

I rolled my shoulders to relax the clenching muscles. "Of course, I did. That's a fucking disaster waiting to happen."

"I knew I shouldn't have left you two alone last night." He shook his head. "She's twenty-two and fully capable of making decisions for herself."

I didn't need him to tell me her age. I'd memorized every last detail of her life, and it changed nothing. As far as I was concerned, she would never be old enough to share herself with a club of perverted men, myself included.

"Easy for you to say." I motioned to the bartender for another drink. "How I feel about it is irrelevant, though. She'll be back."

"Oh, yeah?"

I heaved out a heavy sigh. "That kitten has claws and the determination of a pit bull on steroids."

Dante threw his head back and laughed.

"I don't see what's so funny," I grumbled. "She swore she'd just go to a different club if I kept her from the Den. Then she threatened to get me kicked out of here if I told her father what she was up to."

More laughter, completely unaffected by my murderous glare.

"I could wipe that smile off your face real quick." My voice hardened with a menacing edge, choking off Dante's mirth.

"I'm not sure I've ever seen you agonize over a woman." He eyed me with the perceptive intensity of a man who dissected people for a living—broke down their barriers and gained access to their deepest desires. He was intuitive, and right now, he was making me question why I'd ever befriended him.

"You know it's more than that."

"Yes and no. You could have looked the other way and

feigned ignorance. Instead, you invested yourself in the outcome. *Your* choice," he mused as if analyzing a character from a movie. But this wasn't a damn movie. This was my life, and what he insinuated rang true, though I'd never admit it aloud.

I glanced away, irritated with my friend, and observed the scenes playing out in the main room. I envisioned Camilla strung out and on display with a room full of hungry eyes drinking her in.

I'd rather burn the place to the ground first.

Fuck, I'm in trouble.

I downed my drink and returned my attention to Dante. "Would you do it? Would you kick me out if I broke the NDA and told her father?" If I was smart, that was exactly what I'd do.

He never even flinched. "In a heartbeat." Not a hint of humor in his baritone voice.

I scowled. "Good to know our friendship means that much." I was being petty, but I needed someplace to direct my irritation. Dante seemed like a perfect fit.

"Sorry, man, but this club is everything to me. Not all of us are gifted the world upon birth." He smiled as if to soothe the burn of his comment, but the gesture didn't reach his eyes.

It wasn't often the differences in our backgrounds came between us, but every now and then, I detected the chip that sat heavily on his shoulders. He'd come from nothing, and while my own background was complicated, I never wanted for anything. I'd be an asshole to hold it against him if he tried to protect what he'd created with his own two hands.

I stood and tossed some cash on the bar. "I hear you, and I wouldn't want to jeopardize the Den." I patted a firm hand on his back to ensure I smoothed over any sharp edges between us. "I'm out of here."

"You back tomorrow?"

"Hell if I know," I threw over my shoulder without looking back.

THE NEXT DAY, I found myself at my next favorite haunt. If I wasn't working or relaxing at the Den, I was most likely hitting the heavy bag over at Mighty Mick's Gym. I'd spent most of my night lost in thoughts revolving around Camilla that morphed into obscenely detailed fantasies. By morning, it was obvious I had to clear my head.

Every time I imagined her smooth skin under my fingertips, I forced myself through a punishing combination of punches. I might not have eradicated her from my mind completely, but I had hopefully ensured I'd sleep well that night out of utter exhaustion.

Had she slept well after her epic orgasm? Or had she lain awake as I had, playing over the night?

Fuck.

I forced my body through a series of blocks and dodges. Those thoughts were exactly what I was trying to snuff out. Who cared what she did when she went home? As long as she wasn't getting into trouble, that was all that mattered.

My phone ringing was a welcome interruption until I saw the name on the screen. My brother, Matteo.

I groaned.

What would it be now? I'd been acting as his errand boy for so long, I wasn't sure he saw me as anything more. I tried to be easy-going because getting angry wouldn't change anything, but my agitation simmered below the surface.

"Yeah," I answered. No matter my issues with him, I always answered my brother's calls.

"I need your help. Maria has a doctor's appointment tomorrow, and I can't make it. I want you to drive her so she's not alone. With this cartel action unsettled, I want eyes on her at all times."

Chauffeuring his pregnant wife. Perfect.

"Yeah, no problem. Although, I'm pretty sure your wife can take care of herself." I had to add that last part because it was true. While I didn't blame him for wanting his wife to be protected, Maria was probably more deadly than either of us. I'd seen her in action, and it didn't matter if she was going hand-to-hand or was armed, that woman was lethal.

"She can, and she's pissed I'm making you go with her, but I'm not giving in."

Even better. Chauffeuring an angry pregnant woman.

I grunted.

"I'll text you the info," he added.

"Sounds good." I hung up, not waiting for a reply.

The tension I'd worked through began to seep back into my shoulders. Normally, my work situation didn't bother me all that much, but with the added stress of Camilla, being asked to do an ordinary soldier's job seriously chaffed. Of course, that was all I was at this point—a fucking soldier—and that was the whole problem.

I was ready for more responsibility within the family. I had yet to be named a capo. At first, being Matteo's right hand felt like an honor, but my role often devolved into handling his affairs like some glorified personal assistant. I was going to have to ask him outright what his plan for me was. If our expectations didn't mesh, I would have to challenge him in a way I rarely did. He was eight years my senior, my boss, and the patriarch of my family. His word was the law. But if I brought up the subject, and he tried to give me some meaningless promotion with no real advancement, that pent-up frustration might boil over.

CHAPTER 7

Camilla

Monday, January 27ᵗʰ

Me: Do you go to the club during the week or just on weekends?

I had no clue when Filip expected to meet up next. It had been a couple of days since our night at the Den, and the uncertainty was making me crazy. He said to reach out if I needed anything, but what did that mean? Text when I had an itch to scratch? I needed a clear plan, an outline for how this was supposed to work. Did we meet once a week? Twice? Every other night? I needed to know what he expected from our arrangement.

Filip: I'm busy this week.

Okaaaaay. My initial response was annoyance that I was being given the brush-off, but I tried to remember that not everyone was a proficient communicator over text. Maybe he was super busy at the moment and couldn't give me more of an explanation. I'd give him a chance to clarify.

Wednesday, January 29*th*

TWO DAYS since my text and no word from Filip.

I was a strong, independent woman who had no problem being persistent. I'd allowed ample time for him to communicate before making another attempt myself. I boxed up my insecurities that insisted I was being a harpy and got out my phone.

Me: What's the plan for this week?

Thursday, January 30*th*

FILIP: **Tomorrow.**

Maybe he paid for texts by the word? What the hell was his problem? Would he have texted at all if I hadn't reached out?

Settle, Cam. He did respond, and now you have a specific date. You can discuss the plan with him in person.

I did a bit more grumbling about how I had a life and shouldn't have to wait around for his inconsiderate ass to make my own plans, then moved on and began to plan my outfit for the following night.

Friday, January 31*st*

FILIP HAD SPECIFICALLY INSTRUCTED me not to go to the club without him, yet he'd failed to tell me when to arrive. It was easy enough to text and ask, but I was starting to resent having to extract information from him. Would it kill him to give me more than the bare minimum? I'd given him my word, and I intended to make a good-faith effort to comply, but he wasn't making that easy.

Me: What time tonight?

Filip: Going to have to cancel. Ended up going to the Hamptons for the weekend.

Slumping back in my office chair, I dropped my hands into my lap. We'd been scheduled to meet up in a handful of hours. Would he have stood me up if I hadn't texted? Maybe it wasn't a big deal to him, but I'd spent all week planning what I would have worn this weekend and imagining how the night would have gone. The highlight of my entire week swirled down the drain with a single impassive text.

I was just another canceled appointment to him.

Years of doubt and uncertainty were now history, but the enlightenment I was so close to achieving was being held captive by a six-foot brute who wanted to keep me safe in a glass case. He was moderating my time at the Den by denying me access. Despite our agreement, I was back in the same place I'd started. My fingers twitched with the need to lash out. I despised having something I wanted dangled in front of me only to be pulled from my reach by a beautiful bully.

You're jumping to conclusions again. Maybe he truly was busy.

Damn voice of reason. That uppity bitch was seriously annoying. While there was a slim chance she was right, I doubted it. Fortunately, the issue was easy enough to resolve. My cousin Maria and her husband Matteo had a house in the Hamptons. When they resided in that home, Filip often accompanied them. I could text her and see what I could learn.

Me: You guys in town this weekend or in the Hamptons?

Maria: The city. Too boring out there. Why?

Me: Just curious.

Maria and Matteo were in the city. Filip could have gone to the Hamptons alone, but I doubted it. In theory, his avoidant texts and sudden cancelation of our plans had any number of possible explanations. However, considering the circumstances, Occam's razor was particularly applicable—the simplest answer was most likely correct.

1. Filip didn't want me at the club.
2. Filip told me I couldn't go to the club without him.
3. Filip had hardly texted and now canceled our plans.
4. Filip was keeping me from the club.

I had truly tried to give him the benefit of the doubt, but he made that increasingly difficult. He was stalling at the very least, and quite possibly attempting to renege on our deal entirely.

White-hot anger clawed its way up my throat and stung the back of my eyes.

I will not cry at work. I will not cry at work. I will not cry at work.

My boss was impossible in the best of circumstances. I wasn't going to give him any reason to berate me, but my anger festered deep in my belly. I'd been thinking about my next meeting with Filip all week. The promise of his dark brand of seduction had gotten me through a hellish workweek, and now, my guiding light had been snuffed out.

Fine. Two could play at this game.

I might have agreed not to go to the Den or any other club, but that didn't mean I had to sit at home. If he was going to find loopholes in our arrangement, so could I. I refused to be strung along. The club meant more to me than a passing fancy, and if he couldn't respect that, then fuck him.

I pressed the call button and dialed Trent's extension. His office was only a few doors down, but I didn't want to risk running into my boss in the hallway.

"Yes, ma'am?" Trent was my closest friend at work. I adored him, though we didn't ordinarily hang out outside of work. That was about to change.

"You have plans tonight?"

"I do now. Where're we going?" he asked in a conspiratorial voice.

"Somewhere with hot men. Straight, preferably."

"Ugh, you're no fun," he groused playfully. "Actually, I know the perfect place that has a decent mix of both. I'll text you the deets."

"Eight work?"

"You on a curfew or something?"

I rolled my eyes. "Nine then?"

"That's a little more like it, granny. See you then."

I hadn't had much luck with random hookups, but a week of fantasizing about the Den had me worked up enough to power an entire city block. I needed an outlet, even if it wasn't a Filip-grade release.

With a new plan in place and a grin on my face, I jumped back into work, hoping the rest of the day would pass quickly.

"WE HAVE to start the night with a shot," Trent announced the moment we arrived at our bar table.

"Are you trying to get me sick?" I scoffed.

"Just one to celebrate our first night out together. What took us so long?"

"I don't know. Guess I'm kind of a hermit."

"That's a travesty looking the way you do. That top is absolute perfection on you."

I grinned. "You're just buttering me up to get that shot, aren't you?"

"Is it working?" He peered at me coyly.

"You better believe it." I dug my card out of my clutch. "I'll grab the first round."

"You sit. I'll get the drinks." He grabbed my card, then disappeared into the crowd. A steady thrum of people moved to and from the bar in this huge place, providing ample people-watching entertainment. The selection of available men was more than adequate for my needs. Some were a bit douchey, but I wasn't looking for a relationship. They didn't have to be perfect to scratch my itch.

Trent returned in a matter of minutes with two shots in one hand and two mixed drinks in the other. He placed them on the table, then handed back my card.

"You *are* trying to kill me, aren't you?" I asked with a laugh.

"If these fruity little drinks scare you, we're going to have to work on your tolerance level."

"Whatever. Let's just drink. I need some liquid courage."

"That's what I like to hear." He picked up his shot and clinked glasses with me.

I'd never been much of a drinker, so the liquid burned all the way down. I shook my head and squealed.

Trent threw his back and laughed deep from his belly. "You *are* a lightweight. That tequila sunrise wasn't half as bad as it could have been."

"Tequila! Jesus, Trent. I'm going to be dancing on the table before the night even gets going."

His eyebrows danced on his forehead. "That's the idea."

Shaking my head, I took a sip from my cocktail in an attempt to ease the burn in my throat, only to find the pink drink was just as potent as the shot. I did a full-body shiver, sending Trent into yet another fit of hysteria.

Once we finished our drinks, we joined the crowd on the dance floor for a couple of songs before a few of his friends joined us. They insisted on another round of drinks. I tried to nurse the drink as best as I could but had so much fun listening to their banter that I was sucking air through the straw before I knew it. The heavenly buzz taking over my body magnified the delicious heat that had been simmering in my belly for days. I scanned the crowd for someone to take home, taking in each specimen with a critical eye.

Too tall. Too hairy. Too much ... just, too much.

Each man I assessed failed my evaluation, one flaw at a time. What was wrong with me? I wasn't picking out the father of my children. The image of Filip floated unbidden into my head. My nipples tingled, and my breath caught at just the thought of him.

"You okay, Cam?" asked Trent.

"That rat bastard hijacked my hormones!" I shouted.

My new friends burst into laughter, and I followed right behind them.

"No, listen. This is serious."

More laughter. I almost tinkled in my dress.

"Okay, okay. Who is this rat bastard, and how did he hijack your hormones?" Trent asked, bringing our group back to its senses.

The room dipped and swirled, but it felt in sync with the energy pulsing all around me. I brushed it off and tried to explain. "Flip. He gave me the orgasm of my life, and now my girl parts only want him."

"Flip?"

"*Fil*-ip," I mouthed exaggeratedly. "He had no right! Now I can't have him or anyone else. It's not fair at all."

"I think you should tell him exactly how you feel." One of Trent's friends pointed his drink at me with raised brows.

He wasn't wrong. Filip should know exactly how much he'd pissed me off. Someone should hold him accountable for his cruel games.

"You're right." I yanked open my purse, but a hand clamped down over mine before I could remove my phone.

"You sure you want to do that, Camilla?" Trent peered at me warily.

"I appreciate you looking out for me, but I can't possibly make matters worse. Why shouldn't I call him out for being an ass?"

Trent lifted his hands with a thin-lipped grimace. "Don't say I didn't warn you."

Whatever. He didn't know Filip like I did.

Me: This is some bullshit. You don't own me.

Filip: Excuse me?

Me: You heard me. I decide who I have sex with. My pussy. I decide.

That'd teach him. I hit send and sat taller in my chair, smiling when the response dots bubbled to life.

Filip: Not when you're drunk, you don't.

Drunk? I glanced back over my text and tried to see if I'd given myself away over my wording. I was tipsy, but I could still tell autocorrect had ensured my messages made sense.

Filip: Three drinks in an hour. That's too much for you, Camilla.

A burst of adrenaline battled with the alcohol in my veins, giving me a moment of startling sobriety. Filip was here, watching me. My eyes widened as I swept the room in search of him. In cinematic fashion, the music faded into the background, and the swarms of people became an amorphous blur. Only one man stood out in perfect clarity.

"He's here," I breathed.

"What?" Trent asked, peering around. "Who's here? Filip?"

I nodded, not taking my eyes from the fiendish demigod now closing the distance between us.

"Sweet mother-of-pearl, he's gorgeous." His voice dropped an octave.

Trent didn't know the half of it.

Filip flashed a cavalier smile at my new friends, joining us as though a natural member of our little party. "Hey, guys. It seems Camilla's had a little too much to drink. I hate to break things up, but I better get her home." He cast his god spell over the table, ensnaring all four men in a fog of voodoo lust. All four nodded, not one asking my opinion.

"Oh, no. I don't think so." I pressed my finger into Filip's rock-hard chest, slipping from my chair onto unsteady feet.

Filip lowered his lips to my ear. "You fight me on this, and I'll tan your ass."

My lips smacked shut.

"You guys have a great night." Filip nodded and tugged me toward the entrance.

I waited until we were outside to demand answers. Yanking my hand from his, I asked, "How the hell did you know where I was?" I swayed, wrapping my arms around my middle and wishing I'd brought a coat.

"Because I was following you." He lowered his body and flung me over his shoulder.

"You were … what? You can't just—put me down!" I smacked his back, and the world spun. "Filip, I don't feel so good," I groaned from the pressure of his shoulder pressed deep in my stomach.

He slowed and lowered me to my feet, steadying me with his warm hands on my arms. "Better?"

"I think so."

"My car's right across the street. We can argue once we're in there with the heater on." He led the way, his hand firmly clasped around mine. It was freezing out, so I didn't protest.

Once we were in the sleek sportscar, I angrily buckled my seat belt and glared at him. "You *lied*. You weren't in the Hamptons."

He didn't comment.

"You going to say anything? You could at least tell me why the hell you were following me."

Silence.

Fine, I could play the quiet game, too. I crossed my arms over my chest and glared out the passenger window. The second we approached my building, I unclicked my seat belt and tried to bolt from the car.

Filip grabbed my wrist, his eyes sharp as a steel blade. "Wait," he ordered.

I rolled my eyes but complied, waiting until we were on the sidewalk to charge in front of him. He'd infuriated me in every way possible, and I wanted nothing to do with him. I pressed the elevator call button but froze when the door opened, and a question floated to the surface of my tequila-laced thoughts.

I slowly faced my broody companion. "How did you know where I live?" The alcohol was caving under the barrage of adrenaline and emotions, bringing me much-needed lucidity.

Filip pulled me inside the elevator and pressed the correct floor button.

"*Answer me*, goddammit," I barked at him, my patience wearing thin.

Six feet of angry muscle backed me against the wall in a breathtaking show of dominance. "I know where you live because I looked you up. I know your college GPA and the name of your pediatrician as a kid. I followed you because I fucking *wanted* to and because you obviously can't take care of yourself. Those drinks you had were doubles, Camilla. Did you know that? You never even had a fucking sip of water with them. And what did you plan to do? Go home with some pussy thug from the club?" He shook his head slowly. "I lied because you twist my head in fucking knots. You make me crave what I shouldn't and do things like wait outside your apartment to make sure you're safe."

Each shuddered breath I took pressed my chest against his.

Each of his confessions weakened my knees.

He took in the effect he had on me, his nostrils flaring as the elevator chimed. The doors were fully open before he eased away from me, eyes only leaving mine when I crossed by him toward my apartment.

I was speechless. I didn't know what to say or even think.

I twisted him in knots? A suspicious fluttering warmed my chest.

Filip took my key from me when I fumbled with the lock. He let us inside, took my purse, and tossed it on the counter before leading me back to the bedroom. I followed in a cocoon of numb confusion. Filip had me out of my clothes and lying across the bed diagonally in a matter of seconds. He yanked his tie off, then slipped the silk fabric through a slatted hole in my wooden head-board before winding the tie around my wrists, securing my hands in a knot above my head.

His searing gaze appraised his work, lowering greedily from my hands and over my exposed chest down to the small patch of neatly trimmed curls at the apex of my thighs. He positioned himself between my legs, encouraging me to spread my knees wide. When his mouth lowered over my slit, he didn't just lick at my core; he devoured me whole. Flicking and sucking, Filip rained down an assault of pleasure. He consumed me as though I were his final meal on this earth, and he'd never tasted anything more divine.

Within minutes, I was gasping and writhing, sure I couldn't handle the explosive pressure building in my core. The intensity was overwhelming. Cataclysmic.

I wanted to scream for him to stop and beg him to continue,

the two conflicting desires leaving me mindless. Raw with emotion. I was drunk on Filip and totally at his mercy.

Filip yanked himself away just as the wave of promised pleasure began to spill over. Instead of breaking with mighty thunder against the rocks, the wave fizzled and died beneath its own dark surface.

"What? No, please. I need more." My voice cracked with strain, but my cry fell on deaf ears.

Filip eased from the bed, straightening his collar. "Think about this the next time you consider letting another man touch you." Then he walked away without another word.

I gaped at his retreating form, only gaining use of my words when I heard the front door open. "Filip, my hands!" I cried out. "You have to untie me before you leave. Filip?" My ears strained for any hint of sound, only to be met with silence.

Monday, February 3rd

I APPROACHED my Monday morning work with the detached efficiency of a coroner performing an autopsy. I'd packaged up all my raw emotions and tucked them safely away before subjecting myself to the psychological warfare ensuing each day in the executive offices of my bank. When I first realized the toxicity of the environment, I knew I wouldn't stay. However, for resume purposes alone, I convinced myself I could withstand one year at National Bank. I didn't want my work history to show that I'd left my position mere months after starting my very first job out of school.

I'd survived difficult times before, so I could manage until June.

I'd always been ambitious, and I loved the complexity of financing. The manipulation of money involved structure and regulations—clear-cut rules and numbers—so it suited me perfectly. While my parents had always had money, I never entertained the possibility of not working. My mind wasn't wired to live that way. I needed the distraction. Something purposeful to focus upon.

Had my boss not been an absolute dick, I would have loved my job. As it was, I did my best to keep to myself in my office. Normally, I kept my phone on silent to refrain from coming under fire for disrupting the office. Today, I was off my game, despite my great efforts. My phone chimed with a text, letting me know I'd forgotten to silence it. I snatched the device to turn off the sound and discovered Filip had messaged me.

Filip: I want to see you at the club on Friday.

The fucking nerve. It had taken me thirty minutes to realize the knot he'd used could be loosened with a simple tug of one end. I'd begun to spiral into a panic attack, thinking I was stuck there before pulling on the two ends. As if that hadn't been enough, he'd worked me into a frenzy before walking away. What he'd done had bordered on cruel.

I wasn't ready to talk to him yet, and I certainly wasn't going to surrender myself to that storm of emotions while I was at work. I slid my phone back into my purse without a response.

Tuesday, February 4ᵗʰ

"They were FDIC auditors, sir. I had to turn over the records," I explained to my red-faced boss after he'd charged into my office and accused me of breaching our confidentiality requirements to our customers. I couldn't understand why he was so upset. The Federal Deposit Insurance Corporation, or FDIC, was an agency of the federal government. We provided them documents all the time at their request in regard to insuring our customer deposits.

This particular request was a bit more specific than most, but I didn't see any reason to deny them the documents. There was no good excuse for my boss to yell at me.

The only explanation was that Donald Carter was a dick.

"You damn well should have run it by me first," he shot back at me, finger jabbing in my direction. "I want to know exactly what you sent over and the contact information for whoever you spoke to. This gets priority, so don't be screwing around on social media or gossiping in the break room until you're done." He stormed out, leaving a minefield of emotional shrapnel in his wake.

It was going to be another lovely week.

Wednesday, February 5th

AFTER CLOSING out an arduous day at work, I made the hour commute to my parents' place on Staten Island. My mother tried to coordinate a family dinner once every couple of weeks, and tonight was the lucky night. I would have preferred to hide in my apartment with a bottle of wine, but no luck. I'd been trained well to comply with the wishes of my elders.

"Camilla, you haven't been to Mass with us in over a month. You used to be so good about that." My mother scrubbed a plate in the sink as she delivered her honey-coated barb.

Just what I needed. A guilt trip. That's what I get for helping clean up.

"I know, Ma. I've been insanely busy. It's harder and harder to make short trips out here." I couldn't necessarily blame her for expecting me to go to church with them. I'd been the one to create that expectation by not refusing to go years ago. By not telling her about my loss of faith and doubts in the Catholic church, or any organized religion for that matter.

I avoided conflict because it was just easier.

"I guess I understand, but I sure miss having you there with us."

"You still have Val. She's not done with school for another few months." I handed over two more plates as she scrubbed.

"Just because she's still living at home doesn't mean I can't miss you being here, too." She gave me a sad smile that only made me feel worse.

"I'll try to make it back out here soon." I watched my mom as she made quick work of the dishes and wondered about the woman I'd thought I'd known so well. This was the first time I'd seen her since she revealed that she'd had a secret baby when she was younger and given it up for adoption. I hadn't spoken to her about it since.

Was that part of the reason she was so devout about going to church? How deeply had she been scarred to give up her first child? Would she make any attempt to find him?

"Ma, what's going to happen with the baby you gave up? With … our brother?" I gave voice to my questions, hoping they wouldn't upset her.

My mother kept her eyes trained on her task. "What do you mean?"

"Are you going to try to find him?"

Her movements slowed, the only sound in the room the hum of bubbles popping in the sink. "I can't decide. And it won't matter what I want if he doesn't want to be found." She slowly returned to her work without her original vigor.

"I know it's up to you, but if it matters at all, I think you should try."

Her gaze finally lifted to mine, eyes suspiciously glassy. "Yeah?"

"Yeah." I wasn't particularly comfortable with displays of emotion, and while the moment had been touching, awkward unease circled in around me. I peered back into the dining room to see it empty. "I'm gonna go find G and Val, unless you need any more help." I hoped she didn't because I needed an escape from the mounting emotions. I'd hit my capacity for difficult emotions dealing with my own issues; I couldn't take on any more.

"Nah, you go see what they're up to." She waved a soapy hand in my direction. "I saw them scurry off with their heads together when I brought in the salad bowl."

Scurrying off? Giada and Val didn't normally hang out, mostly because of their age difference. Curiosity and the greasy tinge of jealousy sent me in silent search of my sisters, hoping to catch them unaware. I found them in the study, huddled together cocooned in secrecy.

It stung more than I'd expected.

"Everything okay in here?" I asked, announcing my presence and putting a quick end to their counsel.

They both jumped.

"Yeah, just checking in with Val. School stuff and all," Giada shot back. She'd never cared about her own schoolwork, let alone any of ours.

Valentina glanced at Giada before weaving her own explanation. "There's this new guy at school. He thinks he owns the place and is a bit of a bully, but it's no big deal. You guys get the dishes all done?"

They both stared expectantly at me like world-class amateurs. Had I thrown them off their game that much? My sisters could lie better than that. The question was, why did they feel they had to keep something from *me*? Our parents were one thing, but I was a fellow sister. What could they possibly need to hide from me?

"Yeah … Mom was just wrapping up. I thought I'd let you two know I was heading out." I gave them a tight smile. It was all I could muster through the hurt. I knew I didn't exactly fit in among them, but I rarely faced such a stark reminder.

"Okay. Be safe on your way home." Giada wrapped me in a quick hug, followed by Val.

I said my goodbyes and went outside to request an Uber. As I filled in the necessary information, a text notification appeared at the top of my screen.

Filip: Camilla, don't ignore me.

Why not? So you can bully me some more?

It was too much to deal with on top of everything else. His oppressive agreement. My narcissistic boss. Guilt trips from my mother and a secret half brother. Being ostracized by my sisters.

Filip's demands were more than I could handle.

I dismissed the notification and placed my Uber order. My heart ached for so many different reasons that I could hardly see through the darkness that descended around me. A thundercloud of anger and remorse lingered ominously over my head with no sign of sun to chase away the storm.

When my ride arrived, I slipped into the back seat and wrapped my arms snugly around my middle to help hold myself together until I was home. There was only one way I knew of to release the swell of emotions and keep them from consuming me —to free myself from the oppressive weight of the world—and I had denied myself that comfort for too long. I needed it, no matter the resulting shame.

With or without Filip's help, I would find what I was after.

That promise to myself was the single flickering flame that kept me from being swallowed by the darkness. I focused all my attention on its unsteady light and greedily consumed its warmth to fortify myself. The moment I was home, I crawled into bed and welcomed the oblivion of sleep.

Thursday, February 6ᵗʰ

FILIP: Do I need to come find you and force you to talk?

I'd obsessed over my situation with Filip all morning. His domineering behavior was more than I knew how to handle, but his words had resounded somewhere deep inside me. A bond linked us together—something dark and elemental.

The unsettling demand of desire.

The insidious whispers of torment.

I couldn't put a name to the connection between us. There were no words or explanations. He was drawn to me the same way I was to him, and it was making both of us crazy. Could something so powerful ever be good? Neither of us was a match for the unspoken chemistry that sizzled and popped in the air around us. As though fate charted our course, and we had no say in our destination.

The prospect was terrifying.

Would it be better for us to sever ties? Should I abandon my mission and admit defeat before I ended up hopelessly broken? I had no answers, so how could I possibly respond to his texts?

A knock sounded at my office door before Trent leaned around the doorframe and poked his head inside.

"The Marshall Group just moved our lunch meeting to dinner tonight. Seven o'clock at Fiorino's. It's a little Italian place not far from here. Can you make it?" Trent was the only reason my job was remotely tolerable.

"Yeah, I can do that."

"Great. I could manage it alone, but I'd rather not. I'll see you tonight if I don't see you before then." He rapped his knuckles against the doorframe and disappeared.

A working dinner wasn't my ideal way of spending the evening, but discussing a new construction finance project over dinner could be worse. Donald wasn't involved with this particular project, so my boss was not scheduled to join us. The outing would also help distract me from all things Filip, though he did his best to deny me even that one bit of solace.

At four thirty that afternoon, another text came through.

Filip: Last chance.

I heaved out a sigh and gave in. **I need time to think.** It was the best I could give him.

I tossed my things in my purse and left work early to freshen up and change before dinner. My bank attire was stuffy for an evening out, even if it was a business dinner. When the time came, I changed into a scoop-neck black sweater that revealed a touch of my shoulder on each side and a sleek pencil skirt in the perfect shade of red. I applied a matching shade of smudge-proof lipstick and twisted my hair up into a loose knot with a few tendrils hanging free.

I felt sexy and confident while still maintaining a professional vibe. Trent confirmed that I'd hit my mark when his eyes bulged as I joined him inside Fiorino's.

"That's it. I think you may have just turned me." Trent's gaze traveled down the length of me.

I grinned, my cheeks heating. "You're looking rather dashing yourself. Great pocket square."

"Oh my God, isn't it great? It had the perfect tones of fuchsia and taupe for this tie. I couldn't believe it when I found it." He lifted his eyes from the neatly folded satin and paused, brows raised. "Nope, still gay, I guess."

We both burst into a fit of giggles. It was exactly what I needed.

"Come on, let's get our table. The others will be here soon." He tugged me over to the hostess station, where we claimed our reservation.

The two gentlemen representing our client joined us shortly after. Our conversation had a life of its own, evolving naturally from one topic to another, only stopping for brief interruptions by our server. When all eyes lifted to a presence behind me, I assumed the young waitstaff had simply come by to check on us.

I was wrong.

A rumbling, assertive voice addressed my companions from above me. "Excuse me, gentlemen. May I steal this lovely young woman for a moment?"

Embarrassment and outrage colored my cheeks.

What the hell was Filip doing here? Had he followed me again? Did he realize he was interrupting a business dinner? With each second that ticked by, my pulse rose until my heart tumbled over itself in a rush to leave my body.

"No problem at all," offered one of our clients.

Trent's eyes were as round as golf balls.

"Please, excuse me," I murmured, unable to find my voice. I slid back my chair and rose with a grace and ease that effectively concealed the chaos rioting inside my head.

Filip placed his hand on my lower back and guided me to the back of the restaurant, where he ushered me into the women's water closet and locked the door. The restroom wasn't my ideal location for a confrontation, but at least it was relatively private.

I spun around as soon as we were alone and glared at him. "What the hell are you doing here? And how did you even know where I was?"

"Don't look at me like I was stalking you. Your phone location services are on."

Ugh. My father had insisted on that ages ago. I'd completely forgotten.

"My turn." Filip took a single intimidating step forward. "Why the fuck are you ignoring me?"

"I'd say it was obvious, considering how you left me tied to my bed."

His eyes narrowed to angry slits. "You were perfectly capable of getting free."

"A fact it took me thirty minutes of fear-induced panic to figure out."

His head lowered, and his hands came up to cup my face. "You're right," he murmured. "I was angry, and I lashed out. It won't happen again. If it's any consolation, I didn't leave until I knew you'd freed yourself."

"What? How?" If he'd planted cameras in my apartment, I would run screaming straight to my father. A girl could only take so much.

"Twentieth floor, master bath in the southeast corner of the building. I watched for the light to come on from my car."

Well, that wasn't too stalkerish, and it assured me he hadn't been totally heartless when he'd left, but it wasn't enough. "How can I trust you when you hurt me like that?"

Deep mocha eyes studied me beneath furrowed brows. "I'm sorry, Camilla," he conceded quietly. "This arrangement has proved more complicated than I anticipated."

"Well, it's not ideal for me either," I murmured. "You don't have to do it, you know. You could look the other way. No one has to know." I peered up at him, drinking in his disarming features. While I'd asked for my freedom, I wasn't entirely sure I wanted him to grant it. His commanding presence called to me in ways I hated to admit.

"No." His answer was resolute, resounding in its finality.

"Then I need more from you. Better communication. More understanding. Otherwise, this isn't going to work." I spoke calmly but with a pleading tone in an attempt to make him understand how important this was to me. "I'm new to club life, and I get that I'm not supposed to expect a normal relationship, but our arrangement isn't totally casual either. It's complicated, and I can't be punished for rules I was never made aware of."

Filip seemed to war with himself, a myriad of emotions crossing behind those calculating eyes. "I've already fucked up more times than I can count over the past two weeks. I don't know what this is either, and I don't handle that uncertainty well. I like to exercise control in my life, and with you, I'm fucking helpless. I hate it, but I hate the thought of losing you more." His thumb caressed a path over my cheek. "Give me another chance, Camilla."

I swallowed the heap of emotions lodged in my throat and nodded. How could I not? I knew precisely how unsettling our attachment had become. Some might say it was unhealthy, but I was messed up already. Why should I expect anything less?

Filip dropped his hands, and his gaze traveled leisurely down my body, heating my skin just as thoroughly as any tangible caress. "Turn around," he ordered gruffly.

I paused only briefly before complying, the air in the room becoming dizzyingly thin.

Filip eased behind me, placing his hands on my hips and pulling me flush against him, his rock-hard length firm against my ass. "I want you at the club tomorrow night. Eight o'clock. And the next time you're pissed with me, we talk it through. Understood?" His softly uttered words wrapped me in a comforting embrace. I wasn't sure why, but he simply had that effect on me.

I nodded in agreement.

Filip buried his nose in my hair for a moment before pulling away. I turned to face him in time to catch him adjusting himself with a grimace. He shot me a raised brow when the corners of my mouth twitched with a grin.

"One more thing before I go," he drawled, eyes growing hooded. "Take off your panties."

My eyes darted around the room, and a host of concerns shot through my mind. "I need to get back out there, and—"

"Camilla, look at me." He waited until he had my full attention. "All I said was take off your panties. I know I've damaged your trust, but I won't hurt you again."

I took in a steadying breath and eased my hand up under my skirt, hooking the edge of my black lace thong and slipping it off. Filip held out his hand. I placed the scrap of fabric in his palm and watched in shock as he deposited it in his jacket pocket.

"But ... I'm at a work dinner. I can't ... It's not ..." I failed to string together a complete sentence in my bewilderment.

Filip stepped closer and clasped his hands around my arms, bringing his mouth close to my ear. "You can, and you will. You wanted this, remember? And I want you to spend the rest of your dinner consumed by thoughts of what tomorrow will bring." He slowly pulled away and reached for the door.

My mind was so overwhelmed by everything Filip that I wasn't sure I could remember how to walk. He was a force of ruthless masculinity that disabled my every defense. He wanted me to think about our upcoming rendezvous; I doubted I'd be able to think of anything else.

It was a good thing dinner was almost over.

I followed Filip back to the dining area, where he gave me one last penetrating glance before disappearing around a corner.

CHAPTER 8
Camilla

F ilip messaged me just after lunch with instructions to text him when I arrived at the club. I took it as a good sign that he was trying. On the ride over, I struggled to squash my mounting nerves. At least I didn't have to stress about what I was wearing now that I was more familiar with the club standards. I'd chosen a dress similar to the one I'd worn the first night, but this one was a rich forest green and not so short. It was sexy yet sophisticated, and I felt as confident as possible, considering the circumstances.

Filip waited for me in the entry when I arrived. His ravenous gaze drank me in from my upswept hair down to my black-patent stilettos in an unhurried homage to my efforts. Heat blossomed beneath my skin everywhere his eyes lingered. When he completed his survey, he slowly stalked forward and slid one hand around to the back of my neck, pulling us close. His thumb caressed a possessive path over the corner of my jaw while his eyes dropped to my lips. I couldn't breathe with him so close or while the intensity of his stare devoured me whole. For a fleeting moment, I got the sense he was going to say something, but he pulled away instead.

"Let's head upstairs." The dark timbre of his voice brought to mind the deep resonating warning of a panther hidden in the shadows.

Filip was ready to play.

We went directly to Filip's room where the curtains were drawn and the haunting strains of a string quartet played softly in the background.

"No window tonight?" I asked as the door clicked shut.

"I don't want to share your attention tonight. You'll concentrate on me and only me." He had me intrigued, only adding to his alluring mystery when he prowled in a small circle around me. He closed in behind me and lowered the zipper to my dress. "You look stunning." The whispered words kissed my ear and warmed my chest.

Filip slipped the shoulders of my dress down and guided the fabric to the floor, revealing that I'd been bare underneath. His chest rumbled with masculine approval as he stepped around to my front and pulled something from his jacket pocket. Without a word, he ripped the small scrap of fabric—my thong from the night before.

Knowing he'd kept it did strange things to my insides.

With one more quick jerk, the garment was reduced to a ribbon of lace. He closed the distance between us, making my naked skin tingle with awareness.

"Hands," he ordered.

I peered up at him warily, unsure I wanted to comply. His answering stare unraveled me at the seams with its raw honesty, rife with pleading and apology.

"Please, Camilla. Let me show you how good it can be."

I extended my hands and reveled in his confident touch as he secured my wrists. The lace was the perfect length. His hands were strong and adept, the rough pads of his fingers surprisingly delicate against the sensitive underside of my wrists.

How fast could a heart beat before it gave out? Mine was experimenting on the matter.

Filip nodded toward the chaise in the corner. "Lay yourself over the arm."

The large, tufted piece was designed with a wide, rounded back and arm perfect for draping over. I doubted it was a coincidence.

Resting the weight of my upper half on my arms, I followed his instructions and lay over the soft velveteen fabric. Off to the side, Filip removed his jacket, rolling up the sleeves of his shirt. The muscles in his neck flexed as he stared at my exposed backside and legs. When he moved from view, each of my senses strained and stretched to ascertain his next actions. Anticipation nudged me further toward a precipice. A cliffside overlooking the unknown.

My breath shuddered when his warm hand rested gently on the curve of my ass.

"We're going to test a new limit tonight. See how you do with a little pain." His hand slowly swept down the length of my legs, then signaled me to shift my weight as he removed my heels one at a time. From where he squatted, he had a perfect view of my folds.

My position left me vulnerable. On display. I had to focus in order to remain relaxed.

"Your skin is flawless. It's going to look incredible reddened with my marks." He nipped at my buttocks.

My back arched in surprise. "If it's too much, you'll stop, right?" A tendril of panic wound its way around my throat, making it hard to breathe.

Filip came to the side of the chaise and squatted until we were eye level. "Camilla, this is all for you. I have no intention of going beyond your comfort zone. You say the word, and we're done. Period. Okay?"

I nodded, my heart rate easing back to a healthy jog rather than a dizzying sprint.

Filip used his thumb to tug at my bottom lip before standing and resuming his stance behind me. "For four days, you ignored my messages. As I'm the man who has pledged to see to your needs and keep you safe, that is inexcusable. You will communicate openly with me at all times. Is that clear?"

"Yes."

His hand made a caressing circle around one globe of my ass. "Monday." It was the only thing he said before his hand disappeared. Just as quickly, a stinging palm branded my backside.

I stilled, hardly breathing as I absorbed the mild pain.

Filip caressed over the sting, his hand then traveling to the other cheek. "Tuesday."

Thwack.

This time, the sting triggered a tiny trickle of endorphins. *Yesssss. There it is.*

"Wednesday," he barked, the intensity in his voice building.

Thwack.

I moaned, feeling a tiny taste of euphoria just out of reach.

Filip switched back to the original cheek. "And this is for your silence when I specifically warned you Thursday."

Three strikes in rapid succession.

The slight spike in pain heated and cooled my blood at the same time. I focused on the sensation, absorbing every ounce of my body's reaction to the firing nerves. When the initial wave crested and I coasted back down, my body melted into a puddle of relaxed tissue. The pain was so short-lived, and the subsequent high was only momentary, but it was enough. I languished in the tiny taste of release I'd gone so long without.

The ecstasy of letting everything else in the world fall to the wayside.

Too quickly, I was tugged back to reality.

"Camilla, that was a very unusual response to being spanked for the first time. You haven't lied to me about being new to this, have you?"

"I haven't lied." Not exactly. Besides, my past was irrelevant.

"Considering your response, I should go harder on you after forcing me to go without for two weeks, but your actions weren't entirely unjustified."

"Go without?" I glanced back to where he was unbuttoning his shirt, allowing a mesmerizing peek at the taut skin beneath.

He tugged on my middle, lifting me up to stand with him at my back. "If I wasn't with you at the club, then I wasn't with anyone. That's how this works."

So he hadn't gone back in to fuck another woman after I'd left the club? He hadn't been with others while he kept me at bay? I was stunned. Was that why he was so upset that I might have taken a man home from the bar?

A damnable fluttering warmth filled my chest. It would do me no good. I was absolutely not allowed to develop any feelings for this man.

"I didn't know," I sputtered.

His nostrils flared. "Now you do. I may not have been clear at first, but this agreement extends beyond the walls of the club." It almost sounded like it angered him to say the words.

"Okay," I whispered soothingly.

The sudden fire inside him eased to a molten glow at my reassurance. "Hands against the wall."

I did as he said, hands raised just above my head. Filip shadowed my every movement. The moment I stilled, his warmth was at my back, his hands reconnecting with my skin.

"I should make this last longer tonight. You deserve that at least, but it's been two weeks, and seeing your ass red from my hand while hearing the sweet sounds you made when I touched you ... I can't hold myself off any longer." His hands swept around to massage my breasts, plucking sharply at my pebbled nipples.

I arched into the sting, eliciting a groan from behind me.

"You ... you don't know what you do to me." A whispered admission I doubted he would have shared had he not been in such a state.

One hand trailed with a tremor down my belly and slid easily into my folds.

"*Fuck*, you're ready. So wet and ready for me." His voice was strained, his lust stirring the molten lava pooling in my belly.

"Please, Filip. I need more."

A grunt. His hands left me, and I could hear the clinking of his belt and the rip of foil. He placed one hand at the nape of my neck and guided me a few inches lower against the wall. His other hand pressed against my lower back, encouraging me to arch and present my ass for his pleasure. For my pleasure.

I was completely drunk on lust. Nothing else existed in that room but the two of us and our pursuit of physical bliss.

Filip eased inside me, soothing the pulsing need that clambered to be filled. His hand clamped harder around my neck as he sheathed himself fully inside me.

"*Fuck.*" The curse tore from his lips with unrestrained violence. It wasn't a benediction or praise. The expletive was a pure curse.

I didn't have time to question his outburst. The second he recovered from whatever had overcome him, Filip began to pound into me. With one hand at my neck and the other on my hip, he burrowed deep into my soul where the darkness lived. He was a musician playing the perfect chords to make my heart sing.

I pressed my hands against the wall and met his every stroke. Harder. Faster.

"Yesssss!" I cried out, well on my way to abandoning my sanity. To embracing the animal instincts inside me and relishing my ruination.

Filip roared behind me. "*Now*, Camilla." His palm connected again with the already tender skin on my ass, a sharp slap that electrified my body. White-hot energy radiated from my core into every extremity.

Filip hissed as his hands clamped down and his motions slowed. I was only vaguely aware, adrift on a chemical high no drug could ever duplicate. His scalding body folded over mine, our heaving chests aligning. My legs grew shaky, but Filip supported me, one hand propped on the wall and the other secure around my middle. He lowered his lips to my shoulder and hovered. His panted breaths cast warm swaths of moisture across my skin before his mouth opened and clamped over the sinewy muscle at the base of my neck. Pain blossomed. I gasped, and my inner muscles squeezed around him viciously.

Filip groaned as he released me, standing us both upright before determinedly pulling up his pants and avoiding my gaze. When I turned and our eyes collided for an instant, he cursed again under his breath.

"Is everything okay?" I asked, confused.

He exhaled loudly and ran a hand through his tousled hair. "I'm sorry about that. I got carried away." His gaze lingered on my shoulder before shuddering, all traces of his irritation locked securely behind a stoic mask.

"Don't be sorry. I liked it."

"I've got to go." He snatched his shirt off the ground. "I'll walk you out."

What the hell just happened? Filip was the most mercurial man I'd ever met, and it was contagious. After only a short time around him, I was such a bundle of competing emotions that I didn't know how I felt. Excitement? Relief? Anxiety? Anger?

I slipped on my dress, and Filip helped with the zipper.

"That won't work," he ground out before attacking my updo and releasing my hair to cascade over my shoulders. He stalked around me and studied his work. "The mark can still be seen, but it'll have to do. Come on."

He was trying to hide the bite mark? What did he care if someone saw it? I was so confused.

Filip led me into the hallway, but I yanked my hand from his when we passed the main gathering room.

"I'm not ready to go home. I'd like to have a drink and relax for a minute first." Just because he needed to leave didn't mean my night had to end.

He eyed the doorway where pulsing music was the backdrop to an erotic orchestra of sounds. "No. You don't have anything on under that dress, and you have no reason to be in there without me." He was clearly agitated. I didn't know exactly why, just that our time together continued to upset him.

I eased close to peer up at him, speaking softly just for his ears. "Please trust me, Filip. I won't touch anyone, and I won't let anyone touch me. One drink, then I'll go home."

His piercing stare blasted me with frustration and pleading, then confusion and surrender. "One drink," he bit out.

My face lit with a hesitant smile.

Dante chose that moment to come strolling off the elevator. "Everything all right here?"

"Yes," I assured him. "Filip was just heading out, and I was going to have a quick drink at the bar."

Dante glanced at Filip as if for confirmation. Filip merely grunted and stalked to the empty elevator.

Well, that was interesting.

I shook my head, bewildered. "Care to have a drink?" I asked Dante.

"That sounds perfect."

We zigzagged through the bustling room to the bar and snagged two seats.

"It's been a while," he mused. "I was starting to wonder if we'd scared you off."

"It's complicated."

Dante smiled. "Always is. Everything okay between you two?" His eyes traveled down to where I'd inadvertently exposed the bite mark on my neck by tossing my hair over my shoulder.

I replaced the curtain of hair to regain some semblance of privacy. I realized Filip hadn't been so unreasonable with his desire to hide the mark. He'd done it to save me from this precise feeling of awkwardness. I hadn't considered I'd see anyone I knew well, and I didn't think Dante would judge me, but it still felt personal. Intimate. What had happened between Filip and me wasn't meant to be shared with the world.

"Everything is fine, promise." I infused a healthy dose of reassurance in my smile.

"Okay, but if he gets too rough, you know you can always come to me. You should always enjoy what's being done to you, even punishments."

We placed our drink orders and watched the bartender as she quickly threw together our drinks.

"The physical aspects aren't an issue. It's understanding how to manage this type of relationship that's the struggle, if that makes sense," I tried to explain.

"Absolutely." He sipped his gin, ever the consummate gentleman, allowing me the chance to speak rather than offering solutions or mansplaining.

"I thought joining the club would mean casual sex with no strings attached. With Filip in the mix, that's changed. He insists on exclusivity both in and outside the club, which implies a certain degree of commitment, so I'm not sure where that leaves me. How do you not form a bond with someone you are intimate with exclusively?" I finished airing the jumbled thoughts swirling in my head and turned to Dante.

His features were inscrutable. Blank. "Filip instituted a mutual exclusivity between you?"

Had I said more than I should have? Suddenly, I wished I could gobble all those words back in my mouth. "Yes? He implied that was normal for him."

Dante raised a single brow. "Is that so?"

Was that not true? Had Filip lied? Why would he do that? I'd never implied a need for exclusivity. In fact, he was the sole ardent proponent. None of it made any sense.

A large hand settled warmly over mine, and Dante's features softened. "I didn't mean to imply anything. I only want you to be comfortable here. Filip can be … intense. When I offered my help in handling him, I meant for any physical and emotional issues that might develop. If you came here to explore yourself, there's no reason he should limit you. He may be a bit of a bully sometimes, but I assure you, I have no problem standing up to him."

Did I want the freedom to explore? I shifted my weight in my seat and felt the residual warmth of my spankings. Everything about our time in that room had been perfect, aside from the awkward ending. The only exploring I wanted to do at the moment was between Filip De Luca and myself.

I offered Dante a tight smile. "I appreciate that." Pulling my hand from his, I glanced down and noticed an intricate gold initial ring engraved with a lion's head on the thick sides and the letters D and L stacked together on the flat face of the ring. It was an odd design, considering the initials seemed backward, but it was clearly a tribute to the club. "This place is your baby, isn't it?"

"It's been my life for the past five years." Five years? He

couldn't have been much older than me when he started the business. How intriguing.

"Sex club owner isn't the average career choice. What made you decide to open the Den?"

His face split in a devious grin. "They say do something you love, and you'll never work a day in your life."

I chuckled and took a sip from my drink.

"Actually, that's not that far off. I wanted to do something I enjoyed, and I hated school. Got into trouble all the time. I'd rather work with people than numbers. And what better business than sex? There's a ton of money in it, and it didn't take me long to figure out this city needed a high-end place people could trust to protect their secrets and provide a clean, safe environment to explore their sexuality."

"You almost make it sound charitable," I teased.

Those twin dimples made an appearance. "That's me. I'm a charitable kind of guy."

I shook my head with a laugh. "All right, Saint Dante, I better go. I promised Filip one drink only."

Dante's smile faded. "If that's what you want." His hand gently closed around my upper arm. "Just remember, you always have options."

Was Dante making a move on me? He'd been nothing but professional upon meeting him, but maybe he dabbled in club life more than he let on. I didn't know how I felt about his advance. It was flattering, but my interest was focused elsewhere at the moment.

I cleared my throat. "I'll keep that in mind."

He nodded once, his thumb giving me a single gentle caress before he slipped from his seat. "Come on, I'll walk you out."

CHAPTER 9
Filip

What the fuck was wrong with me? I questioned my sanity as I stalked away from Camilla and Dante.

From the moment she'd walked into the Den, my control was shredded. She was a vision—a fucking temptress—and the yearning she stirred within me was terrifying. I battled against my instincts the entire time we were together. The need to claim her. To assure and protect her.

I'd marked her as though she were already mine. A few more minutes in that room with her and I would have catapulted us down a road we couldn't come back from. It was bad enough I'd instituted exclusivity beyond the club. I'd never intended to set such a restrictive standard, but watching her eye the crowd at that bar and imagining her taking home some asshole made me furious. I couldn't let it happen.

Each step I took to control the situation only left me feeling more disoriented and powerless. My life was a runaway car barreling down a mountainside, and I couldn't convince my foot to ease off the gas. As if I had a death wish.

If I allowed my hunger for her to take root, I would succumb to the emotion. My need for her would govern my thoughts and color all of my choices, and her presence would completely upend my life as I knew it. I could sense the change with a growing certainty that engulfed me in a storm of unease. If I bound myself to her, my life would never be the same.

I was being ripped apart by two competing desires, neither rooted in an ounce of logic. The result was a desperation that permeated my entire being. An insidious compulsion tugging me to have her was as strong as the one to walk away. I needed both at the same time—couldn't breathe without them—yet there was no middle ground.

If I didn't find a way to control myself soon, I'd drive myself insane.

Perhaps it would be best to just tell her father. He'd make sure she never left home again, guaranteeing she couldn't disrupt my life any further, and I would have no choice in the matter. The prospect was tempting. Anything to end my torment.

I blew through the front door of the club, almost careening straight into a woman reaching for the door. She gasped as she stumbled backward, nearly tumbling to the ground.

I clasped her arms, steadying her as recognition set in. "Liana, I apologize. Are you all right?"

"No harm done." She grinned broadly. "It's lovely to see you, Filip. Are you leaving so early?"

I dropped my hands when I sensed a rising heat in her gaze. Liana was frequently at the club, and we'd been known to entertain one another when the mood struck. Not exactly regularly, but often enough that we shared a certain familiarity. More than I did with most women.

She was beautiful, petite with a curvy body that she worked to her every advantage. But her most striking features were her green eyes and natural red hair that sparked in the light. She possessed an enchanting beauty, yet she'd never tempted me half as much as Camilla.

If I were to suggest it, I had no doubt Liana would join me inside and do her best to eradicate all thoughts of Camilla from my head. The idea was appealing. An escape might provide relief from the ever-worsening bisection taking place inside my mind —two warring desires wrenching me apart in a most violent fashion.

As much as I craved an escape from myself, breaking my pact with Camilla would only inject further venom into the festering wound inside me.

"Yes, I'm afraid I have to go. Things are in full swing, so I'm sure you'll have a lovely evening."

Liana's smile wavered. "Yes, of course. See you soon, then."

I nodded my goodbye and fled for home.

THE NEXT DAY I came to with a splitting headache. Polishing off half a bottle of scotch on my own had not been my brightest idea ever. It had seemed necessary at the time to dilute my thoughts. Now, I wasn't so sure. I'd slept half the day and felt like shit for more than one reason.

Images of the mark I'd left on Camilla haunted my dreams.

It was my responsibility to see to her pleasure and to care for her when the pleasure involved pain. Never in all my years at the club had I ever been so callous to a woman as I'd been when I up and left Camilla. Shame was a heavy boulder on my chest, the constant pressure a reminder that I needed to fix what I'd done.

I rolled out of bed and showered the scotch from my saturated pores. As the scalding water cleansed my body, I thought about my father. In his prime, he'd been a fierce enforcer for the Gallo family. A legend of loyalty and brutality. He'd been a good father—though tough on us boys—who prized honor and courage above almost everything. I'd strived my whole life to live up to his legacy, but I also witnessed the way my mother's death had destroyed him. Destroyed our entire family. I had pledged I wouldn't allow myself to fall victim to that weakness. The lives we led were dangerous, and bringing a woman into the mix was asking for misery. Between that promise and my need to maintain control of my life, having a wife never made sense.

How could I be adamantly against something yet cling to it with such ferocity?

I never wanted to end up losing the love of my life like my father. Yet what kind of man would I be to ignore how I'd treated Camilla? I had to go check on her and give her some semblance of an explanation. My sense of duty demanded it, but there was more. I had to go because I wanted to. Because I felt guilty about what I'd done. Because I cared about her feelings.

Hell, I'd been staking out her apartment like a total creeper. I told myself I was keeping her safe from the cartel and her own brashness, but there was more to it. I wanted to know her patterns. See where she went and who she talked to.

Motherfucker.

I was in far deeper than I wanted to admit, and it didn't change a damn thing.

Less than an hour later, I was knocking on her door. Her surprise at my visit quickly morphed to wariness. I hated that—despised that my behavior could make her feel uncomfortable in any way.

"Can I come in?"

She widened the door and stepped back. I was surprised to

discover her place was almost as orderly as mine. In my experience, women's apartments were often canvassed with clothes, papers, and all sorts of miscellaneous debris scattered everywhere. Camilla's tabletops were barren save for a single vase of pink roses.

"I hope I'm not interrupting. I needed to make sure you were okay. I should never have left you like that last night." I drew closer and lifted her hair from her neck, grimacing at the sight. Purple smudges marred her delicate skin where my teeth had been. It served as a reminder of my primal response to her.

How could something that tempted me to a point of madness also be the source of such torment?

"It's really not that bad," she murmured.

I lifted her gaze from my chest. "If anyone else had been so rough with you, I would have killed them."

"Is that why you left so quickly?"

"That was a part of it." I had to avert my gaze. We were touching on uncomfortable territory.

"What was the other reason?"

I sighed, trying to keep my irritation at bay. It wasn't her question that bothered me. I was frustrated at myself for being messed up. For freaking out and having no control over myself. Camilla wasn't going to judge me, I didn't think, but admitting I didn't want to want her felt shitty.

I pulled out a jar of salve from my jacket pocket and swiped some to rub on her wound. "You're just more than I expected," I offered softly.

"More?"

"I like things a certain way in life, and when something threatens to change those things, it throws me off." I wanted to explain further, but I also didn't want to hurt her.

"Oh." Sadness saturated her voice.

I slipped the jar back into my pocket and wiped my fingers on my jeans before clasping her face in my hands. "Sometimes change, no matter how disorienting, can be good. Yeah?" At least, that was what I tried telling myself. I'd spent so many years refusing to consider love or marriage that altering that mindset, no matter how deeply I craved Camilla, was still a struggle. "Be patient with me, little warrior. Not everyone is as brave as you are."

The air around us flickered and flamed with an electric attraction. She angled her chin ever so slightly toward me, sensing this was the perfect moment for a kiss, but I couldn't. I didn't kiss the women I was with. Ever. It was too intimate. And while she was different from the rest, I couldn't bring myself to do it. Like a line in the sand, allowing such intimacy would be the ultimate surrender, and I wasn't ready for that.

I dropped my hands and allowed an ocean of unsaid words to filter between us. "I have to get going, but I'll be in touch."

She nodded, a lopsided smile assuring me she hadn't given up on me.

My heart thudded like an angry bass drum as I left her apartment, but the beat had rhythm. No thundering chaos. Maybe I could find a way to push past the anxiety and keep her without hurting us both in the process. I wasn't giving her up, so we'd know soon enough. Either I'd find a way to live with her in my life, or I'd shred every ounce of my sanity trying.

The moment I stepped onto the sidewalk outside her building, my phone began to vibrate. Matteo was calling. I expected it to be yet another errand, but his clipped tone had me immediately on alert.

"I need you here. We've got a big problem."

"Be there in ten."

I raced to his apartment, my mind buzzing with questions. When I arrived, I let myself inside and found him in his office staring intently at his phone.

"What's up?" I asked, announcing my presence.

"Have a seat. I've just received notice there's going to be a meeting of the Commission. A bad batch of product made it into circulation, and there have been six deaths so far. The feds are in an uproar, and cops are all over the streets asking questions."

"Where?" The Five Families had divided the city into sectors and industries, allocating a portion to each family. A problem in one area should have indicated which family was having issues.

"That's the thing. There was a string of incidents over in Brooklyn, which is Giordano territory, but there are also cases up in the Russo neighborhoods. You know we respect our borders. Product from one family shouldn't have migrated like that. We think it's an outside source. Someone framing the Families to draw attention."

"The Russians?" They were the second most active organization in the city, and though we'd had a long-standing agreement with them, things could always change.

"They stick with firearms and dope. Besides, they know not to cross us. Whoever this is was looking for a fight by drawing attention to us like they did. The newest Chinese Triad leader was arrested a month ago, so they're back to feuding over leadership. Don't think they're in a place to make a coordinated attack. The only thing that makes sense is the cartel."

"Has anyone spotted Vargas in the city? Do we know if he's still in Mexico?" A couple of months before, several families, including our own, united in sending a message to the Sonora Cartel after they made a play for turf in our city. It appeared they didn't heed our warning.

"All reports indicate he's still south of the border, but he's clearly still in play here as well. We're gathering tomorrow to discuss our strategy."

If the cartel wanted a war, it was war they would get. The

families didn't care much what went on in the rest of the country, but we ruthlessly protected our rights to the city.

Oddly enough, the chaos of violence and turf wars didn't bother me at all. Something about strategy and battle gave me a sense of purpose and thus control. I had no doubt we would bury those cartel fuckers, and I relished the opportunity.

CHAPTER 10
Camilla

I was left reeling after Filip's visit. I'd been halfway through a new series on Netflix when he showed up, totally unexpected. Even after he left, I still couldn't wrap my brain around all that had transpired within a few short minutes.

Filip said I was more than he expected.

He didn't explain what he meant, but his thoughtful actions and heartfelt words were all the context clues I needed. He cared for me more than he anticipated he would and possibly more than he wanted to. It was clear he was still struggling, but his appearance at my doorstep was a genuine, caring effort. His earnest plea was a display of vulnerability I would never have imagined, especially less than a day after his curt dismissal.

It struck me as incongruent that someone so self-assured could struggle with change. His limited explanation only stirred my curiosity further. Why did he struggle with change? Not just struggle, he'd seemed as though he were furious at the club. Like he wanted to crawl out of his own skin.

I wondered at the source of his fear. Most people didn't respond so violently to the prospect of caring for another person. Evidence of my own disfunction, his turmoil endeared him to me. Made him real. I had my own challenges and appreciated what it took to battle one's inner demons.

There was no light without darkness.

No bravery without fear.

It was our imperfections that defined us—made us stand out from the crowd. Would we vanquish those demons and be seen for our strength or succumb and become notorious for our weakness? The answer lay in the choices we made each day.

I wanted to choose strength, but that path was challenging. I had yet to arrive at my destination. Filip was clearly on a journey of his own. I wanted to help him, but he would have to let me in first, and I wasn't going to preach the merits of opening up when I wasn't ready to do so myself. Instead, I would simply have to try to be patient and understanding to the best of my ability.

My phone buzzed with a text from Giada, drawing me from my thoughts.

Giada: Can I come by?

That was strange. G didn't come by all that often, and she certainly didn't ask before showing up. What other surprises did this day have in store for me?

Me: Come on over.

Less than five minutes later, knocking sounded on my door. Now *that* was more like Giada. She probably texted from the lobby downstairs.

"Thanks for the warning." Sarcasm dripped from my tongue whenever she was around like some kind of Pavlovian response.

"Whatever. You don't have anything going on, and this is important." She made herself comfortable on my sofa and looked at me expectantly to join her.

"What's so important it couldn't be said via text?"

"I wanted to make sure you're careful. Bad things are going on with the cartel."

Oh. Well, that *was* important. I fell back into my blanketed spot on the opposite end of the couch. "What kind of bad things? I thought the cartel left the city."

"They were told to leave, but it looks like they aren't giving up. I don't know all the details, but they've done something to stir up the authorities. There have been some deaths, and Javi is concerned." Her boyfriend had been a part of that cartel only a few months earlier. He understood better than any of us what they were capable of, and after his defection, he had a right to worry.

"What does that mean for us?"

"Well, Dad is watching over Val, and the other girls and I all have guys who will make sure we're safe, but you're unprotected. I wanted to make sure you understand the dangers. Dad hasn't assigned a bodyguard yet, but I think it's important for you to know what's going on to keep yourself safe. I saw these men in action down in Mexico. They're monsters."

I appreciated Giada looking out for me but also noted the stark reminder of how different I was from everyone else in the family. I was the lone deer separated from the herd. An easy target.

"Thanks for the heads-up. I'm not sure it changes anything, but at least I'm aware." What did she think I was going to do? Hide in my apartment indefinitely? As she so kindly pointed out, it wasn't like I had someone else I could rely upon to help me unless Dad assigned a bodyguard.

"Are you brushing me off?"

"No, I just don't know what you expect me to do. I still have to go to work and live my life."

"You could text me or someone else so we know if you go out alone at night. Take extra precautions."

Hey G, I'm headed out to the sex club. Text back when I'm done getting fucked.

I huffed a wry chuckle. "Yeah, that's not going to happen."

Giada scowled. "Val was right. You are moody lately."

"Is that what you guys talk about in your little secret gatherings?" My voice drained of all levity.

"Secret gatherings? What the hell are you talking about?"

"The other night after dinner, you and Val huddled in the study whispering. You guys don't have to include me in your little secrets, but you might at least make an attempt not to rub it in my face."

"We weren't hiding from you," she shot back, hands waving in the air. "We were hiding from Mom and Dad."

"Oh, yeah? Then why wasn't I in on your little meeting?"

"You want to know what we were talking about? Fine, but you cannot breathe a *word* of it."

I didn't know why it mattered so much to me, but hell yes, I wanted to know.

"G, you have no idea just how good I am at keeping secrets. If there is anyone in this room who has a propensity to squeal, it's you." I glared at her.

"That's ... probably right," she conceded, unable to deny the truth. "Okay, so a while back, I figured out that Val had befriended the daughter of the cartel boss. She's trying to help the girl and knows that if Dad found out, he'd forbid any interaction between them. I told her I'd keep my mouth shut as long as they only saw each other at school. I was just checking in to make sure she was being safe. That's it. That was the big secret."

My stomach clenched. "Are you sure she's okay? I don't want her getting hurt." It had been all too recently that we'd gone through the horrific experience of Giada being taken to Mexico. I didn't want Val wrapped up with those people. It was easier to worry about my little sister's safety than my own.

"I think it's okay. Javi knows about it and is keeping an eye on things. I worry about her, but I also worry about *you*. That's why I'm here. I don't mean to be the safety police, but I'd never forgive myself if something happened to you when I could have prevented it."

Where had this protective side been years earlier? She'd been too wrapped up in her friends to see anything outside her immediate bubble. I squashed down the resentment and tried to focus on being appreciative. No matter our past, I was still glad to have her looking out for me now.

I scooted across the couch and hugged my sister. "Thanks, G."

"Always and forever. You know I love you."

I pulled back before I caught too many feels. "Yeah, and I'm sorry if I've been on edge. My boss is a dick and has been making my life miserable. A few more months and I'm out of there."

"Need me to key his car?" she asked with one-hundred-percent sincerity.

I couldn't help but laugh. "Thanks, G, but not this time."

"You know my number should you change your mind. I better get going. Please be safe out there!"

"I'll do my best," I told her honestly.

Giada smiled warmly. "That's all I'm asking." With a quick wave, she took off just as suddenly as she'd arrived.

I RECEIVED a text from Filip later that afternoon asking me to meet him at the club that night. I was surprised he wanted to go again so soon after the explosive ending to our night not twenty-four hours earlier, but I wasn't going to question it. He wanted to see me. To be with me.

A chorus of exultant butterflies swarmed my stomach.

I took extra care getting ready, making sure to leave my hair down and cover my bruising with concealer so that the reminder didn't ruin our evening. Just as he had the night before, Filip met me at the entry to the club. There was an edge to him, as always, but it was less pronounced this time. He had already removed his jacket and had the sleeves of his pale silver dress shirt rolled to his elbows. His shoulders were relaxed, and he moved with the predatory grace of a man who had all the time in the world.

"You look mouth-watering, as usual," he murmured as he clasped my hand in his. "Come with me."

Stepping into the elevator, we stood with our backs to the far wall, our gazes locked on the closing doors. I half expected him to release me, but instead, his thumb rubbed gentle circles across the back of my hand. I basked in the affectionate touch and reveled in our nearness. I'd been cautiously hopeful about our evening, but under the nurturing glow of his attention, unrestrained excitement blossomed in my chest.

When the doors opened, we were met with an unusual silence on the second floor. As we neared the main room, I could hear a man's voice rumble like distant thunder. I was surprised to discover the room was full of people. They watched the stage raptly, some engaging in silent acts, but most were too engrossed in the scene being played out before them.

A shirtless man, clad only in jeans, stalked around a naked woman who stood with her hands tied behind her back. Just behind him was a sturdy wood table lined with instruments and restraints. They appeared to be playing out some kind of kidnapping fetish scene. That type of erotica wasn't something I'd put a great deal of thought into, but seeing it in person, I was instantly engrossed.

"Do you want to stay and watch?" Filip asked softly.

I nodded, unable to take my eyes from the couple. All of the seating areas were full, so he led me behind one of the sofas where we could stand and observe.

The well-muscled man stalked around the woman, who exhibited the appropriate amount of fear without diminishing from the fantasy. The scene wouldn't have been enjoyable had it been overly realistic. This wasn't about realism or any kind of statement on consent. It was about embracing the darker side of our fantasies in a safe manner. Acknowledging that people had a variety of appetites, and that didn't make us bad or wrong.

"I'm going to teach you to be my perfect slave," the man stated plainly just inches from her. "You'll beg to please me." His hand reached for her curls at the apex of her thighs, stroking her slow but firmly.

The woman whimpered, fear colliding with pleasure.

It felt so taboo to be watching such an intimate scene. Despite the crowd and open stage, the performance seemed shockingly real and fascinatingly raw.

The man cooed at the woman, reassuring her that she was allowed to enjoy his touch. "You'll come to crave this. My cock in your throat. My cum dripping from your skin." He continued his rhythmic motions, causing her breath to catch and shudder.

She appeared torn. His actions brought her immense pleasure when she knew they shouldn't.

I understood her conflict. It was like being spanked and bitten. Those things shouldn't have felt as good as they did. Sometimes enjoyment came from the most unlikely sources.

The man squeezed her breast, twisting her nipple, and I could almost feel the delicious friction in my own breasts. Hearing the sounds and seeing their bodies react, I found it was easy to imagine myself in her position.

"When I tell you to suck me, you will salivate at the chance. When I tell you to spread your legs for me, you will ask how wide."

"No, never," she gasped, shaking her head.

A dark chuckle rolled from his lips. "But, kitten, if you don't, there will be consequences. You should choose your battles wisely." He stepped back, his hand leaving her mound. "We'll start simple." He towered over her by nearly a foot and appeared to enjoy the disparity.

The crackling tension in the room mounted with heady anticipation. No one made a sound save for the woman's affected breaths.

"Kneel," he said firmly.

Her eyes darted around, looking for a way to escape. Finding none, she met his gaze and shook her head reluctantly.

The man crossed his arms over his broad chest and glared at her, his eyes traveling down her lithe frame. "Kneel." This time, there was an iron force to his order. A threat and a promise.

The woman still refused to concede. "No, please don't do this, Matthew."

The use of his name enraged him. He slammed his hands on the table beside him with a thunderous clap against the wood, and roared, "*Kneel!*"

It happened so quickly that I could hardly believe what I'd done. The scene had been too engrossing, and the memories too real.

My reaction was visceral.

On instinct, my knees dropped me to the floor with a crack. My heart raced in my chest. My vision blurred as my breaths became shaky pants.

What had I done? Had I just ruined everything?

I warily lifted my gaze to where Filip stared down at me in horrified shock.

CHAPTER 11

Filip

I'd been curious how Camilla would respond to a scene involving questionable consent. It was a hard limit for many women. I could tell by her wide eyes and shallow breaths that she'd been engrossed, but I never imagined what she'd do next. The second the command to kneel had ricocheted through the room, Camilla was instantly on her knees as if she were the one on stage. A response so innate, it implied a degree of conditioning. What other explanation was there?

Someone could scream all sorts of commands at me, but not one would incite my compliance. Any number of women in that room had participated in submissive relationships or scenes, yet none of them had reacted as Camilla had. Not one.

I was stunned. Confounded and horrified.

When our eyes met, my heart twisted painfully in my chest. All of her characteristic strength had melted to a warm puddle of uncertainty and embarrassment. There on her knees, she'd never looked more innocent and broken.

Two of the people on the couch in front of us turned back to see what had happened. The movement snapped me out of my shock and hurtled me into action. I lifted Camilla into my arms like a child and whisked her away to my room, away from prying eyes. Away from whatever memories had triggered her response.

I set her on the chaise lounge before going to the window and drawing the curtain shut to make the room feel more private. It needed to be just us for the conversation that was about to take place. No crowded room of people and certainly no distracting kidnapping scene.

"I'm sorry about that. I don't know what ... got into me." She shook her head, eyes averted. Her voice was a wisp of its usual strength.

I began to pace, battling a mounting sense of unease. I debated how to handle the situation, but before I could make any decisions, Camilla spoke and derailed my intentions to be patient and nurturing. Her claim of confusion appalled me.

"You don't know what got into you? Are you saying you have no idea why that happened?" I tried to keep my tone as calm and reasonable as possible, but I was reeling on the inside.

"I just got so consumed in the scene ... and the way he yelled ... It was just intense, that's all." She shivered in recollection.

Frustration seethed just under my skin. She was lying. There was no way that response wasn't elicited by something from her past. "Camilla, you dropped to your knees like your life depended on it. That wasn't a normal reaction."

Her eyes finally found mine, a spark of anger blistering behind those mocha irises. "Sometimes people have odd reactions to situations. *You*, of all people, should understand that."

"I never claimed my behavior lately was unfounded. I have my reasons. I want to know what the fuck would make you respond like you did. You said you didn't have experience in an alternative, erotic lifestyle. I'm asking you one more time. Was that a lie?" That kind of stuff was important to know as her partner. If she had triggers or trauma from a past relationship, it was my job to be sensitive to those subjects.

Camilla surged to her feet, now openly glaring at me. "Oh, so now I'm supposed to just bare my soul? You hardly explained anything about why you freaked out, but I'm supposed to spew all my secrets? I don't think so. You haven't come close to earning that."

I crowded her, my own fury blazing down on her. "If someone hurt you, I need to fucking know."

"No, you don't. My past is none of your fucking business."

"What if I make it my business?" My voice went deathly calm, conviction crystalizing in my veins. There was no way in hell I wasn't going to get answers.

"You stay the fuck away from me, Filip De Luca." The words were a venomous threat, her voice cracking with emotion.

She bolted for the door and fled from sight.

I took one lunging step to go after her, then froze with the overwhelming certainty that following her was a terrible idea. No good would come from pressing her now. I knew what it was like to be irrationally upset. If I followed her, I'd only make things worse.

I would give her time to calm down, but she wasn't going to avoid me forever. Camilla had seared herself into my being, branded herself in my thoughts, and planted roots deep inside my soul. There was no walking away now.

I tried to take a few minutes to calm down, but I wasn't going to be able to stop my racing mind without a distraction. Something far from the Den where I wouldn't keep replaying what had happened. I needed to take a drive and let fresh air filter through my lungs.

Set on my own escape, I yanked open the door to find Dante on the other side with a dangerous glint in his eyes.

"What the fuck did you do to Camilla?" he growled, pushing inside my room and slamming the door shut behind him.

"What happens between Camilla and me is none of your concern." He never meddled in member drama, so I saw no reason for him to take a special interest in our situation.

"Bullshit," he spat. "Not when I see her running from my club with tears streaming down her face."

I'd known she was upset, but it still gutted me to hear it.

Fuck. What had I done? Whatever her past entailed, I was sure it hadn't been her fault. She'd been lost in her own turmoil, and I'd gone and acted like a caveman demanding answers.

I dropped my gaze to the floor and sighed. "I fucked up."

"No shit, Sherlock. The question is, how bad? If I need to beat the shit out of you, I will."

"I didn't do anything physical if that's what you're implying. We were both upset, and I should have been more understanding. I don't know what it is about her, but I lose my head when I'm around her."

"You want me to talk to her?"

"*No,* I'll fix it."

"You better. She's not just some club bunny looking for a little kink."

The skin on the back of my neck pricked with awareness. Why the fuck was he talking about Camilla like he knew her? Like he was some kind of honorary older brother looking out for her. Maybe I was being overly sensitive, but I suddenly felt an intense need to piss a circle around her and claim my territory.

"I think I know Camilla a hell of a lot better than you."

His lip fish hooked in a sneer. "Good, because lately, I can't tell what the fuck you're thinking."

"Not your problem." I might have berated myself over how I'd treated Camilla, but I was done taking shit from him. "There's no reason for you to be in my head or meddling in my relationship. If we're done here, I'm leaving." I headed to the door, not waiting for his response.

"Make things right, dickhead."

I would. Soon.

CHAPTER 12
Camilla

It'd been six days since I'd run from Filip. Six long, confusing days of reflection and a full gambit of emotions. At first, I bathed in a vat of embarrassment and self-loathing—for what I'd done at the club and for what I hadn't done so many years before. I wallowed in uncertainty, wondering what assumptions Filip might have made, then questioning why I cared. I felt anger at Filip for pushing me but mostly at myself for unveiling my secrets. Who needed enemies when I was so proficient at airing my own dirty laundry to the world?

When I finally sluffed off the sweltering blanket of emotions, I was left feeling numb. Without Filip around me, I was free of the torment. Free of the memories and pressure to share them. Locked in my apartment, I was safe. I could pretend nothing had happened and my life was just as it was before I'd ever stepped foot in the club.

Filip had texted once, asking if he could see me. I told him I needed more time. I couldn't talk to him yet because I wasn't sure what to say. I wasn't sure I ever wanted to see him or the club again. A small voice urged me to take a chance and trust him with my story, but I trapped her in a Mason jar and vacuum-sealed the lid. I didn't *owe* him an explanation—I didn't owe him anything.

If I told him about my past, he would undoubtedly see me differently. How could he not? I didn't think he was the type to judge me, considering he had his own issues, but my past would color the way he perceived me. Instead of headstrong temptress, he'd cast me in the role of a wounded bird and try to cage me. Protect me.

I craved his dark intensity, and I didn't want him to sheath those sharp edges.

If he couldn't see me as more than my past, I wouldn't give him my present.

Plus, telling him would breathe life into the memories. I'd never told anyone, ever.

As much as I wanted to believe I could slip into oblivion and never see him again, that would never be an option. Filip would demand to see me at some point. Talking to him was inescapable, and I hated that the outcome of that conversation was a complete mystery to me. The uncertainty was daunting, but as each day passed, a fissure in my heart cracked and deepened. Down in an emotional abyss I'd created to hide the pain, longing clawed its way out and seeped back into my thoughts. I missed him as though I'd banished a piece of my own soul.

I was a living, breathing conflict of interest.

When Friday rolled around—a day we would have likely been together had I not been in hiding—remorse over not seeing him made my limbs feel heavy. We'd only had sex one time. Would that passionate handful of minutes be our last? Was I willing to allow fear and embarrassment to steal away our Friday night at the club? To steal everything that could develop between us?

There was a chance, no matter how small, we could resolve

our differences. Wouldn't I rather get it over with and see him than miss a chance to feel Filip's heady touch forever?

The inner debates were exhausting, and the looming solitude sucked every ounce of joy from my week. The cherry on my shit-show cake was that today was Valentine's Day. Normally, the commercialized event didn't register on my radar, but somehow, this year's celebration magnified Filip's absence from my life.

An email from the club had outlined the special Valentine's event they were having. Would Filip participate without me? The possibility alone made me want to crawl under my desk and cry.

I made a mental note to grab more cookie dough on my way home that evening.

"Camiiiiillaaaa." Trent sang my name from the hallway before poking his head inside my office. "You have a delivery." He stepped back and made room for a man carrying a striking arrangement of roses in varying shades of pink.

"For me?"

"You Camilla Genovese?" the delivery guy asked, reading from a small clipboard.

"Yeah."

"Then these are for you. Just sign here, please."

I scribbled my name, hardly taking my eyes from the bouquet, then thanked the man before he left.

Trent buried his nose in one of the roses. "So, are they from Filip?" His question was loaded with a ridiculous amount of innuendo.

Filip? Flowers were awfully romantic. Surely, they weren't from him. But if not, then who? Maybe they were his way of apologizing. Warmth radiated from my chest, heating me down to my toes. The mere possibility of contact from Filip thawed the frost-filled emptiness I'd lived with for the past week.

"I have no clue who they're from." I rotated the vase a full three hundred and sixty degrees in search of a card but came up empty.

"No card? How mysterious!" Trent grinned. "Someone has a secret admirer."

I rolled my eyes. "With my luck, it's probably a stalker."

Trent raised a brow. "As cute as you are, I'm not sure I could blame him. Or her. You never know."

I chuckled and shooed him out. "Go on, before we start to draw attention."

"Good call." His eyes cut to the door before he lifted his chin, his face falling in a dramatic rendition of professionalism. "Keep me informed of your progress on the investigation. That is all." He strolled from my office, bringing a smile to my face, as always.

We hadn't garnered our boss's attention, but that didn't mean my afternoon was free of Donald's vile presence. An hour after lunch, he stalked into my office and closed the door behind him. He rarely took measures for privacy. I got the sense he liked people to know his business to impress his importance upon others. His sudden interest in confidentiality had me instantly on guard.

"Camilla, you've gotten the bank into an embarrassing situation. The auditors have got it in their pea-sized brains that they've found some minor discrepancy with those accounts. They've frozen all of them until the matter can be sorted, which could take weeks. Valuable customers are unable to access their money because you decided to send out documents to any old person who asked." Donald's face was an angry shade of crimson, and his blood pressure had popped out a throbbing vein on his forehead. "I need you to sign these affidavits to resolve the issue." He tossed a stack of papers onto my desk.

It didn't surprise me that I was being blamed for something that wasn't my fault. If there was a problem with the accounts, that was on someone else. I was obligated to be transparent with the FDIC, and he wasn't going to bully me into believing otherwise.

I skimmed the top document, my lunch growing rancid in my stomach. "Donald, this statement claims I met with people I've never heard of. I can't sign these."

"The hell you can't. You're the reason I have customers breathing down my neck. How would you like it if a bank held hundreds of thousands of your dollars hostage?" He pointed a finger at me and glared. "If you have any aspirations of running a bank someday, you have to work to protect your customers. If you're not willing to make things happen, maybe you're in the wrong field. Money involves power and influence. If you can't handle the associated pressures, maybe you should find a husband and just stay home."

An eerie calm settled over me as Donald's tornadic tantrum raged around me. As if I were safely in the eye of the storm, impervious to its battering winds.

I rose to my feet and handed Donald his papers. "Take these and get the hell out of my office."

One of the few perks of hating your job was being able to stand up to the boss and not give two shits if he fired you. I was done. If Donald wanted to fire me, my integrity was a sword I would happily die upon.

His purple lips thinned, and I could almost see cartoon clouds of steam billow from his ears, but he didn't say a word. Yanking open my office door and throwing it back against the wall where the doorknob gouged a hole in the sheetrock, he simply left.

That was it. Whether he fired me or not, I was looking for a new job, starting today.

I slumped back into my chair, my legs growing more unsteady by the second. What the hell was that? Donald was an ass, but he'd never verbally assaulted me in such a way or asked me to do anything illegal. What the hell had come over him? Was

I supposed to report him? Why the hell was he willing to break the law for a customer? None of it made any sense.

"You okay in here?" Trevor whispered, poking his head into my office.

I sucked in a lungful of air. "Yeah, I think so, but I need a soda." Sugar. I needed lots of sugar.

"I bet. That was intense."

"God, did the whole office hear?"

"Only that he was yelling. What got him so upset?"

"I can't talk about it here." I shook my head, eyes glancing in the direction of Donald's office. "Maybe later, okay?" I grabbed my purse out of a desk drawer. "If anyone comes looking for me, tell them I'll be back in five."

"Absolutely. Take all the time you need."

I took one more glance at the exquisite bouquet on my desk and fled my office. We had a break room in the back, but I wasn't going to risk running into Satan incarnate. Instead, I slinked toward the lobby with the intent of grabbing a drink from a nearby street vendor where I could get some fresh air. Alone.

Lost in my distracted thoughts, I almost didn't notice a woman lift her chin at me to gain my attention. Not just any woman. The woman I'd seen on my first night at the club. She'd been restrained on stage with clamps on her nipples. She was fully clothed now, but her unique beauty was easy to recognize.

Holy shit, what is she doing here?

My frayed nervous system, still buzzing from my confrontation with Donald, elevated itself back to high alert in an instant. Maybe I was an alarmist, but I couldn't imagine a good scenario involving my sex club life bleeding into my professional life.

Fortunately, the woman didn't appear intent on a scene. She was lovely with long red hair and mesmerizing emerald eyes. She looked like a movie star and walked with the regal swagger of an aristocrat.

Who was she, and why had she flagged me down?

"Hello." I displayed my most professional grin. "Can I help you?"

"Yes, actually. You're just the woman I came to see. Liana Bissett." She extended her perfectly manicured hand, wearing a vitriolic smile on her face. Came to see? How did she know where to find me or even who I was?

We shook hands, and I got the distinct feeling I was being assessed by the eyes of a hungry predator.

I'd been right to worry. Liana was up to no good. Unlucky for her, she picked the wrong damn day to mess with me.

"I'm Camilla Genovese. What can I do for you, Liana?" Polite yet direct. This feral cat wasn't catching me off guard.

"I was curious to meet the woman who's been sequestering Filip all to herself. You must be rather gifted to keep him so entertained."

Oh, Jesus. Was she seriously trying to have this conversation right there in the bank lobby? And she sought me out, so she knew this was my place of employment. How she'd known where I worked was an entirely different problem.

My heart thudded in my ears, but I maintained a perfectly cool façade. "Liana, this is where I work. I hardly think it's the time or place for this conversation."

She waved a patronizing hand. "I forget that you working ladies are always so sensitive about your jobs. I just wanted to warn you that tying down Filip is the wrong strategy. You're not the first who's tried. He gets bored easily. Locking him down will only backfire on you."

What a load of bullshit.

As if this crow would ever go out of her way to help another woman. Every word out of her mouth was seeded in jealousy and spite.

"I appreciate you sharing. Now, I have to get going."

"I'm sure I'll see you around," she purred.

Unfortunately, she was probably right, assuming I eventually made my way back to the Den.

I tossed her a thin-lipped smile and walked away, ready to put her and her baggage in my rearview mirror. I mean, what the hell was going on? Had I worn a drama magnet to work this morning? I was the last person to stir up trouble, but at this rate, trouble seemed to be drawn to me like flies to a barbecue.

If I'd had plans to go out, I would have canceled them for fear of inciting a riot with my presence alone. Lucky for the NYPD, I had no plans of leaving my apartment. It looked like another evening in, just me and my cookie dough.

HIDING in my apartment proved an effective strategy for avoiding further conflict. Friday night was blissfully quiet, and my Saturday morning excitement was limited to getting an extra shot of caramel in my macchiato.

However, the world couldn't be held at bay forever. Just after lunch on Saturday, I had an unexpected knock on my door. My first thought was that Filip had finally come to force me to talk. I was inundated with a barrage of emotions and warring desires. I contemplated not answering but decided now was as good a time as any to confront him.

As it turned out, my panic had been for nothing. A glance through my peephole revealed Dante had paid me a surprise visit.

I opened the door and stumbled for words. "Dante! What are you …? I mean … hey. You're here."

He smirked sheepishly. "I'm sorry for showing up unannounced. I hope I'm not interrupting."

"No, not at all. Come in."

"Thanks. I've been worried about you all week after I saw you leave the club so upset. I wanted to make sure you were okay."

He'd been worried about me? I couldn't imagine Dante made house calls. Did he think I was going to sue the club or something? Had Filip sent him? What exactly was going on?

"Um, that's kind of you. I'm okay, though. Can I get you some water or a soda?"

"No, I'm fine, thank you."

I led him to the dining table and took a seat. "I take it you got my address from my paperwork?"

He bit on his lower lip with a guilty smirk. "You're correct. It's not something I'm in the habit of doing, but you're ... you're not the average woman."

I'd heard that a lot lately but wasn't sure if it was a good thing or not.

"You wouldn't happen to have provided my information to anyone else, would you? Say, another member?"

Dante sat taller in his chair, his face growing stern. "I absolutely did not. Has someone else contacted you?"

I sighed. "Some woman named Liana showed up at my bank yesterday. She didn't seem to like me very much."

"I'm so sorry about that. It won't happen again." His midnight gaze went glacial, broadcasting a scathing intolerance for the woman.

"She didn't do anything outrageous, just caught me off guard." I wasn't sure why I was defending her except that I'd always been taught snitches get stitches. It went against my upbringing to get her in trouble.

Dante quickly thawed and waved me off. "Don't worry. I won't do anything rash, but I believe I know what happened, and it's an issue that needs to be sorted. I appreciate you bringing it to my attention."

I gave a tight-lipped smile. "No problem."

"Is there anything else I should know about? Perhaps what happened last weekend?" He peered at me from beneath a forest of lashes.

"No, really. I just needed some time to think." Dante was sweet, but I wasn't talking to him about my issues with Filip before I even talked to Filip about them. It would be a betrayal, and I wasn't that type of person.

Those perceptive eyes studied me, searching and analyzing my every tell. Before he could dig for more, I turned the tables on him.

"Dante, why exactly are you here? I know this isn't normal protocol. You don't go check on every member who has a rough night."

He sat back in an open stance and regarded me as if debating what to tell me. "I see all sorts of people walk through my doors at the Den. Many are curious about a kink or bored with their lives. A select few are addicts, and sex is their drug of choice. But you, dear Camilla, you are a rare flower where before there were only vines and weeds. I sensed from the moment I met you that you were worth nurturing. That your growth would be something to behold."

I was speechless, struck dumb by his unabashed confession. "I don't know what to say," I whispered, my eyes darting to his only briefly. The intimacy of eye contact after such a personal admission was more than I could bear.

I'd been so caught up with Filip that I hadn't given Dante a second thought, but I'd clearly been on his mind. The disparity was uncomfortable. What did he hope to achieve by coming over and sharing his feelings? If he'd just wanted sex, he could have approached me at the club. Was he asking for something more?

My stomach dipped and swerved at the prospects.

"You don't have to say anything," he offered. "I only want you to know I'm here for you." He reached over the table and wrapped his large hand around mine, giving me a gentle squeeze. "I won't bother you anymore, but please tell me I'll see you again at the Den. I'd hate for one bad experience to bar you from other … possibilities."

Possibilities? As in, a relationship with him? He was definitely interested, but I wasn't sure how I felt. I'd already been overwhelmed with how to handle Filip, so throwing Dante in the mix made me positively dizzy.

"I'd love to reassure you, but I'm just not sure at the moment. Thank you, though." I pulled my hand out from beneath his.

His smile faltered ever so slightly. "Well, I don't need to keep you. It's a relief to know you're okay, and I'll remain hopeful that I'll see you again soon."

We both stood, but before leaving the table, Dante's eyes tracked to my kitchen island where my vase of roses was on display.

"Your flowers are lovely." He turned back to me, stepping in and placing a gentle kiss on my temple. "Just like you," he breathed, then made for the door and let himself out.

I never budged from the table.

When I decided to become a member at The Lion's Den, I never imagined I'd be complicating my life to such an extreme. Between Filip, the catty Liana, Dante, and my own sordid issues, I was embroiled in more emotional angst than I cared to experience in a lifetime.

Proverbial waters were inching up and over my nose. Any higher, and I wouldn't be able to breathe.

I'd opened Pandora's box when I joined the club. What if I put the lid back on and walked away? I'd never have to see Liana and Dante again. I wouldn't have to tell anyone about my sordid past, and Filip would eventually give up trying to see me. I could pretend none of it had ever happened.

Filip and I only seemed to hurt one another. Maybe it would

be merciful to put an end to our relationship. The whole point of the club was to seek out pleasure and learn more about myself. A place I could go purely for my enjoyment. At this rate, the Den had stirred up more strife than pleasure.

It would be so much easier to walk away.

Would that be so bad? If I needed that to support my own mental health, it had to be the best course of action, right? If I still wanted to pursue my erotic exploration, I could join one of the other clubs. Despite what Filip implied, the Den wasn't my only option. There were two other elite clubs in town that could provide what I was seeking without the other entanglements.

My phone vibrated back on the couch, and I rushed to grab it. Mom calling.

Can't a girl catch a break?

I took a deep breath—good air in, bad air out.

"Hey, Ma. What's up?"

"You know, it's Saturday, so I just wanted to see if you'd be able to come to Mass with us tomorrow. It's been ages since you've come." Somehow, the universe knew my emotional cocktail was one bitter flavor shy of a complete recipe. Guilt. The secret ingredient to a world-class case of emotional instability. Just what I needed.

"Sorry, Ma. Not this week." There was no way I could handle family interaction after the week I'd had. "I'll try to come out next weekend, I promise." Why did I just promise something I had no intention of doing? It just set her up for disappointment and armed her with more ammunition to make me feel guilty. I couldn't help myself. I wanted to want to please her. I wanted to be the kid whose parents boasted about them at every chance, but my efforts felt more cumbersome and less effective with each passing year.

"Sofia's birthday dinner is next Friday evening, so I guess we'll see you then. Remember, you never know how long we'll be around. We're getting older every day, Cam."

The death blow. The threat of an early grave and a lifetime of guilt.

I heaved out an exhausted sigh. "Don't talk like that, Ma. You're not even sixty yet."

"You never know what could happen."

"Okay, I hear you, and I'll do my best."

"That's my girl." So much pride. I just wished it wasn't conditional.

A fissure of pain lanced through my chest. "All right, Ma. I gotta go." If she truly listened, she would have heard the discordant strains of heartbreak in my voice.

"Love you, Cam. See you soon."

"Love you, too."

I hung up and sat for long minutes in the vacuous silence of my apartment. Such a stark contrast to the cacophonous voices in my head. So many people wanting me to fall in line with their expectations. To dance like a puppet in their narratives without any consideration for my needs.

I circled back to my question from moments before. What if I didn't allow myself to care what others desired from me? What if I focused on meeting my own needs and put myself first? In a way, we were taught as women that such a mindset was selfish. Was it, though? Who said I couldn't be the captain of my own ship?

A whisper of energy trickled through my veins at the prospect of such empowerment. Could the answer be so simple?

I loved what I found at the club, but so many complications had arisen. Filip demanded so much more than I'd expected to give. I'd seen the look in his eyes. He wouldn't give up his fight to uncover answers to his questions. My past was never a part of our bargain, and he had no right to change the terms of our agreement.

I didn't have to give him anything if I didn't want to.

I could chalk up my experience at the Den to the learning process and try one of the other clubs on my list. Maybe I'd find the perfect atmosphere for personal enlightenment, growth, and discovery at the Omega. It had been the next club I planned to visit if the Den hadn't panned out. What was stopping me from at least checking out my options?

Me. I was the only obstacle to my own happiness.

Just the thought of walking away from Filip and the Den gave my body a sense of weightlessness. The prospect of escape was intoxicating. Deep down, I knew avoidance would come at a cost, but I couldn't bring myself to care. The immediate sense of relief was too great to ignore.

It was decided.

I would call and set up a meeting for tonight, if possible. No more wallowing. No more stalling. If I didn't want to give Filip more of myself, I didn't have to. It was time to take the reins and chart my course. There was no shame in abandoning one path and branching out on a new one. I would see what the Omega might offer, then let Filip know our experiment was over.

Five hours later, I was crossing the threshold at the Omega after submitting the paperwork and setting up a visit. I was anxious, but nothing like I'd been that first night at the Den. Having a general idea of what I would encounter gave me a good deal of comfort.

The Omega was located on the top floors of a high-rise building. When the elevator doors opened, I found an ultra-modern lobby all in white with a built-in fireplace burning orange flames over turquoise glass shards. The feel was elegant, if not a bit cold despite the fire.

"You must be Camilla," said a man stationed in the lobby. He was older, perhaps close to fifty, but still handsome in a professor sort of way.

"Yes." I smiled and reached for his offered hand.

"I'm Niall. It's lovely to meet you."

"Thank you. I'm pleased to be here."

He pressed his palms together and grimaced. "About that, I'm afraid there's been a change of plans."

"What? I just set this up earlier today."

"Indeed, but we didn't realize who you were at the time."

Wariness twined with annoyance to stiffen my spine. "And who exactly is it that you think I am?"

"You're Filip De Luca's woman, and we'd be in a great deal of trouble if we let you step foot in our establishment. I apologize for the confusion, but you'll have to leave." He lifted his hand and gestured to the elevator. I'd been blacklisted.

Venomous talons of rage clawed beneath my skin.

Scathing accusations danced on my tongue, but Niall didn't deserve my wrath. I excused myself politely, pulling out my phone the second I was back in the elevator.

Me: Meet me at the club in ten.

I wasn't crazy about hashing out my grievance in public, but I didn't know where else to do it. I had no idea where he lived, and I certainly wasn't inviting him to my place. The club would have to do because I needed to have words with him. Now.

I threw my phone back in my clutch handbag, uninterested in his reply. If he was busy, too bad. He could damn well make the time to talk to me. It was the least he could do. I couldn't believe he'd clipped my wings and prevented me from joining Omega. Had he executed similar warnings at the other clubs in town? Undoubtedly.

That *bastard.*

Just when I started to regain control of my life, he went and swept the rug out from under me. I was livid. Filip had stolen my escape plan. If I wanted to have access to a club, he was my only option. The thought of giving up on my exploration when it had only just begun was a hammer straight to my gut. I desperately wanted more of what I'd experienced at the club, but not if it resulted in the extortion of my secrets. Filip would pry each of my ugly truths from my clenched and bloodied fists.

He held all the cards, and it made me furious.

The Uber ride to the club felt like an eternity. I envisioned countless renditions of what I wanted to say. Argued points and spat accusations. I gathered the courage to stand up for myself as I never had before.

When I stepped from the car in front of the Den, my heart began to stampede in my chest. My palms tingled from adrenaline, and my tongue was sticky against the roof of my mouth.

I didn't let any of it deter me.

Filip must not have been far when I sent my text. He stood inside the lobby when I wrenched open the door, waiting coolly with his shoulder propped against the wall. He quickly took in my fierce expression and stretched to his full height.

"We need to talk. Privately," I told him.

He nodded and motioned to the elevator. When his hand grazed my lower back, I stiffened. His touch was too seductive to be allowed. Not when I had more pressing matters to delve into. I would not allow lust to break down my resolve. Nothing would come between me and what I had to say.

I charged past the main room, not taking notice of the activities within. I had one purpose, one directive, and I wasn't interested in distractions. When the door to his room closed behind us, a swell of words and emotions wedged a knot in my throat. I wasn't the crying type. I couldn't remember the last time I'd shed a tear, yet my nose began to sting with the telltale signs.

I took a deep, steadying breath before meeting Filip's wary

gaze. "How *dare* you blacklist me from another club." My words were unsteady but still laced with venom. "You had no right."

His eyes narrowed to angry slits. "You went to another club without even trying to talk through this with me first?"

"I don't owe you *anything*. If I want to join another club, that's *my* choice. *My* life." I jabbed a finger at my chest, my voice growing stronger.

"I was trying to keep you safe, Camilla."

"You were trying to control me!" I shouted back.

Filip charged, pinning me against the wall. His shallow breaths came unevenly through parted lips. The jagged flint in his eyes sparked as his gaze bore relentlessly deep into my soul. "I've always been perfectly honest with you about my need for control. I never pretended to be a saint, and I certainly didn't give you the impression I was some kind of fucking Boy Scout. I do whatever is needed to protect what I value. My family. My home. *You.* Not to mention the fact that we made an agreement, and under the terms of our agreement, every inch of this body is *mine.* I'm not letting another man anywhere near you."

"You don't *own* me," I hissed back, shoving my hands hard against his chest.

Filip clamped his hands around my wrists and subdued my assault with ease. "No, I don't own you, but I do have a responsibility to protect you. You won't always like my methods, but at least I know I've done my job."

"It was a simple arrangement! It wasn't like we signed in blood or something, which was evident since you've changed the terms. And besides, it sounds like this is more about you than me. It's your duty that's important to you, your ability to control those around you, and not my actual safety that's so critical."

His nostrils flared, and I got the sense I'd struck a nerve.

He took in three even breaths before delivering a devastating defense. "My mother was killed when I was only five," he deadpanned in a hollow voice. "I spent the next half a decade being tossed from one relative to the next with zero stability in my life or control over what happened to me. I don't just have a need for control; I can't survive without it. When I feel the things that mean the most to me slipping from my control, I become crazed, and I can't think straight. You, more than anything else, cause me to lose my fucking mind."

"Filip," I breathed, overwhelmed by his admission. Hearing the reason behind his domineering behavior cast a new light on the situation but didn't change how we continued to inadvertently torment one another. "I hate that you went through that, but my life isn't yours to control. I think we may be hurting each other more than helping." I tried to explain my perspective with as much compassion as I could. The discord between us was truly neither of our faults. We were doing the best we could. I just wasn't sure it was enough to overcome the mammoth hurdles between us.

"What are you saying?" he rasped.

My eyes dropped to his full, biteable lips, and I suddenly became acutely aware of his hardness pressed against my belly. I wanted him with every fiber of my being, but I feared we'd only bring each other heartache. "I love the things we've done in this room. I love the way you touch me and the feel of you moving inside me, but the expectations are too much. I'm not sure I can give you what you need."

The muscles in Filip's jaw flexed and bulged. His lips thinned, and the glint of fire in his eyes smoldered into ash. "So, you want what we have here in this room without commitment or expectation."

Wasn't that the terms he'd initially set out? Why did it suddenly sound so callous when he said it now? Was that even what I wanted?

"I don't know exactly. I didn't necessarily have a problem with agreeing to intimate exclusivity during the arrangement," I conceded.

"Then why were you so upset about being denied access to another club? If you were okay being monogamous, you had no reason to be at that club in the first place."

"Because you took away my options. You were going to make me give you everything, and I couldn't handle that. It may sound weak, but I ran."

"And were you planning to tell me you were leaving?" His question was tinged with the faintest touch of pain.

I was hurting him. He'd opened up to me, and I was still hurting him. Would the cycle of injury between us never end? I wanted to throw myself at his feet and beg for his forgiveness, but that would only perpetuate the problem. We were both better off keeping our relationship purely physical, but I wasn't sure that was even possible.

A rogue tear slipped from my lashes and tumbled down my cheek. "I'm so sorry." My voice was no more than a cracked whisper. I didn't want him to think of me as broken, yet that was the picture I painted. My heart clenched even more tightly as the realization hit me. Maybe I was just a little more damaged than I'd wanted to admit. "I never meant to hurt you."

His stoic expression never faltered, but he released my hands and coaxed my legs up around his hips. He carried me to the bed, laying me down reverently on the soft cotton sheets. His hands went to my waist where he undid my pants and tugged the fitted fabric down my legs. I hadn't paid attention to my wardrobe choice, but it suddenly occurred to me that I'd worn pants to the Omega when I'd only ever worn dresses to the Den. Had I subconsciously made it more difficult for myself to stray from Filip when I dressed that evening? Perhaps I wasn't quite as heartless as I was acting.

All I knew was that it felt right for his hands to be the ones that lifted my blouse over my head. For his eyes to drink in the sight of my nipples peeking through the white lace of my bra.

I wanted Filip just as desperately as I needed to keep my secrets securely locked away.

But in that room, when the gentle strains of a piano played in the background and the world fell away, *all* I wanted was Filip.

All that mattered was Filip.

The emotion was too intense to share, but I could feel the sentiment shining in my eyes as he stripped me bare. A week of mental agony had been too much to process without the overflow of emotions pouring out. Now that he was there with me, dropping his last articles of clothing and pressing his naked body against mine, the relief was overwhelming.

A second tear leaked from the corner of my eye. Filip lifted my hands over my head and ran his lips down the column of my neck. When he lifted his head and met my gaze, he used one hand to gently swipe the moisture from my temple.

"Are you on birth control?" His hand slowly trailed along my jaw to my chin and down my sensitive throat. It was such an intimate gesture. Everything about this moment felt so much more personal than our times together before. I couldn't fathom how that could be. We'd argued. It was clear we weren't compatible and would likely only hurt one another, yet the confrontation had somehow pulled down a veil from between us.

Now he was wanting to have sex without protection. It was foolish and unnecessary and exactly what I wanted—to feel that connection with him re-established.

"Yes," I answered, giving my permission to feel him bare inside me.

Filip wasted no time. He pulled one of my knees up, then rocked himself inside me one inch at a time. His breathing shuddered while I gasped, in awe of how perfectly our bodies fit together. My insides felt stretched and full in the most delicious way. I lifted my hands to wrap around his neck, but he stopped me, taking my wrists back into one of his hands and securing them above me.

His body hovered over mine, filling me and soothing away all the torment from the days before, but he never lowered himself close enough for my lips to seize his. I desperately wanted to taste him—to feel his velvet tongue glide against mine—but it hadn't escaped me that we'd never kissed. And while one of the many barriers between us had fallen, others were still firmly in place. I had essentially told him that he hadn't earned my trust, but it would seem that the reverse was true. I had not proven worthy of his faith in me.

That hairline crack in my heart blistered open further.

Of all the people I was close to, Filip had become the very last person I wanted to let down. I'd hurt and disappointed him, and that sin felt unforgivable.

He wouldn't let me kiss him or hold him, so I did the only thing I could. I wrapped my legs around his middle and met his every thrust. I held his fierce stare and allowed him to see inside me to the depth of my remorse.

I wanted to be worthy of him. I wanted to please him yet maintain my own autonomy, but I didn't know how to achieve those two things concurrently. Could it be I hadn't given us a fair chance? My baggage might have made me oversensitive to the threat of being controlled. Could I find a way to keep Filip in my life? Would he even want to stay with me when he learned the darkest of my secrets?

"Camilla," he called softly in a strained voice. "Stay here with me. Don't lose yourself in those thoughts of yours." He knew. He sensed my panic and had drawn me from the edge.

I discarded my worries and focused on the delicious rhythm of our bodies. His flexing abdominals and the tempting way his chin pushed toward me with each thrust, almost as if he craved my taste just as much as I craved his.

He lowered his head to suck one of my nipples into his mouth, tugging the sensitive flesh taut before releasing it with a pop. I moaned, and my internal muscles clenched, chasing the cliffside that remained just out of reach. Sensing my desperation, Filip increased his speed, hissing when my muscles clamped down impossibly hard.

"*Yes*, Filip. Yes!" My eyes shot to the ceiling, but all I saw was a blinding white light as my body plummeted into an abyss of pleasure. I fell endlessly, lost in another dimension.

Filip squeezed me closer, burying his face in my hair as his body found its own release buried inside me. His lips drifted down and hovered over the spot at the base of my neck that had only just healed from our last joining. Though I was still drunk on my own release, I was aware enough to sense what he was doing and angle my head to give him room. To encourage him to mark me. Instead, all I received was a hollow sense of disappointment. Filip pulled away and rolled us over, situating me close against his side while he lay on his back, eyes trained on the ceiling.

We lay like that for minute after minute. Neither of us said a word.

What we'd just shared had been more than sex, but there was still so much to resolve.

"Where does this leave us?" His voice was hollow steel, cold and empty.

My whispered reply was just as broken. "I don't know."

CHAPTER 13

Filip

How was it possible to cover so much ground yet resolve nothing? In fact, I was more confused than ever. Camilla and I had parted the night before without any promises or new understandings, and I'd spent every minute since wondering what it all meant. Nearly a day later, I was still lost in thought parked along the curb at my brother Gabe's house. For almost ten minutes, I'd sat in the dark searching for answers.

I couldn't believe Camilla had tried to get into the Omega. Every time I thought about what she'd tried to do, my fists clenched with the need to tear something apart. Or someone. She'd been willing to walk away without a word, and I couldn't have done anything to stop her. I wasn't sure if I was angrier at her or my own lack of control over the situation.

Normally, I was excellent at reading people, but I never expected her to abandon our arrangement without telling me. We didn't just have an understanding regarding the club; our connection ran far deeper. There was no doubt she felt it too, yet she was willing to throw it all away.

Is that really so hard for you to understand? Hadn't you done the same thing when you discovered how much you wanted her? You avoided her for a solid week.

Fuck.

She had panicked just like I had. My overwhelming emotions had sent me running from her. I'd never considered pushing her away entirely, but what I'd done was in the same vein as her attempted escape. The question was, did she truly want freedom, or were her actions defensive in nature? Was she pushing me away out of fear—to keep me from learning about her past?

I had no idea.

What I did know was that she was a skittish rabbit ready to bolt at the faintest whiff of danger. I could ease off my domineering tendencies if I could trust she wouldn't run, but how did I get to that point when she was so unpredictable? One of us had to make a sacrifice, or we'd never get anywhere.

Was there any possible way for us to find middle ground?

Camilla and I had connected on another level in that bed. We'd expressed our remorse physically. Our pain and frustration. What we'd shared had been a deep level of communication, not just sex. Something so pure and raw was surely a sign of our rightness. Yes, we'd hurt one another, but it was never out of malice. We never meant each other any harm.

The road to hell was paved with good intentions.

My father had never intended for my mother to get hurt, but that didn't stop her from being shot. Just because Camilla and I didn't want to hurt one another didn't mean the pain would stop. Was I perpetuating the problem by not letting her go?

During the past week, whenever I envisioned her, a drowning sensation crept in to constrict around my chest.

The fear of losing her.

The fear of loving her.

The two grappled for dominance, severing me into two minds warring against one another. A schizophrenic pendulum swinging closer and closer to madness. If I made a push to claim her, I would grow more invested and risk utter annihilation. If I walked away now to save myself the misery, I had a terrible premonition that I would be abandoning an intrinsic part of my own soul.

Her tears had been evidence that she was just as torn as I was.

She didn't want to push me away, but she also didn't want to commit. To bind herself to me or open up about her past. She wanted the sex and our time at the club without any further entanglements.

I wasn't sure that was an option for me anymore.

Camilla would be all or nothing. If I was willing to push past my own fears and bind myself to her, I refused to share. I wouldn't just want her body or our time in that room.

I would want all of her.

Every ounce of her perfection and each painful crack that lay beneath.

If I was willing to take the chance.

If I was willing to risk my own heart when she had explicitly told me she wasn't willing to give her own. I'd been known to play the odds, but never when my life was at stake. Was I willing to gamble my sanity on the off chance that Camilla would change her mind?

My father always said to listen when a man tells you who he is. Camilla had told me she was willing to walk away if I pushed her for more. It would be my own fault if I expected anything different. If the only way I could proceed in any sort of relationship with her was to have all of her, and that was something she would never give, then I was left with no options.

I would have to cut ties before it was too late.

My mood instantly descended into darkness, and I decided I would bow out of dinner with my family. I had no desire to be around anyone.

Banging on the car window told me I'd narrowly missed my opportunity to flee. Matteo peered through the window with a smirk, amused that he'd startled me.

There was no backing out now.

"What the fuck, man?" I groused at him as I stepped from the car.

"You were sitting in the dark like some kind of fucking creeper. You're lucky the neighbors haven't called the cops."

If he only knew the extent of my stalker tendencies lately.

"Jesus, you're a pain in my ass." I shook my head and turned to his wife. "Hey, Maria. You're looking lovely, as always."

"Fuck off," she grumbled back at me.

"What the hell did I do to piss you off?"

Matteo chuckled. "She's outgrowing her maternity clothes and couldn't find anything to wear."

"As if being pregnant doesn't make you feel enormous enough, they don't make the clothes sufficiently expandable to last the whole pregnancy. It's ridiculous."

"Well, only about two months left. That's not too long," I offered in an attempt at reassurance.

Matteo cut his eyes to me, then shook his head before walking toward the house.

Maria's eyes went feral. "Not too long? I ought to break both your kneecaps so you end up in a wheelchair, and then we can talk about time, you insensitive *prick*." She pushed past me and followed her husband to the house, muttering, "Indigestion and pissing myself. Can't sleep and my fucking back aches all the time..."

My bad. I hadn't realized I was walking through a minefield.

Gabe opened the door and welcomed us inside. He was the middle brother, although he and Matteo were so close in age that they were always a package deal. At five and seven years older than me, I'd always been the odd man out.

Gabe never wanted anything to do with the mafia and Dad's dangerous lifestyle. He'd gone to school and settled down. His wife, Mia, was a great woman, and they had two adorable kids. I was happy for him and glad that despite our occupational differences, we still remained close.

"Hey, man, it's been a while." I hugged my brother and kissed his wife's cheek.

"A month." Mia grinned. "You need to come around more often. The kids ask about you all the time."

"Yeah, yeah. Nona coming over?"

Nona was my maternal grandmother who became a cornerstone in our family when my mother died. She took in my brothers when my father was working. I stayed with her and my brothers at times, but since I was so much younger, I was often sent to stay with aunts and cousins. Nona had six children and ten grandkids, so she did her best to help when she could. I understood as an adult why it was easier to keep a ten- and twelve-year-old rather than a five-year-old, but when I was little, all I wanted was to stay with my brothers.

"Not this time. She had a cold this week and wasn't feeling up to getting out."

"She okay?" She was usually in good health, but at eighty-three, she was getting up there.

"Yeah, I checked on her earlier today. She's doing a lot better."

"Good. She needs anything, you let me know. I'm happy to help."

We filtered into the dining room and took our seats while Gabe and Mia brought out the food.

"Filip, I almost forgot," said Maria. "My parents are throwing a dinner party this coming Friday for Sofia's birthday. They want you to come, said you're part of the family." She rolled her eyes.

"Me?" That was a surprise. I wasn't sure I'd considered myself a part of their family, but I had seen a lot of the Genoveses lately.

"Yeah, Dad said you've been a big help to the family watching over Giada. With you being Matteo's right hand and brother, they want you to come."

Matteo gave me a pointed look as if he expected me to decline. A personal invite from Enzo Genovese wasn't something to shrug off. It annoyed me that he thought I wouldn't grasp the importance of such an offer.

"I'd be honored. Just let me know when and where." I smiled at her, then shot a glare at my brother.

A family dinner with the Genoveses.

A plan suddenly came together. I would bring a date to dinner

I didn't want to add more grief to our already turbulent relationship, but this would be the perfect opportunity to give Camilla a small dose of reality. It would be a last-ditch effort to see what she truly wanted. If she maintained her need for distance, I wouldn't ask her to change. I would listen to what she was telling me and make a clean break before either of us was irrevocably injured.

If things didn't work out, I'd have to find a way to convince Dante to keep her from the club. She would eventually accept her ousting and settle down with a decent, respectable man.

The thought made my skin crawl.

Would seeing me with another woman make her jealous? I didn't want to hurt her, but I wanted her to realize she needed me. I was the perfect reflection of everything she wanted, if she allowed herself to see it. It was manipulative, but I wasn't the type of man to shy away from a challenge. I could see with more clarity now that I wanted Camilla—all of her—despite my fears. This was likely the only way to bring her around. Learning she'd gone to the Omega had been instrumental in changing my perspective. A similar reality check might be just as effective on her end.

Whether it was owed to simply having a plan or my sincere belief in my success, my spirits lifted. I wouldn't focus on the possibility that Camilla might be indifferent to seeing me with another woman. Holding onto such a tenuous hope was danger-ous, but I couldn't fully irradicate the emotion. Hope was insid-ious—the birthplace of expectation and anticipation—and the foundation of crippling disappointment.

I would cross that bridge only when I had no other option.

When I considered who I might bring with me, Liana was quick to surface as a prime candidate. I'd known her for years and didn't think a night out would confuse our relationship if I was clear about my intent. The last thing I needed was more rela-tionship complications.

As soon as dinner was over, I would send her a text and set my plan in motion. By the end of the weekend, Camilla would either be mine or remain a painful memory of my past.

CHAPTER 14

Camilla

I arrived at Sofia's birthday dinner a few minutes early. I'd needed to get out of the house in order to stop thinking about Filip. I hadn't heard from him and wasn't sure where we stood. It was my fault. I'd put him in an awkward position, and I knew it. My emotions were such a jumbled mess that I didn't know what to think. Nothing about the Den had gone as I'd expected.

It was a frigid February evening. I had dressed for a casual family dinner out—fitted slacks with booties and a devilishly soft cashmere sweater. I piled my hair in a messy bun and added long dangly earrings. I wanted to look cute, but comfort was my primary goal for a night with the family.

"Hey, Ma. How are you?" I greeted my mother when I arrived by giving her a warm hug. I wasn't normally big on hugging, but I'd hoped to stave off impending questions about Mass by getting on her good side.

"I'm good, honey. You look beautiful." She smiled with more enthusiasm than normal.

"You okay?"

She glanced to where some of the others were chatting and pulled me aside. "I decided to submit my information to the adoption database, the website that links adopted kids with their birth parents, and I consented to the release of my information. They'll let him know, but he may not respond. We just have to wait and see." Her hands clutched one another, twisting in a worried knot that projected just how anxious she was on the inside.

"That's really exciting, Ma. I hope you're able to connect one of these days."

Her smile faltered. "I know I've been a little intense lately, wanting you and Giada to visit and all. It's just that having this all out in the open has made me a little emotional. I just want to have *all* my babies close for once."

I hadn't considered how hard it would be for her to have a kid out there, let alone to have kept it a secret. Now that the truth was out, she probably had twenty years of repressed emotions bubbling to the surface.

"I'd say I understand, but in all truth, I can't imagine what it's like. I think you're doing an amazing job sorting through it, though. Let's hope he reaches out. You're not the only one who wants to meet him."

My mother's face lit with happiness. "You really want to meet him?"

"Of course! He's my brother. I've never had one of those." I was being honest but threw in the last part to be cheeky. I wasn't sure she even heard it.

She threw her arms around me and squeezed. "Thank you, Cami," she breathed through an onslaught of emotion.

"We're family, Mama. Always." Was it possible for me to cry

twice in twenty-four hours? My sinuses appeared interested in finding out. I breathed through the burning in the back of my throat and used a smile to ward off the impending emotions when we pulled away.

"Okay, enough before we ruin our makeup. Let's grab our seats."

I ended up sitting next to Giada, which I normally preferred because she carried the conversation. Tonight, she was so preoccupied with ogling her new boyfriend that she could hardly hold a thought.

"You keep staring at him like that, and I'm going to have to wipe the drool from your cheek." I clinked our glasses together and downed the rest of my wine.

"If something that scrumptious was yours, wouldn't you want to lick the wrapping?" The salacious innuendo in her voice caught me off guard enough that I choked on my last swallow of wine, sending her into a fit of laughter. My own laughter made the coughing worse. Fortunately, someone arriving drew everyone's attention from me, so I was able to recover without the heat of a spotlight.

"Check it out," Giada hissed next to my ear. "Filip just showed up, and he's got a gorgeous redhead with him."

My entire body fossilized to pure stone as I lifted my gaze to the newest arrivals. There was Filip, looking positively edible, and on his arm was Liana, the seductive goddess who hated my guts. Not only had he not told me he was coming to one of *my* family functions but he'd also brought *her.*

She shot me a satisfied smirk.

That bitch.

My mother rushed over to welcome them. I used the distraction to steady myself and school my features. The last thing I wanted was either of them seeing how profoundly they'd upset me.

"Is something going on between you and Filip?" Giada asked in a hushed whisper.

I did my best impression of a woman utterly confused. "We hardly know one another." I glanced over at his sly smile as he helped his date into her seat. "Besides, look at how cocky and … and smarmy he is. He's probably been with a different woman every night." The words tasted bitter on my tongue. I didn't believe a word of what I said, but between my anger and the cavalier reputation Filip had garnered, it had seemed like the right thing to say to avoid suspicion.

My family knowing about Filip and me was one thing, but no way would I allow him to humiliate me in front of them. If they could see on the outside how wounded I felt on the inside, I'd be mortified.

Why are you so upset? Didn't you just tell him no commitments?

Yeah, but I didn't think he'd run out and fuck someone else. I told him I was okay with being exclusive. I let him see me cry.

But you also pushed him away. You suggested the relationship may not work.

Yeah, but Liana? Why did it have to be someone from the club? Now I would spend the rest of the night wondering if he was having sex with her. She'd indicated he wasn't as monogamous in the past as he'd implied. Had he grown frustrated with my mixed signals and moved to greener pastures?

My stomach climbed to my throat about the same time as obnoxious laughter assaulted my ears from down the table. Liana tipped her head back and cackled at something Matteo had said. Was she part hyena? What the hell was up with her laugh? How could he stand that?

The grating sound clawed at my ears every few minutes throughout dinner. Chinese water torture would have been less painful. I could only take so much.

As soon as the dinner plates were bussed away, I placed my

napkin on the table and stood. "Sofia, I'm so sorry I have to cut out early, but I told someone I'd meet up with them tonight."

I gave my cousin a hug and did my best to politely ignore the protests of my leaving. Meeting someone had been a total fabrication, but I'd needed a reason to get out of there. I couldn't stand seeing Filip and Liana together one second longer.

My feet carried me without instruction from my head, weaving through the restaurant and depositing me into a passing cab. I gave the driver the address of the club, unsure of my intent but not knowing where else to go. It seemed pathetic to lick my wounds at home alone. At the very least, I'd go to the club and have a drink. Or ten.

I was growing more comfortable with the club already, walking past people openly fucking in the main room with a mildly curious glance. I ordered a vodka tonic at the bar and had only taken my first sip when Dante joined me.

"I'm not sure Filip will be in tonight, if that's why you're here."

"Actually, I'm on my own tonight. Just thought I'd relax for a bit after a long day." I lifted my drink in explanation.

He studied me for a drawn-out second, the weight of his stare warming me. "In that case, the Den is at your service." He gave me a seated bow and a playful smirk.

"Good. Don't let me drink alone. People will talk," I teased, forcing myself not to sound as depressed as I felt.

Dante ordered himself a drink. "Long day, huh. Care to tell me about it? I'm an excellent listener."

"Not really. I'm here to drown my troubles, not wallow in them." The vodka tonic was quickly doing its job, warming my insides and lifting my spirits.

"Well, then. What shall we discuss? The weather? Perhaps the current political climate?"

Damn those dimples. They were utterly irresistible.

"How about you and Filip. I understand you two have been

friends for a long time. I'd love to hear how you met." I hadn't meant to bring up Filip, but the two men were so drastically different. I was intrigued to hear how their friendship had started.

Dante leaned back in his seat and pursed his lips. "I'm not sure it will cast either of us in a flattering light."

"Oh, no. You can't say something like that and not tell me more," I goaded.

"You win," he said with only a mild amount of reluctance. "It all began when Filip started an underground fight club at our high school."

My jaw dropped to my chest. "You're shitting me."

He sipped from his drink and studied me. "No, unfortunately. Filip has always had a taste for trouble."

"Did you guys get together just to beat each other up?" The concept completely evaded me. I could understand the perks of a spanking with an orgasm, but a full-on fight was another matter entirely.

"I wasn't exactly a member of the club. I had a beef with Filip, and when I heard about the fights, I decided to use the opportunity to show him how I felt." He was so nonchalant about wanting to fight someone. Men were so weird.

"I don't understand how that led you to being friends."

"Well, we pulverized each other. Went at it for ages, but we were an even match. His buddies pulled us apart and told me I needed to come by more often. I discovered how therapeutic a good fight was, and we formed a certain respect for one another."

"I can't say I've ever befriended someone I wanted to beat up."

Dante's eyes lowered to half-mast. "I bet I can do a lot of things that you'd find interesting."

I shook my head with a chuckle.

"See, just like that," he crooned. "I made you laugh. Somehow, I suspect that's not always an easy feat."

I sobered but offered a gentle smile. "You're not wrong. Thanks for cheering me up, Dante. This was exactly what I needed."

His hand found my knee and gave me a light squeeze. "Anytime."

The dynamic between us was quickly shifting as his hand lingered. Was he flirting? If he was flirting, was that such a bad thing? No, but I wasn't going to return the energy just to spite Filip. It wasn't fair to either of them.

"Okay." My cheeks flooded with heat. "I better get going. I'm sure a good night's sleep will turn everything around. Thank you, again." I slid from my chair and set a few dollars on the bar.

He followed my lead. "Let me get you a cab."

I smiled graciously before walking to the elevator. When we were alone together in the enclosed space, I was engulfed in awkward awareness. Had it been a mistake to have a drink with him? I didn't want to lead him on. He seemed so cool and unaffected, but could that be a front? Instances like these gave me the distinct sense he was exponentially more invested in gaining my attention than he let on. Was it my imagination?

My self-doubt hissed at me that he was simply being polite. *Not every man is in love with you, Camilla.*

Great. Thanks for the vote of confidence.

I tried to breathe through my insecurities and not borrow trouble. Dante walked me outside and flagged down a cab.

"Come back tomorrow, will you? Our visits have been the highlight of my evenings." He opened the car door for me and waited for my reply.

I had no idea what to say. "I'll have to see. I talked to my mom about visiting out on Staten Island." I placed my hand on the door to slip inside when my eyes were drawn down the sidewalk about fifty feet away to where Filip stood next to his car. I held his furious stare, not giving him an ounce of emotion before smiling up at Dante and slipping inside the car. "Thank you again, and enjoy the rest of your night."

The driver took off as soon as the door was closed.

My pulse pounded in my throat. I kept my eyes trained straight ahead, not allowing my gaze to stray to Filip—the man who crafted my fantasies and tormented my every waking thought. If anyone had a reason to be angry, it was me, not him. What he'd done had been insensitive. I didn't care if the parameters of our relationship were murky; bringing *that* woman to my family dinner was out of line.

Filip was angry he'd seen me with Dante? Good. Hopefully, the incident would help him realize what an absolute ass he'd been. He could fester in his anger, for all I cared.

CHAPTER 15
Filip

"You better not have laid a fucking *finger* on her," I shot at Dante, charging toward him on the sidewalk. A couple of passersby gawked at me, but I didn't give a shit. I was pure livid rage.

"Despite what you may think, you don't own her. She has every right to come to the club and do what she pleases." Dante squared his shoulders, crossing his arms over his chest defensively.

I only pulled up when we were toe-to-toe. My righteous stare assaulted him inches from his face. "Camilla is *mine*, so don't pretend to know anything about her or our relationship." It wasn't exactly the truth, but Dante didn't know that.

A car door slammed somewhere behind me. Dante tilted his head to take in the angry redhead I'd completely forgotten about. I'd stepped onto the curb to help her from the car when I'd spotted Dante with Camilla. All thoughts of Liana had instantly evaporated.

"You fucking prick," he spat at me. "No wonder she was so upset." Dante shoved my chest. I had to take a step backward to remain upright. "You shit on everything you touch, don't you?"

I got straight back in his face and clenched his shirt in my fist. "What the fuck is that supposed to mean?"

"It means she only has eyes for you," he sneered. "But you treat her like shit. You tell her she can't be with anyone else, then you traipse around with *Liana*? What the fuck is wrong with you?"

I'd seen how upset Camilla had been at the dinner. There was truth in what Dante had said, no matter how much it pissed me off. The problem was, he didn't know the whole story. He didn't know she was the one who had insisted on boundaries. That she had attempted to go fuck men at another club.

I released my hold on him and shoved him away. "Not that it's any of your business, but it's complicated."

"My club, my business. My *friend*, my business."

I glared at him. "The only reason I brought Liana here was because she needed a ride after dinner. I wasn't planning on touching her. We've known each other for a long time, Dante. Have you ever known me to be intentionally cruel to a woman?"

"You used to beat the shit out of guys for fun. How am I supposed to know what might get your rocks off?"

"Don't act all high and mighty. If we hadn't been such an even match, you would have killed me that first time we fought. You're no saint, Capello."

Liana strolled over and stepped between us, propping her hands on her hips. "If you two are done making a scene, we should take this inside."

Dante and I never took our eyes from one another.

"No need," I said. "The only reason I was here was to drop you off." I finally turned to Liana, whose green eyes narrowed to twin jade daggers. Rightfully so. "Thank you again for joining me tonight."

"I'm happy to help you any time." The harsh angles of her face softened. "You sure you don't want to come inside? I could help you relax—let go of all of that tension."

My lips thinned. "Appreciate the offer, but that's not on the table anymore. Have a good night." I shot a parting glare at Dante before walking away. The club didn't hold the slightest interest to me when the one woman I wanted wasn't inside, and that infuriated me. I didn't want to want her as much as I did, but there was no escaping it.

I spent the rest of the night agonizing over whether I'd made the wrong move by taking Liana to the dinner. I hadn't considered that she'd run straight into Dante's arms. I debated whether I should go to her and insist she belonged to me because I refused to accept anything less. I doubted pressing the matter tonight would be effective, though she'd given every sign of encouragement. She'd stoked those treasonous whispers of hope when she'd been so clearly upset about Liana. Had she truly wanted no strings attached, she wouldn't have cared if I brought a date. Her cold stare as she slipped into a cab told me she didn't just care. She was outraged.

The memory soothed the angry voices in my head, bolstering my confidence that she was mine, regardless of her claims otherwise. I'd give her the night to cool down before going to her.

Eventually, my eyes closed, and my thoughts settled, but Camilla still haunted my dreams. The gut-wrenching scene was more nightmare than a dream. I walked into the club where I found Dante fucking Camilla. She yelled that it was all my fault. That I'd forced her hand by refusing to maintain our boundaries.

I'd never experienced so much rage in a dream.

When I woke, the sticky remnants of malignant emotions

coated me on the inside. I waded through the tar-like substance, unable to shake free of it. Something about her being with Dante was far worse than simply losing her. I could deal with moving on, but I couldn't stand the possibility of her being with Dante when I couldn't have her.

I had to talk to her. I wasn't sure what I would say, but the nauseating unease from the dream demanded I do something.

I arrived at her apartment at just after ten that Saturday morning, my hands straining and flexing with pent-up frustration. Camilla had been so upset with me that I didn't warn her I was coming. I didn't want her trying to avoid me and denying me the chance to say my piece.

When I knocked on the door, she opened it a crack and peeked out, keeping herself hidden from view.

"Filip, what are you doing here? I'm still in my pajamas."

I pressed my knuckles against the door and eased it open, holding her gaze captive as she allowed me inside. "I hardly think modesty is appropriate between us."

She held her arms tightly crossed over her middle, her oversized T-shirt scrunched to hide the front. "It's not that," she fussed. "This just isn't exactly the outfit I would have preferred you to see, aside from the fact that I don't feel like seeing you at all."

"Camilla, put your hands down," I ordered softly, curious what she could possibly want to hide.

Her gaze lifted to mine, then she heaved a sigh and rolled her eyes before dropping her arms to her sides. The tattered shirt unfolded to reveal a faded set of screen-printed Care Bears. "Happy now?"

Fuck, she was adorable.

I coveted moments like this just as equally as I yearned for our times at the club. How could I possibly push her away and lose it all? Risk someone like Dante seizing what should be mine?

I snagged the shirt in my fingers and tugged her close to me. "You could be wearing a parka with hospital socks, and I'd still think you were the most gorgeous woman I'd ever fucking seen." The truth was a relief. She could run if she had to, but I couldn't deny my desire.

Her lips parted, and her gaze became unguarded before she caught herself and slammed the gate back down. "Is that what you told Liana, too?" she said in a tone so cold it tightened my chest.

I reluctantly released her, my muscles tensing for the possibility of a fight. "Not even remotely. But I am here to address what happened last night."

Camilla's arms crossed again over her chest, but this time, it had nothing to do with her shirt.

"I know things between us are complicated, but I need you to stay away from Dante while we sort through them." I knew immediately that my tactic had been an error, but the words were out before I could stop them.

"I can't believe you're telling me to stay away from him when you were the one who brought that vile woman to my family dinner." Her voice was reinforced concrete without even a hint of softness.

Definitely shouldn't have led with the Dante issue.

I tried not to lash out in response, but my frustration raked along my skin. "Just listen for a minute. I brought a date because you were insistent that I give you space. I never touched her. We're just friends."

Her eyes narrowed to angry slits. "Just friends? That's certainly not how she described it when she showed up at my bank the other day. She's a real piece of work, that Liana."

"Liana came to your office?" My agitation was suddenly doused in a chilling bucket of unease. "What did she want?"

"She told me keeping you to myself was a mistake. That you

preferred to keep your options open." Between the hostile way she imparted this information and her injured response to Liana acting as my date, I was feeling more and more confident that Camilla wasn't as married to her freedom as she wanted to believe.

In my bones, I could sense that this was a pivotal moment in our relationship. That what I said and did next would either drive a permanent wedge between us or help bind her to me. Part of me wanted to bend her over the sofa and fuck her until she admitted she was mine. While I was more emotional around her than any other woman I'd met, I was levelheaded enough to know that the Neanderthal strategy was probably a mistake.

I wove my hands behind her neck on either side and pulled her in close, enjoying the way her breath caught at my nearness. "The last time we were together, you had just taken steps to fuck other men and considered walking away from me. You were furious that I'd overstepped my bounds and insisted you didn't want to give up control of your life. I told you that I've been wrestling with my own struggles about how I feel for you and fighting off the insane desire for you that thrums in my veins. I didn't want to accept it, but I think about you all the fucking time. Learning about you going to the Omega made me realize there's no halfway for me. Either you're mine, or you aren't. I won't share you. If I can't have all of you, it would be best for us to sever ties. You insinuated the same last week when you said all we did was hurt one another. I refused to accept that without being sure there was no other option. Liana was my way of testing if you truly believed we were better off apart. If I had any reason to believe you were willing to be mine, that would change everything. I'm not asking for a commitment, just that you're willing to try."

She bit down on her lower lip, her brows deeply furrowed. "It was a test?"

I nodded.

"I don't know what to say. Part of me wants to kick you for hurting me, *again*, but I guess I understand why you did it."

"We're complicated people, Camilla, but at the end of the day, it's clear we want one another. My blood sings for you, and I know you want me too. There's no time limit for us to sort this out, but I want us to try. I'm willing to set aside my expectations and fears to make room for you in my life if you can do the same. It would mean a mutual commitment to actually give this relationship a chance. A *real* relationship. Tell me you'll try, little warrior. Please tell me you won't give up."

Her brows knotted, and she worried her lower lip between her teeth. "I want to, but what if I can't give you all of me? My past is..."

"I won't demand answers from you. The only thing I would need aside from you is the reassurance that you'll stay away from Dante. Whether you think it's absurd or not, it's important to me. I won't go near Liana or any other woman. I promise."

She searched my face with uncertainty before finally nodding. "I think I can do that. But what about if I'm at the club? I don't want to be rude to him."

I lowered my hands and allowed a few inches of space between us. "I'm not planning to allow you time alone there without me. I don't want that to scare you away, but it's the truth. No more hiding or deception. From now on, I show you exactly who I am and speak from my heart." I waited for her to rebuff me, but the argument never came.

"Okay," she whispered.

I was flooded with relief. That tiny spark of hope leapt to life, sending sultry flames licking through my veins. The prospect was terrifying and exhilarating at the same time. I had a sudden urge to kiss her, but petty fear kept me from bringing our lips together. We were about to take the first step forward and attempt a real relationship. The ground was still shaky beneath us. Despite my bold words, I was riddled with uncertainty.

"Can you meet me at the club on Thursday? Eight p.m.?" The effort of restraint and my growing lust shredded my voice to the coarse grinding of gravel.

Camilla nodded in a distracted haze that made me want to pound on my chest and roar with masculine pride. She was mine in every way that counted, whether she knew it or not.

I LEFT her place feeling like I could breathe for the first time in weeks. Our situation wasn't totally resolved, but we were working in the right direction.

Matteo texted, asking me to come by while I was in the car, so I rerouted myself to his place. I made certain to knock, unsure if Maria was there. She'd made it clear in that homicidal way of hers early on in their relationship that I no longer had an open invitation at my brother's place. I enjoyed having my balls intact more than I wanted to fight over the matter, so I made sure to follow the new rules.

My brother opened the door. "That was quick. You in the area?"

"Yeah. I was out running a few errands. What's up?"

He led me to the living area and took a seat. "First, I wanted to remind you that Wednesday is Mom's birthday."

"I'm twenty-eight, Teo. You don't have to remind me like I'm a kid. I was well aware of the date." Regardless of his good intentions, his continued paternal treatment made me resentful of the smallest of gestures. Each year we got together on our mother's birthday and had dinner to honor her. It was a tradition I'd participated in for over two decades. I didn't need a fucking reminder.

"Don't get all bent out of shape. I helped raise you; I can't just turn that shit off. I was the one who had to keep you from being expelled when your little fight club was discovered at school. I talked to the cops when you went joyriding in old man Carlson's Buick and kept him from pressing charges."

"Well, I'm grown now, so try. I haven't needed your help in a long-ass time." I sounded like a fucking crybaby, but I couldn't seem to help it. He might have seen the reminder as a small thing, but all the small things added up to him not seeing me as a responsible adult. If I didn't point them out, he'd never change the way he perceived me.

He stared at me across the heavy silence in the room. "Fair enough. I also wanted to update you on the cartel situation. Our guys were able to track down a single dealer responsible for the bad product. We got him to talk, and he confirmed it was Vargas behind it."

"You able to find out his game plan?"

"He wants chaos in the city. Thinks it's the best way to steal a piece of the pie. He hasn't pulled his troops back to Mexico, and until he does, he'll continue to be a threat."

"We know where they're hiding?"

"They're scattered, which makes it almost impossible to round them up. I'm not sure we can strike back until he either returns or makes his next move."

I shook my head, unwilling to settle. "I disagree. We got eyes and ears all over this damn city. If the families work together, we can flush them out."

"We're working on it, but they're like fucking ants burrowed underground. We do have one means of leverage if it comes to it, but you know we try not to involve women and children. Vargas makes one more wrong move, though, and we may have no choice."

The man had left his wife and daughter in the city. We'd

learned his wife had been living in a tequila bottle for years, so we hadn't worried about her being an issue, and the daughter was only a kid. I hated to think of using them, but the safety of our families was our first priority.

CHAPTER 16
Camilla

F ilip said he hadn't touched Liana, and I believed him. I
was surprised at the warm flood of relief that melted the
hard pit in my stomach. As I lay in bed the night before,
I realized that going to the Omega had been a cowardly attempt
at escape. It had been more about my fear of telling Filip about
my past than anything else—avoiding the threat of my evolving
emotions and potentially opening up to Filip. My response to his
emotional admission only confirmed that I'd been lying to
myself. I'd been elated when he confessed his feelings for me.

Over the past week, I'd been so concentrated on avoiding my
fears that I hadn't considered what it would truly be like to lose
him. The sight of Filip with Liana had rocked me to my core. And
once he explained his motivations, it was hard to blame him for
his actions.

So, where did that leave us? We were going to see where a
relationship between us could go, but that still left so many ques-

tions unanswered. The most crucial on my mind was whether I could share my past with him. If telling him the truth would remove the main obstacle between us, would it be so terrible to tell him? What would be the worst that would happen? He'd reject me, and I'd be no worse off than if I had walked away on my own.

I didn't like the prospect, but it wasn't so terrible as it had seemed a week before.

Filip was adamant about his feelings for me. The least I could do was trust him with the truth and give him the opportunity to respond without making my own assumptions. I didn't think he'd outright reject me; that wasn't the heart of my fear. I worried he'd think I was damaged, and I couldn't stand for him to coddle me. I didn't want to see my past reflected in his eyes every time he looked at me.

Deep down, I knew I needed to tell him, but I also needed a boost of encouragement. I wasn't normally the type to seek out advice, but when Giada asked to do lunch on Sunday, I decided she might be able to help me sort my feelings. She'd spent a good deal of time with him when he was assigned to protect her, so she just might understand my predicament.

We got a booth at a quaint little diner, and I kept my conversation light at first to keep her from being suspicious. When the opportunity presented itself to inject a harmless question, I jumped at the chance.

"I was curious. What are your impressions of Filip?"

Her eyes lit up like a kid spotting an Easter egg. "I knew something was up with you two."

"There's not. I was just curious after seeing him with that woman."

"Whatever. I was surprised she could still walk out of there considering the daggers you shot her direction all evening."

Oh, God. Had I been that obvious?

"I was just annoyed that he brought some stranger with him to a family dinner." I waved my hand at her dismissively, but she didn't buy it for a minute.

"He's hot. You should totally go for it."

I sighed. There was no use hiding from her. "It's complicated. We both have our issues, and I'm not sure we'd be compatible in the end."

"Why not?"

"Well, he's so damn domineering. He wants to be involved in every aspect of my life, and I can't decide if I'm willing to give him that kind of access."

"You're just scared. The men in our world juggle some serious shit. It may come across as controlling, but they're just looking out for us. I'd say he must care for you a lot if he's wanting more of you. These guys don't open themselves up like that for just anyone."

"I just don't think it's that easy to decide. How much should we be willing to compromise in a relationship? Maybe it's better to keep some things private. Do you tell Javi *everything*?"

"Yeah, pretty much."

I groaned.

Giada leaned back in her seat and shrugged. "Every relationship is different. You're the one who has to set boundaries you can live with. But I have to say, I'm kind of surprised this is an issue. I kind of assumed you didn't have any secrets because you were so perfect and never stepped out of line. Hell, you were such a rule follower that you were Principal Hale's golden child. There was even speculation you were a spy for him."

"People make stupid assumptions when they shouldn't. I have just as many secrets as the next girl." My acidic response was too harsh for her not to take notice. Giada cocked her head as if she were going to delve into the topic, but I cut her off. "Look, I'm not up for talking about that now. I've got too much on my plate dealing with Filip."

Her lips thinned, and she studied me intently before responding. "All right. But tell me this. How deep are you in with him?"

I lifted my eyes to hers. "Too deep to see my way out."

CHAPTER 17

Filip

"There's my little Filip! Come give your nona a hug. I haven't seen you in ages." She pulled me into her deceptively strong arms, not deterred in the slightest by our size difference. Being a foot shorter than me had never stopped her from calling me little, and she was the one person who could do that without pissing me off.

"Hey, Nona. Glad you were able to come. I heard you weren't feeling so great last week." I gave her an extra squeeze before releasing her.

Her face creased with emotion. "You know I wouldn't miss this day for anything. I just wish it wasn't so cold. I'd go take Angelina some flowers if I didn't think I'd freeze to death doing it."

When the weather cooperated, Nona visited her daughter's grave before we all gathered for dinner. She had assumed Angelina's role as mother to us boys without question when her daughter was killed. I was sure she grieved, but she did so in private, knowing we needed her strength. She was an incredible woman, and I would always be grateful she was a part of our lives.

"I'll take some over tomorrow," I offered.

She clasped my hand between her knobby fingers. "That's sweet of you. You know how much it means to me."

"I'm happy to help." I kissed her cheek. "Now, what's for dinner? I'm starved."

She grinned broadly and pulled me farther into the great room. This year, Matteo and Maria were hosting a catered meal. I didn't think Nona was thrilled that someone else had cooked, but she didn't argue with their choice. Mia helped Matteo in the kitchen while Maria sat with Gabe and our father at the table. The atmosphere was warm and inviting. In the early years, the anniversary dinner had carried heavy undertones of sadness, but that wasn't the case anymore. We all appreciated the chance to get together and celebrate a woman we'd all loved.

My lingering tension had eased after making progress with Camilla, but my father's presence never failed to strain my nerves. I wasn't sure I'd ever escape the need to prove myself to him.

"Hey, Pop. How're you doing?" I asked, shaking his hand.

There was no smoking in the apartment, but that didn't stop Valentino from keeping an unlit stogie propped on his lips.

"I can't complain. The water pressure in my building's been shit lately, but I think that's because of the new apartments they're putting in across the street. Already so many damn people in this city, but they keep squeezing more in. It's nuts." He gave off the vibe of a harmless old man, which couldn't have been farther from the truth. His trim body might have softened with age and his hairline receded until there was nothing left, but the razor-sharp glint in his eyes was there for a reason. He read between the lines and could discern a man's character in an instant.

He was also just as deadly today as he'd been twenty years before.

While he didn't have a reason to use those skills he'd honed over the years, he wouldn't blink twice if he needed to manage a situation. Once an enforcer, always an enforcer.

"You could do like Teo and get a place out in the Hamptons. There's more space out there," I suggested, knowing there was no way in hell he'd give up city living.

My father just grunted.

Matteo carried in the main dish, followed by Mia with two bowls in her hands.

"What's on the menu tonight?" Pop asked.

"We decided to have gnocchi." Matteo set the large steaming dish on the table and went back to the kitchen to retrieve another platter. Gnocchi had been Mom's favorite, so it was frequently the main course at our annual dinner. I didn't remember things like what she liked to eat or her endearing quirks. At just five years old, my memories of her were primarily based on the stories everyone told at these dinners.

While the rest of us appreciated the chance to refresh our memories of her, my father never seemed to fully escape the pain. He bore a tremendous amount of guilt about her death. As far as I could tell, he'd never let go of blaming himself.

He was supposed to die that day.

Matteo had been at lacrosse practice late into the evening. Dad usually picked him up but got sick that night, so Mom made the drive in the family car instead. An enemy had planned an attack and shot up the car, thinking they were taking out my father. I went to bed that night completely unaware that I'd never see my mother again. The next day, I was told my mother had died in a car accident, but I didn't learn the truth about her death until years later.

Our family was shattered that day. My father withdrew from us for more than a year. I was passed around my relatives, and even though I wasn't around him often and I was just a child, I could still sense the changes in my father. The seething darkness that overtook him.

Not long after Matteo turned fourteen, there was a second shift in our family dynamic. My father's anger simmered to a noxious melancholy, and the divide grew between my brothers and me. Matteo became more serious. Hardened. And Gabe began to spend more and more time away from us.

I'd only been six and had no idea what had caused the turbulence in our new normal. Not until years later when I learned about the family—the Gallo crime family and the truth behind my mother's death. I discovered my father had gone on a killing spree to avenge her murder, and Matteo had become a made man when he killed the last of the men behind the hit. It changed him, understandably. The ripple effect of my mother's death painted our lives in shades of loss long after her heart stopped beating.

The pain caused by my father's mafia connection convinced Gabe early on that the life wasn't for him. On the other hand, I decided marriage was where the danger lay. I found a source of stability and loyalty among my mafia family and was confident the absence of a wife would only strengthen me. When I was old enough to learn the business, the Gallo family was the reason I regained a relationship with my brother and, to a degree, with my father.

I belonged. I had earned a place among them.

There was nothing I cherished more in my life up until that point.

"That's good. You did good, boys," my father praised with a tremor in his voice as he took in all of us gathered around the full table. Emotion wasn't his forte, and such a display, while seemingly minor, tightened my throat.

We all took our seats around the overflowing table, and the room was bathed in a sense of fellowship, gratitude, and respect. My family was far from perfect, but times like these reminded me just how fortunate I was. That was exactly what my mother would have wanted. I might not have remembered much, but I knew she'd been a good mom. Above all, she would have wanted her family to remain close.

There was no better way to celebrate her life than by being together.

"To my Angelina," Pop began, raising his glass. "There's not a day that goes by that we don't think about you. This year, we brought a beautiful young woman into our family, and I know you would have loved how she keeps our Teo on his toes."

A warm rumble of chuckles embraced the room before he continued.

"I know you're up there watching out for each of them. Especially our little Filip. He's not so little anymore, Ang. You'd be proud. He's turning into a fine young man." Pop continued to praise Mia and Gabe along with their two kids, but I was so stunned at my father's mention of me that I hardly heard his words. I couldn't remember my father ever using the word proud when he'd spoken of me. Not once.

My throat constricted.

The room suddenly blazed with heat. I was immensely grateful when my father concluded his tribute and blessed the food. The emotions overwhelming me were diluted by the clinking of serving spoons and hum of conversation. I tried to be present but remained in a sort of haze throughout dinner.

As soon as it was reasonable, I fled the table and took residence in a living room armchair near the window. A few minutes later, Maria wandered over and leaned against the window frame, peering out over the Manhattan skyline.

"I noticed the funniest thing the other night at Sofia's birthday dinner," she mused, never looking in my direction.

"Oh, yeah?" I knew where she was going but wouldn't give her the satisfaction of owning it.

"I could have sworn my little cousin was chewing on nails from the second you walked through the door."

"Your point?" I asked dryly.

She casually glanced down, meeting my stony gaze. "Hurt Camilla, and I don't care if you are Matteo's brother, I'll make you wish you'd never heard the name Genovese."

There was a side to Maria that remained uncivilized. That feral creature peeked out at me from behind her glacial stare.

"Point made," I conceded.

If I hurt Camilla so badly that Maria got involved, I'd likely deserve whatever she dished out. She would get no resistance from me.

Matteo's phone rang across the room, drawing our attention. The caller said only a handful of words when my brother's posture stiffened.

"Be there in five." His eyes locked with mine. "We have to go."

I was on my feet in an instant and following him to the door. Maria didn't push to join us, which was a pleasant surprise. I wasn't sure what had happened, but I preferred not to complicate things with her presence. She was moody on a good day; pregnancy hormones only magnified her delightful personality.

Matteo and I said quick goodbyes and made our way to the basement garage.

"What's going on?" I asked once we were alone.

"We've got men down. Alonzo took a few guys to the warehouse that the dealer had mentioned to scope it out. All but one were shot. The authorities were called, but that's all I know."

It was never good if an ambulance had to be called. We avoided interaction with the authorities if at all possible.

As promised, we were at the scene in just over five minutes, thanks to some creative driving by my brother. Paramedics worked on one of the guys while two others lay motionless in pools of blood on the icy ground.

We walked to the men to see if there was anything to be done, but they were gone. Nothing we could do would save them. One was a soldier, but the other was Frank Alonzo, a longtime capo.

"I hope I did the right thing by calling the cops. I didn't know what else to do." A young guy came up behind us, his face drained white and blood splattered across his clothes. A soldier no older than I'd been when I first started.

Matteo clamped a hand over his shoulder. "You did fine, kid. Hard to hide a scene like this," he murmured. "I want to know everything that happened, but not here. Go home and clean up. Meet me at Angelo's in an hour, okay?"

The kid nodded, then trudged off with his head down. Behind us, the paramedics clicked a metallic gurney into place before loading their patient into the nearby ambulance.

Matteo took out his phone. "We need a cleanup crew to 51st and First Avenue." His message received, he hung up and began to walk back to the car.

"Without Alonzo, we've got a gap in leadership." It might not be the greatest time for this conversation, but it was fitting, nonetheless.

"I'm aware."

"I want to take his place. I've been at your side for years now, Teo. It's time for me to take my place as a capo."

He huffed out a sardonic laugh. "Can't wait to get away from me, can you?"

I grasped his arm and brought us to a stop. "You can't keep treating me like a kid brother chained at your hip," I shot at him, years of frustration getting the better of me.

"A kid chained at my hip? I've been training you to be my fucking underboss," he hissed back. "Why the fuck do you think I've kept you so close? So you can learn. I know you're capable of more. That's why I've wanted you at my side. I'd already planned to make you the next capo, but I wasn't going to rush your education just because you're my brother. Being close to me wasn't a punishment, and if you'd fucking grow up, you'd see that." He stalked off, sliding into the car and slamming the door.

I was too stunned to follow until the car thrummed to life, and I realized there was a definite possibility he would leave my ass on the street. I rushed over and jumped in the passenger seat.

"I'm not a fucking mind reader, Teo. How was I supposed to know?" I argued.

He sighed and pulled away from the curb. "You're right. I just lost my cool. You *are* my little brother, and it's hard to see you differently, but I do have plans for you. We'll make the announcement about your change in rank to capo after Alonzo's laid to rest."

"I appreciate that. And you know I'm always happy to stand beside you, even when you're a prick."

He smirked and shook his head. "Fuck. What are we gonna do about the cartel? Those fuckers aren't going to disappear without a fight."

"First, I'd say we need to up the threat alert. Women and children need to be protected."

"Agreed. I'll spread the word. Our family is good, all except for Camilla."

"I've got Camilla covered," I offered far too quickly.

Matteo's gaze left the road to assess me. "Care to explain?"

"That an order?" I asked.

He spared another glance in my direction. "No," he answered with a hint of amusement.

"Then no, I don't care to explain."

We made the rest of the drive to Angelo's in silence.

CHAPTER 18
Camilla

Filip texted on my way to the club Thursday night that he was running late. He'd been clear about not wanting me to spend extra time with Dante, so I greeted Beth in the lobby and got comfortable in the sitting area. I was only there for a minute when Dante appeared. Had he known I'd arrived? Had Beth alerted him, or was it pure coincidence that he showed up? I wasn't sure, but I couldn't do anything about it now.

"Camilla, you look lovely. Can I get you something to drink?"

"No, thank you." I smiled, not wanting to be rude but also not wanting to upset Filip by encouraging Dante.

"I take it you're waiting for our mutual friend?" he asked, easing himself into the armchair opposite me.

"Yes, he got caught up with some work."

"I'm happy to keep you company while you wait. Filip is extremely dedicated to his job; there's no telling how long he'll be."

"Are you … do you work with Filip?" I wasn't sure how to ask if Dante was a part of the Gallo family business. I hadn't considered it before, but a sex club was perfectly suited as a mafia operation.

He smirked. "No. The Lion's Den is all mine. While not every dime that went into its creation was purely legitimate, I've steered clear of entangling myself with his type of organization."

"I would imagine the club wasn't a small financial undertaking."

"No, and I didn't have access to the type of funds someone in Filip's business might have had. I lost my parents when I was young, so I was taken in by relatives who never had much money. This club is the product of years of my life. That's why you'll find me here almost every day." His pride was palpable. He enjoyed sharing his achievement, and I couldn't blame him. Establishing a thriving business as he had wasn't easy, no matter the industry.

"It's a wonderful success. You must be very proud of what you've accomplished."

He was at ease in his role as host at the club. Unceremonious and easily approachable. But if he'd come from a modest background, there had to be an extremely driven, ambitious side to him. You didn't build something like The Lion's Den from the ground up without passion and hard work.

"I am, but more than anything, I wanted to make my parents proud. They may not be here with me, but they will always be a part of me, and I know they see what I've accomplished. *That* is what motivates me."

My heart squeezed. I was impressed that he was so open about such a personal subject.

"That's very admirable," I said softly. I was getting the sense that Dante was immensely more complex than I'd realized, and I wished I could get to know him better without upsetting Filip. The two clearly had a murky past, creating a puzzling friendship that I couldn't begin to understand.

He stared at me for a pregnant moment, his fathomless gaze piercing me until I had to glance down at my hands self-consciously. At that moment, the front door pulled open, and Filip's menacing presence saturated the room. His eyes cut to where Dante and I sat and bore angry daggers at my companion.

I swiftly rose to my feet and walked to Filip's side, gently threading my fingers with his. "I'm glad you're here. Ready to go upstairs?" I doubted Filip would harm his friend, but I wanted to defuse the situation regardless.

Filip squeezed my hand but never stopped glowering at his friend. "Dante," he rumbled in a dismissive greeting before leading me to the elevator.

I chanced a peek backward, catching Dante's glare. There was no hiding the menacing energy radiating off Filip, but I was surprised at the intensity of Dante's irritation. He normally shrugged off Filip's possessive outbursts. I wondered if something had gone down between the two after I left the club the other night.

Filip led me from the elevator and straight past the main gathering room, not stopping until we were secured inside his private quarters. He slipped off his suit jacket and turned his blistering gaze on me.

"Strip." The word reverberated in my head and warmed my belly.

I loved the way he dominated me inside these walls, but after establishing an emotional connection between us, I couldn't fully enjoy our time together if he was truly upset with me.

"Are you angry with me? Because it wasn't my fault Dante came to sit with me. I didn't get your text until I was almost at the club, and I didn't go upstairs on purpose, but then he found me."

Filip stalked toward me, his penetrating stare stealing the air from my lungs. He backed me against the wall and pressed his body against mine, rubbing his solid cock into my belly and tracing his thumb along my bottom lip. "Never angry with you," he breathed. His midnight gaze flicked back to my eyes. "Now … *strip*." He stepped back enough to allow me room to move.

His reassurance gave me the confidence to slowly bare myself in an erotic tease by removing one article at a time. Filip drank in my every movement as if I were an oasis in the desert and he feared I might disappear. He clicked a remote once I was done, and the haunting strains of a gospel choir swelled throughout the room.

"Come here." He took my hand and led me to the end of the bed, then went to the chest of drawers and pulled out a pair of leather cuffs attached to cables.

I watched raptly as he secured the cables to eye hooks at the top of the footboard posts. I had not previously noticed the dark hardware that blended with the heavy mahogany wood extending up above my head. As he clipped each one in, he also secured my wrists so that I was prone between the two smoothly carved posts.

When he went back to the chest, I peered over my shoulder to see what he would bring out next.

"Eyes forward," he ordered hoarsely.

I obeyed even though I desperately wanted to see the source of the metal clanking behind me. Within a few shuddered breaths, Filip's quiet footfalls returned. Something soft and cool trailed down my back like heavy ribbons, making me gasp and arch.

"Spread your legs."

I widened my stance, opening myself up. With a swooshing sound, something slapped against my ass and seared my skin in a delicious warmth.

"Wider, Camilla." Filip's voice dipped with the promise of

exquisite torture. He then secured the leather cuffs on my ankles connected to either end of a wide silver bar.

I was totally helpless. Vulnerable and exposed.

Such a risk carried an inherent thrill. A surge of adrenaline teetering on a thin red line between intoxicating elation and nauseating terror. Trust determined which emotions would prevail.

The swelling pressure throbbing in my clit was ample evidence that I trusted Filip.

"I've had a shitty couple of days," he murmured, dragging the strips of what I guessed were leather over my sensitive skin. "Each night when I try to shrug off the events of the day, I find myself lost in visions of your beautiful skin flush from my touch."

The leather streaked across my upper thigh in a zinging whoosh. My skin lit with the sharp sting, tightening my inner muscles and making me gasp from the heavenly pulse of endorphins.

He moaned. "Those sounds haunt my dreams."

Smack. The opposite thigh. Harder. I began to smell my arousal all around me.

"I can't get enough of the way you respond to my touch. You've taken over my every fucking thought—it's heaven and hell at the same time."

Smack. Square across my ass.

"I want to punish you for toppling my carefully constructed world and worship your very existence. You make me fucking insane. And you know the worst part?" he asked, breaths becoming shallow and ragged.

I shook my head, my breasts now aching with need.

Smack. At the apex of my thighs, the leather tips grazed the heat of my core.

Filip pressed himself flush against my back, his hand snaking around to cup my sex. "I want it all. Every bit of madness. I'd rather go fucking crazy for you than walk away and never have this again."

He reached up and freed my wrists, then pressed his hand on my back to lower me toward the bed. With my legs still splayed and cuffed, I folded at the waist, fully open to him. In a matter of seconds, he was at my entrance, his warm cock nudging me open. His hands clasped my hips before he surged inside me.

I moaned loudly at the delicious pressure, even more intense when his body made contact with the skin still stinging from his punishing strikes. The pain melted into pleasure, forming a heady cocktail of savory sensations.

Filip consumed my every sense. His spiced leather scent blanketed me in his presence while the masculine timbre of his voice warmed me from the inside out. The sight of him made my brain misfire and tied my tongue into knots. But it was his touch that drove me to the point of addiction.

His branding touch made my blood sing.

Filip stilled, and my body cried out for more of his punishing thrusts.

"That's why, when I see you with Dante, I crave blood. Murderous thoughts whisper inside my head." He lowered himself until his chest lay snug against my back, his cock still hard inside me. "I need to know that this body is mine. That there is no doubt in your mind who you belong to." His request wasn't just a product of shallow insecurity. The raw vulnerability in his voice spoke to a place deep inside me. An old wound that had left him fragile and scarred.

I often felt so different from the people around me, but when I was with Filip, I saw myself in his eyes. We mirrored one another—different but the same. It was that sense of belonging that urged me to give him what he wanted. To make sure he knew I was just as hopelessly bound to him as he was me.

"I am yours in a way that I have never been anyone else's. It terrifies me." I repaid his unguarded admission with one of my own.

"*Fuuuuck*," he groaned, squeezing my middle and pushing himself all the way to my womb. One thrust after another came faster and harder as if he sought to permanently bury himself inside me.

I pressed my ass upward, doing what little I could to meet each of his thrusts. Filip snaked one of his hands beneath me. When his fingers reached my sensitive bundle of nerves, I heard a click before something on his finger began to vibrate.

The deluge of sensation detonated my body.

My muscles clenched, and the pleasure consumed me. Tears sprang to my eyes, and a guttural cry tore from my lips, becoming an erotic harmony when Filip roared with his own explosive release. We drifted for long seconds on a sea of contentment as our bodies recovered.

How could I have never known it could be like this? I'd been living in a black-and-white world only to discover the wonder of color all around me. Filip wanted to know that I was his. How could I ever belong to anyone else? He possessed the key to my soul.

While I grappled with my chaotic thoughts, Filip lowered to remove my ankle cuffs, then used a soft rag to clean me. Once he was satisfied with his work, he helped me onto the bed and pulled me into his side. We lay in silence for several minutes. With my ear on his chest, I listened as his heartbeat eased to a steady strum, but mine continued to pound because of the words I could sense forming on my tongue.

"I know you want to know about my past. There was something that happened, but I've never told anyone."

Filip became eerily still. "A relationship?"

"Not exactly. It's complicated."

"Will you tell me about it?"

My skin began to crawl with the need to hide from the subject, but I refused to give in. "I will, just not right now. Okay?"

He squeezed me gently. "I can wait."

I lifted up onto my elbow and peered at him, my hair cascading down around my face. "Would you tell me how you got into this lifestyle? Why you joined the club?"

A playful smirk lightened his features. "It's not all that sordid. I'm a guy. I like sex."

"Yeah, but you could get any girl in bed. You don't have to pay for a club to get sex."

He tugged me back down, denying me the pleasure of seeing his beautiful face. "I told you that I like to keep control over my life. Having sex with women at the club keeps everything tidy. There's no confusion about relationships or expectations. Plus, women at the club tend to be more appreciative of my ... dominant side."

As much as I loved thinking about his tendency to be assertive, I abhorred the idea that my experiences with him weren't unique. I'd never been jealous of men in the past, but I'd never been with someone who made me feel the way Filip did. I had a whole new realm of emotions to sort through.

We lay together for long minutes, both lost in our own thoughts. I wasn't sure what came next. Eventually, my insecurities got the better of me.

"I guess I better get going. I have to work tomorrow." Maybe if we'd been at one of our homes, it would have been easier to relax and perhaps even stay the night together, but the club set an artificial expiration on our time. Aside from the unfortunate incident at my place, our time together had been restricted to the club. I wasn't sure if that would change under our new relationship status. The night didn't exactly feel like a date, so I didn't know how it would end.

"I'll make sure you get home safely unless your father has

assigned you protection." He sat up, expecting me to scoot from the bed.

I sat up and studied him. "Why? Has something happened?"

"There's nothing for you to worry about." His hand came up to my jaw, but I deflected.

"Don't do that, Filip. You would want to know if something dangerous was happening. Don't treat me like a child."

He looked like he might argue until I said that last part. Then his lips thinned, and he sighed. "The cartel killed some of our men yesterday. We weren't expecting them to make a move so quickly, so we don't know exactly what they might try."

"I thought the cartel boss left."

"He did, but most of his men are still here following his orders." He lifted his hand again without objection this time. "I need to make sure you're safe. That means I'll be escorting you places and checking in with you. I'd do it anyway just because that's who I am, but this is different. All of you are under increased protection for the time being. Okay?"

I nodded. I had no desire to end up carried off to Mexico like Giada … or worse.

True to his word, Filip escorted me all the way to my front door. I invited him in, but he declined, hovering just outside. Awkwardness wrapped me in its sticky clutches. I wanted him to stay, but he wouldn't even come in. I didn't know what else to say or do. I desperately wanted him to at least kiss me before he left, but considering his lips had yet to touch mine, I didn't think that would happen.

"Text me if you're going anywhere outside of work," he blurted. "I'll have eyes on you when you go to and from work, but I need to know if you are going anywhere else so that I can send an escort or come myself if I can."

"Okay. I'm pretty boring, so it shouldn't be an issue."

Filip's lips thinned. "All right. Good night." He nodded, then stalked away from my door.

Was he upset? Why would he be upset? I got the distinct feeling something was wrong, but I couldn't fathom what.

I locked my door and tossed my purse on the counter. It was getting late, and I did have work in the morning, so I tried not to obsess and began my bedtime routine. When I washed my face, I noticed my wrists were slightly pink from the cuffs. I bit down on a smile at the delicious reminder of my evening. A slightly awkward parting was worth the pleasure, and the night had ended far better than our first few encounters.

Optimism shone down on me like a ray of spring sunshine.

I grabbed my phone from the nightstand and crawled into bed, surprised to see a missed text message.

Filip: Have dinner with me tomorrow.

Had there been a way to measure smiles, mine would have broken the meter.

Me: Are you asking me on a date? I couldn't help myself. I had to toy with him.

Filip: I don't believe I asked a question at all.

I outright giggled like a preteen texting her middle school crush. What the hell was Filip doing to me?

Me: Okay.

I hit send and fell back against my pillows, but a brand-new surge of adrenaline ensured I wouldn't get a wink of sleep.

Filip De Luca was taking me on a date—a *real* date—and I suspected I might even enjoy it.

CHAPTER 19

Filip

When Camilla brought up her past, I desperately wanted to demand more information, but jumping on her admission would fuck everything up. At least now I knew she planned to tell me, eventually. If someone needed to die, I didn't want them breathing any longer than necessary. It was a safe assumption that someone had hurt Camilla, and I would never let such a crime go unpunished.

The night had brought on a barrage of emotions. I was relieved she had agreed to talk, homicidal at the possibility that something horrible had happened, awestruck from our explosive sex, and pissed at Dante for so clearly coveting what was mine. The worst came when guilt wracked me on our way to her apartment. I'd wanted to start a relationship with her, and the first thing I'd done was meet her at the club like any other fuck buddy. No dinner before. No staying the night because we weren't at one of our places. I'd been so caught up with work that I hadn't thought it all through until the moment came for us to leave the Den.

What a fucking imbecile.

She deserved better. I couldn't even bring myself to kiss her good night because I was too annoyed. I needed to do this right and start us off on our new path with a fresh beginning worthy of the fairy tale she deserved. Romance wasn't my forte, but for her, I'd fucking try.

Had I been faced with a gun at my head, it wouldn't have been a problem. Taken into police custody? I could handle that in my sleep. But should I need to foster an emotional connection with a woman, I was a beached orca wondering where the fuck the water had gone.

It hadn't escaped me that my behavior had come off abrasive. Ready to kick-start our new beginning, I immediately texted her about dinner. I hated the way I'd left things, but hopefully, I could make it all up to her the next night.

I spent the better part of the next twenty-four hours planning our date in the hopes I could finish one damn night with her without parting like a buffoon. I walked myself through a myriad of possible conversations and outcomes, hoping I could pull off the perfect evening. I'd never in my life put so much effort into a simple date. Of course, I'd never gone on many true dates. Romance involved emotions, and dates were for getting to know someone. Both had been strictly forbidden until Camilla.

I didn't just want to put a smile on Camilla's face. I wanted to be there for all her smiles. I wanted to know why she cried and wipe away her tears.

I wanted to be her everything because I would be nothing without her.

THE NEXT NIGHT, I picked up Camilla at her office and took her to a steakhouse not far from her place. She looked stunning, as always. Something about the golden shades of her hair made her eyes that much warmer. Her lips weren't marred with sticky gloss, and her lashes were thick without resembling thick-legged spiders. She allowed her natural beauty to speak for itself. Why would a rose need to dip itself in paint and glitter when its beauty was already perfection?

"How was your day?" I asked once we were in the car.

"Not bad. My boss is an ass, but he was busy on a project today, so I didn't have to deal with him. You?"

"Mine wasn't particularly productive. Dinner with you should turn things around nicely." I caught a glimpse of her shy smile and was surprised at how good it made me feel.

I found a spot just down the street from the restaurant and helped Camilla from the car.

"Empire. Excellent choice," she said as the awning drew closer.

"I take it you've been here before?"

"Yes, but not often. I actually don't go out all that often."

Surprising. I would have expected her to have men lined up around the corner to take her out. Was that not the case, or did she turn them all down? Or perhaps she'd been in a relationship until recently. I suddenly realized I had no idea about her romantic past. I'd wondered who had hurt her but hadn't otherwise considered her past romantic life.

"I eat out frequently but not like this," I conceded. "Not on a date." I opened the door to the restaurant, but she paused in the entry.

"You don't go on dates? Not at all?" She cocked her head.

"I told you I've avoided entanglements." I placed my hand gently on her back and encouraged her to step inside out of the cold.

She complied but was still contemplating the new information. "I guess I figured there were at least *some*." She peered up at me, still unsatisfied. "What about me? Am I not an entanglement?"

I leaned close. "Baby, I'm so entangled in you that I don't know which way is up." I allowed her soft floral scent to fill my lungs before straightening. "Now, let's get a table. I'm starved."

The hostess led us back to the candlelit table I'd requested in a far corner. As we walked, Camilla slowed and maneuvered herself behind me almost as if she were using me as a shield to hide from someone. I noted the two men at the table she'd avoided and waited until we were alone to push for an explanation.

"Care to explain what that was all about?" I asked softly, giving her a quizzical look.

She rolled her eyes with a slight headshake. "Just my boss. He's here, and I didn't want him to see me. I have no desire to talk to him."

"Why do you work there if you dislike him that much?"

"Actually, I've started looking for a new job. I like what I do, but he's not worth it."

"What exactly do you do at the bank?"

"Commercial lending. It's a decent mix of numbers and people. I've always liked working with money."

A devious grin spread across my face. "I suppose that's something else we have in common."

Camilla smirked and shook her head. "Yeah, except I don't have to worry about being arrested for what I do."

"Don't knock it until you try it. There's a lot of money in my line of work, and I know you have a healthy sense of adventure." My voice lowered, drawing out the most delectable flush across her cheeks.

"I'll keep that in mind," she said, eyes unable to meet mine.

Our server stopped at the table and took our drink order, giving her a chance to redirect our conversation.

"What about you? What do you do for your brother?"

"I handle whatever he needs me to handle." I stared at the dynamic woman across from me and felt oddly compelled to share more information than I would have with anyone else. "Actually, he just told me the other day that he's planning to make me his underboss in the future."

"That sounds like an enormous responsibility. He must have a great deal of trust in you." Her eyes lit with genuine joy on my behalf. I imagined what it would be like to have someone I could share my accomplishments with and who might help shoulder my burdens. I'd been independent for so long that the notion was totally foreign, yet I found it appealing. If anyone could assume that role for me, it would be Camilla. Her compassion and sincerity made it almost easy to share with her.

"I've wanted to be promoted for a while, so it's a big relief to know he sees me as more than his kid brother."

She lifted her wineglass to her lips and took a small sip. "I can't imagine anyone thinking of you as a child," she murmured. "You certainly don't elicit maternal feelings in me."

I chuckled. "We may have issues, but I suppose it's good to know that's not one of them."

We spent the evening talking about where we grew up, and our siblings and parents. She told me about her interest in reading, and I described my brief stint in professional boxing. She was remarkably easy to talk to when we weren't letting our fears come between us.

Our dinner came to a natural close, and I escorted her back to my car, surprised at the swell of relief I felt knowing our night was only getting started. We were both quiet on the car ride back to her place. It was a comfortable silence, though I suspected she was more anxious than I was. I knew our night wasn't going to end like the others. There would be no angry words or awkward departures.

I was playing for keeps, and she was my prize.

When we reached her apartment door, she asked me to come in as she had the night before. This time, I didn't hesitate. This time, I let the energy between us guide me and gave myself permission to do what came naturally. No uncertainty. No doubts or worries. I surrendered myself to the full spectrum of my emotions.

I closed the door behind me, sealing us in together, then locked eyes with the most mesmerizing woman I'd ever known. The electric current that bound us together sparked to life, drawing me closer. My heart thundered against my ribs, blood whooshing in my ears as I pulled her against me and slammed my lips down on hers.

CHAPTER 20
Camilla

F ilip's kiss was so unexpected that I froze as the world around me came to a screeching halt. My heart stuttered in my chest. I'd envisioned his lips on mine dozens, if not hundreds of times, but nothing prepared me for the rush of the real thing. The joy that shook me to my core.

When his lips began to move against mine, I surged into action as if I'd been drowning, and my head finally burst free of the surface to gulp life-giving air. I needed his taste just as desperately as I needed to breathe. My lips parted, and our tongues began to tangle and dance in perfect harmony. Filip grasped me to him as though I alone kept his heart beating. His violent rejection of control catapulted me off the cliff with him until we were both free-falling into the unknown.

I'd never felt such delight in surrender. Such exalted relief from the attention of a man.

I wanted to take root there in his arms and never stray from the warmth of his touch. If I'd had any inkling of what I'd been missing, I would have started my search so much sooner, relentlessly scouring the earth for a taste of what Filip offered. He was the thrill of walking alone under a moonless winter sky and the soul-deep freedom of absolute acceptance. Encircled in Filip's arms, I felt whole.

"Stay," I breathed when I forced my lips from his. "Stay with me, please." My words were nothing more than wisps of air, barely audible, yet they were laden with desperation.

Filip's forehead gently connected with mine, his eyes drifting shut. "Before you ask for such things, you should know there's no going back. What we're doing—tearing down these walls between us—can never be restored. You've seen my nature. Once you're mine, I won't be able to let you go." His voice was ragged with desolation and uncertainty as though he feared he'd already gone too far. Like a child deep in the forest, miles from the designated path.

I waited, breathing through shaky breaths until his eyes finally met mine. "I don't want to be anyone else's. Your ability to see beneath my surface terrifies me, but I'd rather face that fear than ever have to see you walking with another woman at your side. My need for you is irrational and all-consuming, and I'm tired of fighting it."

Our lips collided in an agreement infinitely more binding than any words could have been. With each roll of our tongues, each glide of our lips, we buried the fear and hurt and uncertainty. Our breaths mingled as one. Our hearts thrummed to the same beat. Our souls synced to the same alluring rhythm that had been calling to us for weeks.

He lifted me in his arms and carried me to the bedroom, where our clothes melted from our bodies. It was the first time I'd had total access to drink him in. To let my fingers memorize the granite firmness of his sculpted form as my eyes traced each tightly corded muscle. He seemed to recognize my need to study him and allowed me time to explore.

When my attention drifted down to his thick, protruding cock, saliva pooled in my mouth. I'd been granted the gift of tasting his lips for the first time; would he permit me the freedom to taste the essence of his masculinity? I hesitantly wrapped my hand around his wide girth, my fingers unable to reach around to meet my thumb. Filip sucked in an unsteady breath at the contact. His abdominal muscles coiled and flexed with strain. I chanced a glance up at him, pulling firmly from his base to his tip, my thumb tracing the velvety softness of the ridge around his thick head. He didn't fight me for control, so I pushed to see how far his generosity would go. I desperately wanted to taste him. The only problem was, that would require me to drop to my knees.

Kneel.

The phantom voice shot an icy blast through my veins.

I refused to give it any power. Instead, I absorbed Filip's endless warmth, reveling in the sheer perfection of his body and the reverence in his ravenous stare. Slowly, I lowered myself to my knees.

Every sinewy inch of his hard body marbleized.

"Camilla—" he rasped. He may not have known my story, but he understood that being on my knees was meaningful to me. He didn't want me to feel uncomfortable in any way.

I appreciated his concern, but I wanted this. I wanted to taste him, but I also needed to do it on my knees. I wanted to create a new association—one of desire and pleasure in this position. I'd given blowjobs before, but never on my knees. This wasn't just about oral pleasure; it was me sharing a part of my soul with him.

I lifted my eyes to his, grasping his base in my hand and tapping his swollen cock against my lips. Filip hissed. My tongue flicked out and licked the length of him before sucking him into my mouth, making him drop his head back. A sound of pure exultant relief tore from his throat as one of his hands gently cupped the back of my head. His touch was supportive and appreciative. Nothing was tyrannical or disrespectful about the gesture. I had no doubt he could be more forceful, but I sensed his desire to protect me was far stronger than his need to dominate me.

His gentle regard was empowering. I began to lose myself in the act of pleasuring him, almost forgetting I was on my knees. When his thighs began to quiver beneath my palms, he pulled himself from my lips and lifted me back to my feet.

"I'm not coming in your mouth. Not tonight." He lifted me just enough to fling me onto the bed, then lowered himself above me.

His eyes bled to black in the dim light. Those fathomless depths stared deep into my soul as his hand eased around my thigh, nudging my knees up above his hips. I took advantage of his goodwill to run my hands through his thick dark hair. He'd never given me unfettered access to him, and I was drunk off the gluttonous banquet of sensation. Adrift on a sea of desire.

Filip's parted lips hovered just over mine as he pushed inside me in two confident thrusts. I inhaled his exhaled breaths. Softened beneath his hard edges. I took every ounce of what he gave and reveled in my riches. Every piece of him was a gift—a precious treasure—and I was the fucking queen. The recipient of all his adoration and devotion. The moon to his sun.

For long minutes, we worshiped one another, a writhing mass of sweaty limbs and heaving breaths. He knew exactly how to touch me. Even without the club or restraints or even pain, he commanded my body with absolute authority, conducting an orchestra of pleasure through my veins.

I had thought I needed some element of deviancy to make my

blood sing, but the truth was all I needed was Filip. I enjoyed the other, but he was the key.

Filip owned me, heart and soul.

As though my body spoke to his, whispered its secrets and bowed to his demands, he drove me straight to the cliff's edge and danced with me along the precipice until he decided it was time to push me over. His ability to sense my growing pleasure and control every aspect of my climb coaxed my climax into a violent detonation of sensation. My body flexed and strained in response to the intense chemical reaction, dowsing my fiery body in orgasmic bliss. Wave after wave flooded my synapses and drowned my consciousness until I was nothing but a feather floating on the wind.

When I came to, Filip had settled on his side, peering down at me with one hand trailing his fingers through my hair.

"I don't think I've ever witnessed anything as sexy as you coming undone."

"I don't know about that. I'm pretty sure I'm a sweaty mess." I trailed my fingers along the stubble on his jaw.

"Sweaty is sexiest of all. It's the sign of a well-fucked woman." He lowered his mouth to lick at one of my nipples.

I gasped and arched, my body still oversensitive.

He chuckled and took my hand. "Come on, let's jump in the shower."

Shower together? I was shocked but scooted off the bed and followed him. I'd never showered with a man. It was so personal. Certainly more intimate than I expected from Filip, considering his aversion to relationships.

He turned on the water to my walk-in shower and set two fresh towels nearby. My apartment wasn't particularly luxurious, but I made sure to indulge in my master suite. The entire room was solid white marble lined with pale gray streaks. I'd personally picked out the fixtures and selected a modern standalone tub as the room's focal point. I adored everything about my bathroom, but I suddenly felt a little awkward in the space, although not so uncomfortable as I would have been without the dopamine and endorphins still saturating my bloodstream.

When steam began to billow from the shower, Filip clasped my hand and pulled me inside.

"Um, I've never actually showered with anyone," I admitted as I stepped under the spray.

Filip grinned down at me, tugging me against him. "Another thing we have in common."

"But you seem so comfortable, and this is awfully domestic. Honestly, it's hard not to worry that you'll reconsider and decide you don't want a relationship." I dropped my gaze to the water dripping down the smattering of hair on his chest.

"You're woven so deep inside me that running from you would be running from myself. As far as I'm concerned, there's no unraveling us from one another."

I lifted my eyes back to his. "So it wouldn't bother you if I ask you to stay the night?"

He turned his head slowly from side to side. "I was planning to stay whether you asked or not. You won't get rid of me that easily. Not anymore." He released me to squirt shampoo in his hand. "Now get that hair wet so I can wash it."

My heart was full to bursting as we took turns bathing one another. His hands were extra attentive when he soaped my breasts, and my fingers lingered over his beautifully sculpted back muscles. It surprised me that his brother was covered in tattoos, but Filip didn't have a single one.

"How come you don't have any tattoos?" I asked, my hand drifting down over his perfectly rounded ass.

He peeked over his shoulder at me with one brow raised. "Why? You prefer tattoos?"

An exhilaration came over me just before I popped my palm against his ass. "Answer me."

Filip froze, then slowly spun. I started to worry I'd upset him, but when I saw the playful heat in his eyes, I knew he was feeling just as lighthearted as I was.

"Excuse me, Miss Genovese. Did you just slap my ass?" He stepped closer, forcing me against the cool marble wall.

I gasped then giggled. "You still haven't answered my question. Do you need another spanking?"

He shook his head but couldn't hide the grin fighting to emerge. Filip yanked me up into his arms, and my legs wrapped around his middle. "My reason for not having tattoos may sound … strange."

I sobered, detecting the subject was somewhat sensitive. "You can tell me," I urged softly.

"I just don't like clutter—in my life or on my body." Control. He liked control, and a close relative of control was order. Organization and structure. I was well acquainted with them and a fan myself.

"I can understand that," I replied softly.

A molten heat blazed behind Filip's eyes. He adjusted his hips just enough to find my entrance and pushed inside me. I clung to his shoulders as he rocked into me, impaling me against the shower wall. He fucked me hard and fast, quickly bringing us both to a second release. We had to wash again, but it was worth it. Shower sex was a new favorite of mine. Although, I had a feeling any sex with Filip would be great sex.

We dried off after using our fair share of the building's hot water then crawled back into bed. I laid my head on his shoulder, my body curled into his side. I didn't think I'd ever had such a perfect night with a man. Filip was everything I'd been hoping to find, but one giant roadblock lingered between us. One thing that might destroy the foundation we'd cautiously been building.

My past.

Would he shun me? Would the truth change the way he viewed me? Would he blame me?

Logically, I knew we shouldn't be together if the answer was yes to any of those questions. There was no loss in parting from someone who couldn't love me in spite of the ugly, yet I still didn't want to take the risk. I didn't want to face the possible heartbreak, so it was easier to procrastinate. But I couldn't. I was falling hard for this man, and I needed to tell him my secrets before it was too late. Before I was hopelessly in love with him.

The room was still and plunged in darkness, distant city sounds the only signs of life. That would be best. I didn't want to see his face when I told him the story. I would pretend I was alone, sharing my secrets with the night.

I took two deep breaths in preparation before I was able to force out the words. "I was a junior in high school the first time I got sent to the principal's office."

CHAPTER 21

Camilla

PAST

"A re you serious? You can't possibly expect us to complete this project before next week." I was so frustrated that I blurted out thoughts I normally would have kept to myself.

Mrs. Andrews' spine stiffened. "Excuse me, Miss Genovese? You're walking a precarious line."

I slammed the instruction sheet on my desk, oblivious to the wide-eyed students all around me gaping as they witnessed my breakdown. "This is fucking bullshit," I grumbled under my breath but apparently not quietly enough.

My accounting teacher shot her finger toward the door. "That's quite enough, Camilla," she barked. "You can take the matter up with Principal Hale. I'm sure he'd like to hear what you have to say."

Great. Now I'll end up in detention with even less time to work on my mounting study list.

I shot off a litany of curses in my head as I slammed my notebook and tablet back into my backpack. I was the good kid, not the troublemaker. Andrews was being absurd to send me to Hale's office—even more absurd than assigning a project the week before the SAT. Did they want us to succeed or not?

I tried so fucking hard all the time, following all the rules and jumping through each hoop, but no matter how hard I tried lately, I felt perpetually beaten down. As though the water I desperately needed kept trickling between my fingers before I could get the life-giving substance to my lips. I was running on a treadmill, but no matter how fast I ran, the machine just kept going faster. At some point, I simply couldn't keep up.

Something was bound to fall through the cracks. Then I'd be a failure.

As far as I could tell, the other kids didn't seem to feel the same pressure as I did. I didn't know how to let go of the expectations. How to coast through school with a focus on friendships and memories rather than grades and aspirations. A part of me wanted to be like them, but I knew if I tried, my entire house of cards would fold. Every time I considered relaxing my standards, my chest constricted as societal pressures clamped down over my ribs.

I tried to take a deep breath before entering the administrative offices, but the stress-induced vise grip wouldn't allow it. A stinging pain shot from the base of my lungs. My shoulders rounded, but I didn't stop my progress. The sensation was nothing new. I would probably give myself a heart attack by the time I was twenty if I remained so high-strung.

Giada would laugh at me when I got upset and tell me to chill as if it were that easy. As if I could simply become someone else. She had no fucking clue what it was like to feel as though the world would come crashing down if everything wasn't perfect. I didn't want to be that way; I just had no idea how to be any different.

Normally, I kept the reins firmly in my grasp to ensure the pressures didn't rise out of my control.

My grip was slipping.

"Miss Genovese, what can I do for you?" asked the school secretary, a kind older woman who was angling for best fur-baby mom bragging rights with a slew of pictures and Pomeranian paraphernalia scattered about her desk.

"Mrs. Andrews sent me over to speak with Principal Hale." My eyes shifted to the students standing near the entrance to the nurse's office. They were younger, so I shouldn't have cared what they thought, but I did. Being sent to the principal's office was for delinquents who were either too dumb or emotionally damaged to keep out of trouble.

I didn't want anyone thinking I was either of those things.

"Oh, well that's a surprise." Her penciled eyebrows mimicked the golden arches high on her forehead. "He doesn't have anyone in with him at the moment, so you can go on in."

My lips pulled thin as I walked to my fate.

The principal was working at his desk. I stopped just inside the doorway and waited quietly until he lifted his gaze.

"Camilla, what can I do for you?" David Hale was close to fifty. He kept in decent shape and wasn't totally unattractive as far as middle-aged men went. He was firm with students but not unliked. I hadn't been around the man much and was almost surprised when he called me by name. I wasn't sure I'd ever spoken directly with him, but maybe it was the principal's job to know each of his students.

"I was sent over by Mrs. Andrews," I explained, my voice cracking with discomfort.

Principal Hale leaned back in his chair, the cheap leather seat creaking in the quiet room. "I see. Why don't you close the door and come tell me about it."

I did as he said, sitting in one of his visitor chairs. His office was spacious but dark. The blinds were mostly shut, only allowing in a soft glow from the sunny day outside. Our school was built decades ago as part of a church, so the offices had rich mahogany paneling. The aged wood gave off a musty smell that permeated the older parts of the school. It was worse in areas where the industrial carpeting remained, but Hale had removed it when he first took over his position. Between the dim lighting and dark walls, his office would have served as a cozy study had there been a crackling fireplace to warm the room.

"Well, I know I shouldn't have said what I did, but it's not entirely my fault," I started. "I just got so frustrated, but that's only because Mrs. Andrews gave us a huge project to do over the next week when many of us are taking the SAT. I didn't do anywhere near as well as I had hoped on the PSAT, so I decided to take the SAT this year for practice before my final test next year. She knows that, and I told her, but she didn't care. National Honor Society just upped their service hour requirement, and student council moved its meetings to the same night as math-letes." My arms waved in emphasis, and my voice rose the longer I spoke. Airing my frustrations brought all the emotions exploding to the surface. When I realized I was ranting, I clamped my mouth shut and shrank in my chair.

My words hung lifelessly in the air around us before Principal Hale spoke. "I take it you disrespectfully expressed your frustration to Mrs. Andrews?"

"Yes, but she was the one giving us a project rather than allow us to prepare for one of the most important tests of our lives. I don't understand it. Does she want us to fail?"

He stayed eerily quiet, his fingers steepled before him. "He that spareth his rod hateth his son: but he that loveth him chasteneth him betimes. Proverbs 13:24." Hale watched me, giving me time to process his words.

What was he getting at? The verse was about discipline. He

made it sound like he was going to paddle me, but corporal punishment wasn't allowed in schools. Suddenly, my frustrations melted away, and my attention was focused entirely on the man before me.

"Camilla, you're not an adult yet. Do you think it's appropriate to disrespect your elders?"

I shook my head. "No, sir."

"My Christian faith won't allow me to send you away unpunished. I would do you a disservice to allow your behavior to continue. But more than that, I can see you're struggling, and I want to help." He stood up, towering over me. "Get out a pen and paper."

Okay, that didn't sound so bad. I did as he said while he made room on his desk closest to me.

"I want five hundred repetitions of 'I will respect my elders as the Bible requires.'"

"Yes, sir." Annoying, but doable.

I scooted to the edge of the seat and leaned forward to write using his desk.

"No, Camilla. On your knees," his dark voice commanded.

I glanced down at the polished concrete floor and my knees, exposed below my plaid pleated skirt, before lowering myself to the ground. My knees protested, but the pressure wasn't overly cumbersome.

Or so I'd thought.

The first hundred lines were manageable. The second hundred, my handwriting grew increasingly illegible. The third hundred, tears welled in my eyes. The fourth set of lines brought an onslaught of vicious anger directed at everything. I felt like a wounded animal lashing out at anything in sight. The final hundred, the skin on my kneecaps screamed as though it had been sliced down to the bone.

For the entire twenty minutes of my punishment, Principal

Hale sat at his desk and watched me through his wire-rimmed glasses. When I finished, I peered up at him with glassy eyes. I hated showing weakness, but more than anything, I prayed my punishment was over.

Instead, he came to my side of his desk and sat in the other visitor chair. I watched him warily, trying in vain to discern his intentions.

"Tell me, Camilla, do you have anyone to share these burdens with?"

"Burdens?" I asked, confused.

"Your stress and worries. I haven't noticed you hanging around any other students to suggest you have a close friend or boyfriend. Is there anyone you're close to and trust to talk with?"

I pondered his question, feeling horribly ashamed to realize the answer was no. Not only that, but he'd intuited my answer long before I had. My family was good, but cold in a way. I always felt like I needed to do better to measure up, which didn't create an environment that fostered open communication. Giada wouldn't understand my issues at all, and Val was just a kid. I had casual friends through my clubs and activities but was too busy with academic pursuits to have bonded with any one person.

"Not really," I whispered past the lump in my throat.

He nodded sagely. "I can help you," he said in a gentle rumble that I felt deep in my own chest. Principal Hale stood and held out his hand to me. I clasped my hand in his and used his help to raise myself. My knees were so stiff that I buckled forward, grasping his hands to stay upright.

"Oh! I'm sorry." I gasped.

"It's not a problem, Camilla. I'll always be here to support you."

I peered up at his stern face. At his square jaw and corded neck. He was stronger than I'd realized and exuded more power than I would have expected from a simple principal, as though he could carry the world on his shoulders.

It was the strangest thought. I didn't know what had come over me.

I quickly pulled my hands away, then picked up my backpack. My knees still ached but had regained their strength. "I apologize for losing my temper. I'll make sure to keep a better lid on it next time."

"Pressure can only build so long before it finds a release, no matter how tight the lid. We'll work through it together." He placed a warm hand on my shoulder. "You should get back to class before you miss any more instruction."

"Yes, sir. Thank you." I scurried from his office, wondering what the hell had just happened.

Relief brought a surge of adrenaline through my veins, making me feel light on my feet as I rushed back to class. I was so glad to be free of his punishment that Mrs. Andrews' project didn't even seem all that awful anymore.

What a strange fucking day.

When I took my seat back in class, I felt as if all eyes were on me even though they weren't. My knees had to be bright red, but no one seemed to notice. No one paid me any mind at all. I took out my supplies and lowered my head, committed to moving on and forgetting my little visit with Principal Hale.

THE DAY BEFORE THE SAT, I received a message in first period to see Principal Hale in his office. I knew exactly what it was about, and my stomach roiled at the knowledge. I gathered my things and made the haunting walk down the empty halls to the front of the school.

I greeted the secretary again, hating the remorseful look she gave me as if to say, what a shame she's wasting so much potential. I shrugged off her ignorance and continued to Hale's office. This time he sat waiting for me, eyes trained on the doorway.

"You wanted to see me?" I asked innocently, hoping my suspicions weren't correct.

"Close the door, Camilla." His heavy disappointment made me feel two inches tall.

I did as he asked, and before I could cross to the visitor chairs, he stood and halted me with a single hand. The stress from the week had left me sleep-deprived and running on caffeine. Hale's intense scrutiny and the impending probability of more punishment made my hands tremble and my breathing grow shallow. I wanted to yell and plead—to beg him to try to understand my position—but I could see that such efforts would only inflame the situation.

My principal crossed the room and came to a stop adjacent to me, his eyes seemingly studying a class portrait hung between the doorframe and a bookshelf. "Two times within the span of a week. That would denote a pattern of behavior."

"No, I—"

His biting stare cut short my reply.

"You skipped class yesterday. Left campus a full period early, did you not?"

I opened my mouth, but my breathing hitched. I had to forcibly swallow before I could answer. "I did, sir, but it was PE, and the SAT is tomorrow. I needed the time to study. Please try to understand," I begged in an unsteady voice. The strain was too great to bear any longer. I carried a great load on my shoulders, standing balanced on a single thread frayed by my weight.

My collapse was imminent.

I'd prayed I could hold out until after the exam, but Principal Hale was a factor I hadn't considered. He threw me off balance, and like a pebble knocked from its resting place at the top of a hill, I began a speedy descent.

"It's my job to guide my students. To help them follow the correct path. When I realized you were struggling, I paid more attention."

Oh, God. I was under his microscope. He wasn't going to let a single misstep go unpunished. What had I done? Why had I earned such scrutiny? I worked so hard to always do the right thing. Why would God want to punish *me*?

"I had hoped that perhaps your last visit was a fluke, but I can see the problem is more ingrained than I realized." Hale picked up a clay jar finished in iridescent jewel tones and lifted the cork stopper from the top.

I watched transfixed as he swirled his hand inside, making a swishing sound with its contents. What on earth was he doing? What was in the jar? It wasn't a liquid and sounded like lots of little somethings—but what? And why?

"Set down your bag," he ordered as he came to stand a few feet in front of me.

I did as I was told, hoping my acquiescence would help commute my sentence.

Principal Hale scooped out a handful of the jar's contents and proceeded to scatter the objects in a small area before me.

Rice. He'd placed a handful of rice at my feet. Was I supposed to pick them up with tweezers or something? Had he come up with some New Age form of tedious punishment?

He walked back to the shelf, not sparing me a glance. "Kneel," he instructed calmly.

I stared back down at the ground, sure he couldn't be serious. "What?"

You know that feeling when you say a word too many times in a row, and it seems to lose all meaning? You think, I must be saying it wrong. That's not actually a word, is it? That was how I suddenly felt about the word *kneel*.

No matter how hard I concentrated, I couldn't make sense of what he was asking me to do. Kneeling on rice would be horribly painful. This was the twenty-first century. Kids weren't supposed to be subjected to this kind of torture.

Had I passed out in class after not getting enough sleep and fallen into some twisted nightmare? What other explanation was there?

The jar slammed heavily onto the shelf, startling me out of my confused stupor. My gaze flew back to Principal Hale, whose cutting glare slashed through me.

"*Kneel*," he hissed harshly.

I could hardly take a breath without my lungs fluttering with the need to cry. I tried so desperately to contain my reaction, but when I lowered myself to the ground and my knees instantly screamed in pain, all of my torment and strain overtook me.

Muted sobs wracked my body.

I wept for the person I wished I could be. I wept for the girl I was. Tears of disappointment and anger, fear and resentment. Each pent-up emotion festering inside me trickled out in salty rivulets down my flushed cheeks.

When I wiped at the deluge, I realized that Hale was there before me, eye level. He'd dropped to his knees and was patiently waiting for my hysterics to subside. Once he had my attention, he held out his palms. I placed my hands in his, and he wrapped his large fingers around mine but kept our hands held aloft between us.

"You're doing so well, Camilla," he urged softly.

"It hurts," I whimpered.

He gave a single nod. "I know it does, but I want you to find a place on the other side of the pain. A place governed by logic. Your knees hurt, but there is no real damage being done. Sometimes the body overreacts to a simple stimulus, like a hangnail or a small blister. Neither is a serious threat to the body, but the nerves fire off messages of injury that trigger pain receptors. You have to find a way to acknowledge the hurt, recognize there is nothing to fear because the signal is a misfire, and ignore the pain like an annoying car alarm that won't stop ringing but has no real purpose. Can you do that?" His words made sense, and he sounded so earnest in his interest to help me that I desperately wanted to please him.

"I don't know, but I can try."

"Good girl. Just keep your eyes on me and focus on where our hands are touching. Feel the warmth of my hand and the pressure as I squeeze your fingers." He gently clenched one hand, then the other, cycling back and forth in a hypnotizing rhythm for countless minutes. "There will always be pain in your life, Camilla. Stress and heartache and anxiety. We have to find ways to overcome those challenges and recognize that pain can sometimes be good. It helps us focus. Grow."

I lost track of how much time had passed. It was impossible to tell when the pain warped my perceptions.

I concentrated on his words and his touch, attempting to separate myself from the pain. I wanted to hide from the discomfort, but I also wanted to please him. My efforts were so extraordinary that I was on the cusp of numbness when he suddenly stood and scooped me into his arms like a child.

"Beautiful, sweet girl. You did so well." He set me in one of the chairs, then gently wiped the rice pellets from my skin.

The sudden release of pressure from being lifted off my knees sent my nervous system into chaos. At first, a surge of pain lanced through my legs, but immediately after, an equally violent rush of euphoria stole the breath from my lungs. It was as though liquid relief coursed through my veins, jump-starting my heart rate and injecting me with a flood of delirious energy.

Back when I went through puberty, I got migraines each month. The pain would cripple me. Even the slightest noise or light would send an ice pick straight through my skull. After a couple of hours, the episode would pass, and I found that not only had my anxieties eased but I also felt amazing. Like my body had released a flood of endorphins to counterbalance the misery from before.

That was the same feeling I experienced inside Hale's office.

I was remade. Fully recharged and capable of taking on anything.

The calloused pad of his thumb wiped at the moisture coating my cheeks. "You might want to freshen up before you go back to class." His voice was shockingly lighthearted, as if what had passed between us was as natural as a spring rain.

I was speechless. Dumbfounded.

I'd discovered the most intense natural high I could imagine. The holy grail of coping mechanisms. I also recognized the broader message he'd tried to get across, but I was too obliterated to process it all. I would in the coming weeks, but at that moment, I was spellbound with what I'd uncovered.

Throughout the rest of my junior year, Hale would periodically call me to his office. He always anticipated when I began to hyper-focus on my fears and brought me down from those precarious peaks. His techniques varied. Each was a challenge that I resented like hell until the sweet euphoric release electrified my body after the pain ended. For days after, I floated on air.

I considered telling my parents on a number of occasions. I was aware that what he was doing wasn't professional and possibly even illegal. I could stop him if I wanted to by opening my mouth and telling on him, but that was the source of my greatest shame.

I didn't want it to stop.

I began to like the pain almost as much as the aftereffects.

Sometimes it was my own guilt that wound me tight enough to land in his office. Like a fucked-up carnival ride in a horror movie, my negative emotions fed my need for pain, which created more negative emotions.

It might have been unhealthy, but it worked for me. Until one day when we arrived at school to learn that Principal Hale was gone. He'd supposedly received an incredible job offer out of state and had been required to leave immediately.

Knowing what I did, I suspected I wasn't the only one receiving special lessons, and the word had gotten out. Regardless of the reason, Principal Hale was gone, and I was never the same.

CHAPTER 22
Filip

One time when I was staying with Nona as a young boy, I found a brand-new skateboard tucked away in her closet. My birthday was only a week away, and I knew the board was for me. I floated on air all week, anticipating my gift. When the day rolled around and I opened my present from Nona, I was stunned to unwrap a new Lego set. I'd been certain the skateboard was mine, but I'd somehow forgotten I wasn't Nona's only grandchild.

That same feeling of bewildered astonishment came over me as I listened to Camilla tell her tale. What she imparted was totally unexpected. I'd known there'd been some sort of trauma in her past, and I had pieced together my own suspected conclusions, but none were even close to the truth.

She hadn't been in some dominant/submissive relationship that had gotten out of hand. In fact, it appeared there wasn't even a sexual component to her abuse. At least, not that she had divulged so far. Her principal had taught her to use pain to deal with her troubles. Exploited her.

I'd met any number of women at the club who got off on all sorts of physical discomfort, but this somehow seemed different. More twisted and unsettling. I'd never asked those women about their predilections, but knowing Camilla's backstory certainly changed the way I felt about the use of pain in our play.

She'd been conditioned, groomed even, to receive pain when she was just a child. The man was a predator. Did she even realize that was the case? I had no doubt his intentions were purely selfish. He might not have touched her sexually, but I would bet my life he went home and nutted all over himself when he envisioned what he'd done to her.

That twisted fuck.

David Hale's days were numbered.

"What are you thinking?" Camilla asked in a whisper.

I'd been quiet as I absorbed the implications of her story, and I could tell she'd taken my silence as a cause for worry. As though hearing what had happened to her would make me think less of her. She couldn't have been more wrong.

"I was just thinking about how incredibly strong you are. It makes me sick that you had to endure that." I rolled to face her and hugged her securely to my chest, pressing my lips to her forehead.

"There are so many worse things out there. You lost your mom as a boy. Some kids are subjected to unthinkable circumstances. My situation wasn't ideal, but I almost consider myself lucky."

That was exactly the attitude that made her so damn special.

And what had I done? I'd fucking spanked her. Used the cat o' nine tails on her. I'd caused her pain just like that bastard and felt like utter shit. "Can you ever forgive me?"

She pulled back, pushing past my resistance to look at my face. "Forgive you for what?"

Putting words to my deeds made my skin itch with self-loathing. "For hurting you. For doing the things that ... *man* did to you. If I'd had any idea..."

"No, nononono." She shook her head frantically, squirming from the bed. "This is exactly why I didn't want to tell you." She began to pace beside the bed. "Yes, I went through something. Yes, it changed me, but that's not necessarily a bad thing. It's taken me years to accept who I am and understand I have different tastes than other women. Why do you think I went to the club in the first place? I tried for years to be a normal girl with normal sexual appetites, but that's just not who I am. Not one sexual encounter I've experienced came anywhere close to arousing me the way you do. My desire for pain may have emerged from a bad situation, but it's a part of me, nonetheless. You can't deny me the pleasure just because you feel bad for what happened to me. This is who I am now. If you can't accept that, then you need to let me go because I'm not changing."

I didn't have to see her in the dark to know angry tears were coursing down her cheeks. I scooted to the edge of the bed and reached for her hand, pulling her onto my lap.

"You're right," I admitted, wiping the moisture from her cheeks. "You're absolutely right, and I don't want you to be anyone but who you are."

"I'm glad you think so, but that doesn't answer my question."

So much uncertainty.

So much heartbreak.

Could I cause her more pain after knowing what she'd gone through? After learning the reason for her desires? If I couldn't give her what she wanted, wasn't that the same as rejecting her because of her trauma? I had my own set of issues. Who was I to reject her for hers? I'd enjoyed seeing her smooth skin red from my hand. There was still pleasure in the act, but now it would go hand-in-hand with a helping of guilt unless I could accept Camilla for who she was.

She enjoyed pain, and there was no shame in that alone. She couldn't change the reason that desire came about any more than I could help my mother's death giving me control issues. We were all products of our circumstances to some degree.

"Are there any limits you have—things he did that would upset you now?" If I was going to take this leap, I needed to know that I wasn't doing more damage.

Her head lowered a fraction, and I hated to think she bore any shame for her situation.

"I don't think so. Kneeling was by far his preferred method, so that's what brings back memories. But that's why I wanted to be with you on my knees. I want the act to bring me thoughts of you instead of him."

That made sense, and it actually helped me see my role as therapeutic. I could help turn her association from that of disfunction to being part of a healthy exchange of pleasure between two people. It sounded far better than the alternative. There was no way I'd ever send her away and risk her being abused by some prick who wanted to use her desires in an unhealthy way. Camilla was mine, and I'd give her what she wanted in a way that was good for her.

"If you're open with me so that I don't worry about overstepping my bounds, I see no reason I can't give you what you want."

Her chest shuddered with relief, and she wrapped her arms tight around my neck in a crushing hug. "Thank you, Filip."

I cupped her head with my hand and trailed my fingers down her long hair until she pulled away. "I think we've had enough excitement for one night. We can see where things take us tomorrow once we've had some rest."

We crawled back into bed, my body wrapped snugly around hers. I wasn't in the habit of sleeping with anyone, so I wasn't sure I'd get much rest, especially after all I'd learned. To my surprise, having Camilla safely next to me eased my anxieties, and I was quickly lulled to sleep after her slumbering form relaxed into mine. My heart soared to know she felt safe with me. Safe enough to sleep next to me and safe enough to trust me with her secrets.

This new path we were forging may have been daunting, but I was starting to suspect her role in my life might be just as important as my place in hers.

THE NEXT EVENING, I picked up Camilla at her apartment and drove us to the club together. There was no denying the nervous energy radiating from both of us. We'd spent the day apart after I'd had to leave early for a meeting with Matteo. Camilla had been exhausted and was peacefully sleeping when I left her a note and slipped from her apartment.

Camilla,

I'll come by at eight to take you to the club. Wear the black dress from our first night. Nothing underneath.

Yours,

Filip

I'd considered texting her several times throughout the day but didn't want to seem overbearing. If she'd had any idea how incessantly she'd been on my mind, she'd probably reconsider embarking on this journey. With every encounter, every bit of information I gathered about her, the more she became an ingrained part of me.

My restless thoughts only calmed when I had her back in my sights. Although, knowing she was bare beneath her dress subjected me to a whole new form of torture. It took all my willpower not to defile her in the entry to her apartment.

She was exquisite—the physical embodiment of graceful sensuality. She deserved to be treated like royalty, but that wasn't on the menu. Tonight was about proving to one another we could still indulge in our darker desires. Now that all our cards were on the table, we would see if I could give her what she wanted without being overcome with guilt.

As a bonus, Dante happened to be lingering in the lobby when we arrived. I took enormous pleasure in seeing his face harden at the sight of Camilla at my side, my hand possessively resting on her lower back.

That's right, dickhead. I know you'd love to get your hands on my girl, but that's not going to happen.

He claimed he wasn't moving in on my territory, but I could sense it in my gut. He might have convinced her that his efforts were mere extensions of friendship or the dutiful politeness of a club owner, but I knew better. He wanted Camilla. Unless he backed off soon, things were going to escalate to a dangerous degree.

Dante greeted both of us warmly, but I'd known him long enough to detect the jealousy wafting off him. I'd have to ask Camilla if the club was a necessary part of her interests or if our relationship could be fully satisfying in the privacy of our own bedrooms. Now that I'd found her, the club itself bore no particular interest for me. I'd just as soon avoid Dante's covetous desires if at all possible.

The only thing we could achieve at the club that was inaccessible at home was other people's involvement. Was that even something she wanted? She seemed to enjoy watching others but had recoiled at the prospect of being seen.

A sudden curiosity took root.

I detoured on the way to my room and led her inside the

gathering room. It was still early in the night. Sexual escapades were minimal, and the room was far from crowded. I led Camilla to a dark place along the side wall. She eyed the room, a wary curiosity in her eyes.

I positioned myself directly in front of her, obscuring most of her from view. "We know you enjoy pain, but what other interests do you have?" I cupped her small waist with my hands, gliding up until my thumbs could brush along the underside of her breasts. "If you were hoping to be fucked in front of others, I'm not sure I can fully consent. I don't like the idea of others seeing what's mine."

Her gaze darted away from me to scan the room, and the pulse point on her neck fluttered. "I like seeing other people, but I don't know that I want others to see me."

"I'm glad we agree." I trailed one hand down between us to the hem of her short dress. "But what if I were to touch you … here?" My hand sought out her warmth between her legs and slid two fingers along her slit on either side of her delicate bundle of nerves. "No one can see, although they're nearby. Just a touch of danger knowing we could be caught."

My fingers were quickly coated in Camilla's arousal.

Her chest pressed outward, and her breathing became uneven. My girl wasn't an exhibitionist, but she liked the thrill of adventure. I could definitely work with that.

I played with her until my cock pressed angrily against the zipper on my pants, and her eyes widened in fear that she might come with an audience.

I slowly removed my hand with a satisfied smile. "Let's get you to our room."

Once we were alone, I slipped her dress down her body and instructed her to lay on the bed. I used cuffs to secure her hands in either corner, then bound her ankles into the spreader bar with her knees bent so that she was beautifully open to me.

When she was in position, I went to the chest of drawers in search of something I'd purchased after our first night at the club —an elegant set of gold nipple clamps linked by a dainty gold chain.

"I think you're going to enjoy these." My voice had gone husky from the strain of desire.

I held up the clamps to display, loving the way her nipples pebbled with excitement. I dangled one clamp, allowing the cool metal to trail over one breast and then to the other, dotting her skin in goose bumps. I waited until she was breathless with anticipation before securing the clamp over her pert nipple, devouring her reactions.

"*Oh, God,*" she exclaimed on a whooshing breath as her body squirmed and writhed to adjust to the sensation. Her eyes fluttered shut, but her lips tugged upward in the corners.

I secured the second clamp and was rewarded with a guttural moan from Camilla.

"I thought you'd approve." Resisting the urge to whip out my cock and fuck her to oblivion, I stepped back and slowly removed my clothes, allowing time for the pain to settle in.

As I watched her continue to squirm and breathe through the new sensation, I discovered that I wasn't at all put off by her pain despite what I'd learned about her past. Camilla was unquestionably in her element. She was thriving, delighting in everything I'd done to her, and I found my heart filled with nothing but satisfaction. There was nothing ugly or sordid about what we were doing. We were two people whose needs were perfectly aligned. I required absolute control, and she needed someone who could make her body sing. I could die a happy man if I did nothing else in my life but usher Camilla to the pinnacle of ecstasy each day. I would own her every release. Command her breathless moans and hungrily consume her throaty pleas.

Her knees tilted inward, attempting to bring her legs together enough to alleviate the growing ache in her core.

"What is it, little warrior. Do you need more?" I crawled onto the bed, bringing my face inches from her dripping center.

Sensing my nearness, she widened her thighs in invitation and whimpered with need. Taking mercy on her, I licked the length of her slit, then circled my tongue around her swollen clit. I distracted her enough with my tongue that she didn't notice my hand reaching up until I tugged on the gold chain. Not hard, just enough to send a jolt to her puckered nipples.

Camilla cried out, her body quaking.

I slowed my efforts, giving one slow lick, then several small touches, keeping my movements light and erratic enough not to push her too far to the edge.

"Filip, *please*. I need more."

I dragged my teeth over the delicate lips of her pussy, softly nibbling the flesh. "I'll decide what you need. Right now, I'm having fun playing." I kissed in the hollow below her belly button, then nipped her hip bone and leisurely worked my way up her body.

When we were fully aligned, my cock at her entrance and our eyes locked on one another, I pressed inside her. She'd already been brought so close to the edge enough times that I slid right in, sheathing myself to the hilt.

"You're so ready. So wet and tight," I hissed, my body tight with strain. "You're a fucking dream, Camilla." I held her gaze captive with my own, commanding her to stay with me. To show me the depth of her pleasure. To give me all of her.

I began to move inside her, gradually picking up my rhythm before lowering my lips to her neck. I kissed and nipped, working my way to her delicate pulse point, then farther down to her chest until I was low enough to take the chain between my teeth. I peered up at her with a devious stare. Just as recognition dawned on her pretty face, I lifted my head to draw a steady tension on her nipples while increasing my thrusts to a punishing pace. Her breasts jiggling from my pounding assault tugged against the shimmering clamps over and over until her head thrust back into the mattress, and a savage scream wrenched from her throat. A violent release exploded through her, catapulting me over the edge as well. Her seizing pussy squeezed me until I thought I'd go blind from pleasure. Not just physical but also the knowledge that I did this to her. I made her wild with desire until she lost all inhibitions and surrendered herself completely. As far as I was concerned, there was no greater satisfaction.

When the last waves of release had eased to a trickle, I lowered my body flush against Camilla, my face a breath away from hers. Without overthinking what I was doing, I brought my lips down tenderly. My eyes drifted shut, and I gave her a kiss laced with the swell of emotions filling my chest. It was slow and sensual but ardent. I kissed her with all the words I didn't know how to say. My adoration and respect. Devotion and loyalty.

The kiss was an oath. A pledge I would keep until my dying breath.

When I drew my lips from hers, a tear spilled from the corner of her eye. My message was received. Camilla was so much more than I ever imagined when we first crossed paths. Like two planets colliding, our budding relationship shifted my center of gravity until my priorities no longer revolved around myself. Camilla was all that mattered. Guiding her, supporting her, protecting her, and making her mine in every way possible.

My life was no longer my own, and for once, that prospect didn't scare me in the slightest because I knew down to my bones that she was meant to be mine.

CHAPTER 23
Camilla

From the minute I agreed to Filip's terms our first night at the Den, I'd wrestled with a nagging feeling of uncertainty. Every day, it preyed on my subconscious like a hungry buzzard, pecking away at my decisions and making me question if I'd done the right thing by entering our agreement. For weeks, the doubts haunted me, but that all changed with his kiss.

A precious kiss fraught with emotion.

Everything that happened that night strengthened my resolve, but it was the kiss that shredded the last of my barriers like a blade through silk. Filip had seen my naked body before, but not until that moment had I been totally bare.

My heart was exposed—raw and vulnerable—with his initials imprinted deep into the tissue.

There would be no erasing him from my life.

He would always be a part of me.

After he walked me home, I lay in bed and basked in all that had transpired, delighted in the bond we'd fortified, and savored the strange new sense of certainty that had overcome me. I might not have known what came next for us, but I was sure good things lay ahead. Now that he'd shown he would respect my needs and we'd demonstrated our ability to work through our differences, I had confidence that he was my future.

I was in such a good mood at the close of our night that I set my alarm early enough the next morning to attend church with my parents. My mother was utterly delighted when I phoned to tell her I was on my way. Surprisingly enough, my positive outlook was so pervasive that it kept the outing from feeling like a chore. I had a good visit with my parents and kept myself distracted from obsessing over Filip. In all, the day was a success.

That evening, I texted Filip to let him know I'd made it home. He'd held true to his promise to ensure my safety, keeping eyes on me at all times. We agreed a trip to my parents' house would be of little danger, but he asked that I text him at the beginning and end of each trip. The cartel situation wasn't resolved, so we weren't taking anything for granted.

Me: Made it home.

Filip: Thank you for letting me know. Have a good visit?

Me: Yes, but glad to be home.

Filip: Wish I was there with you. Matteo needed me out in the Hamptons today, so I had to leave the city. You have plans besides work tomorrow?

My heart tap-danced against my ribs. I wished he was here with me, too.

Me: No, just work.

Filip: Will you go out for lunch?

Me: No, taking lunch with me.

Filip: Good. Let me know if you change your mind, and I'll send someone to go with you.

Me: Will do. ❤

Filip: I'll be out here until Tuesday morning. Have dinner with me when I'm back in town?

My skittering heartbeat gave way to a flooding warmth in my belly. I adored my time at the club with Filip, but dinner and conversation were just as appetizing.

Me: I'd love to.

Filip: Sounds good. I'll touch base later tomorrow.

Me: Night, Filip.

Filip: Sweet dreams. Get some rest. You're going to need it.

The grin on my face would have made pageant queens green with envy.

I put my phone away and tried to go back to reading but could hardly concentrate past the distracting prospect of an evening with Filip. It was a good thing I had faith in our relationship because I was a total goner.

DONALD NEVER OFFICIALLY FIRED ME, so I showed up for work on Monday with an updated resume I'd polished over the weekend. I planned to spend my lunch hour checking out job sites for professionals and hunting down new opportunities.

Aside from an uncomfortable management meeting where Donald berated several team members in front of our entire group, the morning passed without incident. Around eleven thirty, one of the tellers popped her head in to let me know I had a visitor. The middle-aged woman waggled her eyebrows as she passed on the message, making me laugh.

Filip must have made it back to town early and wanted to take me to lunch. I dropped what I was doing and hurried toward the lobby, excited to see the man who had quickly overtaken my every thought. When I stepped from behind the transaction counter, Filip wasn't who I found waiting for me.

"Dante, this is a surprise." My smile faltered as I greeted my unexpected guest.

What on earth was he doing here? Would anyone recognize him? I hadn't known who he was until I joined the club, but all it would take to ruin me was for the wrong person to see us together. I had to get him out of there.

"I happened to be nearby and decided to see if you wanted to do lunch." He was incredibly handsome and had been nothing but kind to me. I hated to be rude to him, but between his profession and Filip's warning to stay away from him, I wasn't sure what to do.

"Um, I was going to work through lunch. I wish I'd known."

Dante's brows drew together, and he stepped closer. "This is rather important. Is there any way you can make time for a quick lunch?"

Fuck. Fuckfuckfuck.

"Yeah, okay. Let me just grab my stuff, and we can go." I gave him a tight smile and hurried back to my office.

He sounded like he had something important to discuss. I couldn't fathom what it was. Filip would be so annoyed if he knew Dante was here. It would be easier not to say anything, but I'd promised to let him know if I went out for lunch. I wanted to be completely transparent with him. If we were going to have a solid foundation for a relationship, we would need to be honest with one another.

I shot him a quick text before tossing my phone in my purse and heading back to the lobby.

Me: Please don't be upset. Dante needed to talk to me, so we are grabbing a quick lunch together.

I trusted him enough to let him know. Hopefully, he would trust me enough not to freak out.

I suggested a café just down the street from the bank. Our conversation on the walk was comfortable and gave me no insight into what he wanted to discuss. We ordered at the counter, then found a table in a corner.

I leaned in and spoke quietly in an attempt at privacy. "So what is this all about? Is everything okay?"

Dante scooted his chair a few inches closer to me, then clasped his hands together on the table. "I can't sit by and watch you get hurt. I see you forming an attachment to Filip, and I know he's going to break your heart ... or worse." His lips flattened to a thin line, all traces of the lighthearted club owner buried beneath harsh angles and an ominous stare.

"Filip is your friend. Surely, you don't think that poorly of him."

"Just because I've known him a long time doesn't mean I agree with the things he does. I've seen how he disposes of women, Camilla, and I don't want you to fall victim to that." He placed his hand over mine, his gentle squeeze meant to be reassuring, but I only found discomfort in his touch.

I slid my hand away from his. "I know your warning comes from a good place, but you don't know anything about my relationship with Filip."

Lightning fast, his hand slapped the table. "No, *you* don't understand what he's capable of." When Dante lifted his angry gaze and saw the distress on my face from his outburst, his hands rose in surrender. "I'm sorry. I shouldn't have done that. It's just that I've seen what he and that *family* of his can do to people. They would send a child into the world parentless rather than accept the consequences of their own actions. You may have been a product of that world, but that same evil doesn't live in you. You are not a monster, and I don't want that horror to touch you."

Had the mafia hurt Dante in some way? I got the distinct feeling his grudge was personal, but why would he be friends with Filip if he disliked that world so much? My heart hurt to see him so upset, but none of it made any sense.

"I appreciate you looking out for me, I really do, but this is my life, and I think I'm on the right path. If you find it that upsetting to see us together, I can stay away from the club."

"No." He shook his head. "That's not necessary. I would feel even worse if my actions pushed you away. I just need to know that I've done everything I can." The fight bled from his face, leaving only pained resignation.

I gave him a smile, though somewhat forced. "Let's hope your concern is unnecessary and everything works out for the best."

He returned a smile even more pallid than my own just as a man behind the counter shouted our lunch order number. Dante retrieved our food, and we didn't speak of Filip again during the remainder of our awkward lunch.

I was at a loss as to how to handle the Dante situation.

He left after escorting me back to the bank, but the dilemma weighed on me for the rest of the afternoon. To top things off, Donald stormed into my office five minutes after I returned from lunch.

"I get that you women are flaky, but if you can't remember to tell me before you take an early lunch, you need to stick to regular lunch hours." The perfectly coifed hair he scrupulously maintained had lost its crispy shell, and several strands had disobediently migrated over his forehead.

"I apologize for the inconvenience. I had an unexpected visitor and didn't want to bother you when I left." Better to ask forgiveness than permission, especially when dealing with a maniacal infant for a boss.

He waved his hand in dismissal. "I need all the paperwork for the Valencia deal from three years back."

"Anything that old would have been archived."

"I'm aware," he deadpanned. "I need you to retrieve it. Everything we have, including notes. This is a priority; I need it imme-diately." He disappeared from my doorway without another word.

I breathed out an enormous sigh, my shoulders slumping with the strain of the last hour. What a Monday.

"Hey, did Donald find you?" Trent asked, suddenly appearing in my office.

"Unfortunately."

"He was raising hell looking for you earlier."

"So I gathered. He wants me to pull up some old file from three years ago."

Trent peeked over his shoulder into the hallway. "Some guy was here earlier this morning asking for Donald. He had a Spanish accent and wasn't familiar. I've never seen Donald be so polite to another human being. I don't know what's going on, but it looked shady as fuck."

"You get the guy's name?"

"Nah, I don't think he gave a name. I just happened to see Donald greet him in the lobby and take him back to his office. It had to either be someone important from corporate or a huge customer. He wouldn't kiss ass like that for anyone else."

I rolled my eyes, fed up with the Donald drama. "I'm over it. I've got my resume updated and am on the hunt. That man is toxic."

"I hate to hear that, but I also understand." Trent pouted. "This sucks. Now I'm sad."

I had to smile. "Well, you can always do the same. Either way, it's not like I'm leaving the city. We can still catch up over lunches."

"You mean wine? Catch up over wine." He dropped his chin to his chest and gave me a devious stare.

Now he had me outright laughing. "Of course. Wine it is. Now get back to your office before I get in any more trouble."

He bent in a flourishing bow, then swept from my office.

My day had been a clusterfuck, and it was only half over. Fortunately, I had an evening with Filip in my sights. One more day and I'd be back in his arms. It was amazing how the proper motivation made everything seem more manageable.

CHAPTER 24

Filip

"What the fuck is he up to now?" I bit out through clenched teeth.

"Someone giving you trouble?" Matteo asked from behind his office desk. We'd just made it out to his place in the Hamptons when Camilla's text came through.

"Not exactly. Dante Capello keeps pissing me off."

"Thought you two were friends."

"Me too, but the guy seems to have a death wish." My eyes were still glued to my phone, but I could sense my brother studying me.

"Not much comes between friends besides money and women. He borrow money from you or something?"

I finally met his curious gaze. "No, he didn't." Things with Camilla were moving in the right direction, but I hadn't considered telling anyone about us.

"This have anything to do with Camilla?" His voice took on a hard edge.

"That's not your concern."

"It is when you throw Dante in the mix. That man practically lives at his club. Can you honestly tell me his involvement with Camilla has nothing to do with the Den?"

Well, fuck. This just kept getting better and better.

"Look, I know it looks bad, but I've got it under control. Camilla is safe. And for Christ's sake, don't tell your wife. If Maria found out her cousin had anything to do with the club, she'd have my balls."

"Maybe she should. You're playing with fire, Filip. You can't just let a Genovese girl get passed around a fucking club."

"Don't you think I know that? It's not an issue anymore."

"And why's that?"

I pushed back at him with a confident glare. "Because she's with me now. Camilla Genovese is mine."

Matteo lifted his chin. "I see. And does Dante know this?"

"Yes, but he doesn't seem willing to accept it. I'll have words with him when I get back to the city." I let out an audible sigh, eyes wandering out the window as I considered what Dante would say to Camilla at their lunch. I stopped myself from falling too far down the rabbit hole when I sensed the heavy weight of Matteo's silence.

His eyes were still intently trained on me. "I wasn't sure I'd ever see the day you settled down, but I suppose the timing is good. One of the reasons I wanted to have you out here was to talk about your promotion. I've got a meeting set up tomorrow evening to announce you as the newest capo. You'll need to attend. I also plan to move you into the role of underboss in the next year. The role has been empty for too long. I need someone I can trust representing the organization, and that's you. I should have been more open with you from the beginning about my intent. Going forward, we'll need transparency between us if we are to stay a united front. I believe we can make that happen.

Growing up, our age difference and Mom's death made it hard to connect, but we're past all that."

While he'd already told me his intent, it still winded me to hear him voice his trust in me. All I wanted from the time I was little was to stand on the same footing as my brothers. To be a respected and reliable pillar in my family. I was sure Nona and others viewed me with such regard, but it was an entirely different honor to receive accolades from my brother.

"I appreciate your trust in me. You know I'd give my life for the family."

"Let's hope it doesn't come to that. We all experienced enough loss for a lifetime when Mom was taken."

"At least you got to be a part of avenging her. That's one of my biggest regrets in life." I brushed out invisible wrinkles from my pants. "That I would have been old enough to help punish those responsible."

He shook his head. "It's best you weren't there. Maybe you would have ended up like Gabe and rejected the family life."

"It didn't stop you."

"Yeah, but killing Rocco Leone still seeps into my dreams. I was young. Too young. I insisted I was ready, but that shit haunted me for a long time even though I felt justified in what I did. He set up the hit that took our mother, but ending his life changed me. I'm glad you didn't have to go through that. That's why I made sure you weren't made until you were older. Until you could handle the consequences."

With each new piece of information, I viewed my brother in a new light. "I thought when I wasn't made until I was eighteen that you and the family didn't trust me."

Matteo slowly shook his head. "No, Filip. I was trying to protect you."

I swallowed past the lump of emotions swelling in my throat.

"I appreciate that, Teo. I appreciate everything you do for me and the family."

He fidgeted in his seat, something I rarely ever saw him do. "All right. Enough of this touchy-feely shit. Let's get some work done so we can celebrate. I've got an unopened bottle of Glenlivet perfect for the occasion."

We got on a conference call with his consigliere to discuss operational matters, then brainstormed ways to draw out the cartel. I got a text from Camilla letting me know she'd made it back from lunch, which helped me relax. I'd intended to call her after dinner to find out about her time with Dante, but Matteo and I were halfway into our bottle of scotch by six that evening. I never got around to calling before I passed out.

The next morning, Matteo shook me awake, informing me that he'd received a call from one of our police informants about a cartel-related shooting. We needed to get to the city ASAP.

I ignored my pounding headache, throwing on my clothes and grabbing a coffee before we jumped in the car. Both hungover, we were mostly quiet on the way. When Matteo pulled up near National Bank, a surge of adrenaline erased all traces of discomfort.

A single cop car remained parked next to a perimeter of yellow caution tape near the bank's entrance. When he said there'd been a shooting, I hadn't panicked because he would have told me if it was someone we'd known. Learning how close the incident had been to Camilla made me overcome with rage.

"What the fuck happened here? This is the bank where Camilla works. Was anyone else injured?" I was out of the car before it came to a rest. Matteo hurried after me.

"Take it easy." He grabbed my arm to slow me down. "No one else was hurt. An old guy was killed, and that's it. We can find out the rest from Danny. I had him volunteer to stay at the scene so we could talk to him."

The cop leaning against the back of his cruiser nodded in our direction. Everything but the caution tape had been removed from the scene once it was processed.

I took several calming breaths, reassuring myself that Camilla was okay. By the time we were at Danny's side, I had sealed off my emotions and become stone-cold efficiency. A red bloodstain on the sidewalk was all that remained of the crime. The cop would have to be our eyes and ears.

"What happened?" Matteo asked.

"Name was Donald Carter. Must have pissed off the wrong people—chopped off his fucking hand right here in broad daylight with some kind of fucking machete." The man shook his head, eyes still seeing the gruesome sight. "That's why they're thinking cartel. Who the fuck else uses a machete like we're in some kind of fucking jungle?"

My brother's eyes slowly swept the area. "I need to see pictures."

"I figured you would. Got a couple as soon as I arrived." He pulled out his phone and brought up an image of a man sliced across the neck, hand no longer attached.

"Christ, that was Camilla's boss." I'd made sure to get a look at the guy when we went to dinner. How the hell was he associated with the cartel? "I need to go inside and find her." She would be an ideal source of information, but primarily, I had to see with my own eyes that she was okay. I'd texted her on the way in but hadn't heard back from her.

Matteo nodded, staying with Danny to get the rest of the details.

I marched through the lobby to an unoccupied teller behind the counter. "I need to see Camilla Genovese."

"Um, I'm not sure she came in today, but it's hard for me to say since I'm not back in the offices much. I can call back to her office." She smiled warmly, but I had no time for politeness.

I bolted past the counter and down a hallway to the administrative offices. When I came to a woman at a desk, I asked her to point me in the direction of Camilla's office.

"Actually, it's right here." She pointed at a closed door, the window revealing a dark office. "She didn't come in today. Don't think she called in sick either, which is strange for her."

My muscles twitched with a need for violence.

Camilla was in danger, and someone was going to pay.

Had the cartel come for her boss, figured out who she was, and taken her as collateral? I pulled out my phone and rang her number. No answer. I left a message, then sent a text for her to call me immediately.

The woman peered at me anxiously. "Is everything all right?"

"Camilla may be in trouble. Did anything happen yesterday out of the ordinary?"

"No, aside from that handsome man who came to take her to lunch. She was in her office most of the afternoon, but that's normal. Nothing else comes to mind." Her hands worried at a twisted tissue. "Should we call the police?"

"No," I shot back. "I'll take care of it. Thank you for your time." I nodded, then hurried back out front to where Matteo waited for me.

"Camilla didn't show up for work today, and I can't get ahold of her. I tried to pull up her phone's GPS, but it's not showing up. Something's wrong." I tried to keep a cool exterior even though I was raging on the inside. If someone hurt her, I'd burn the city down to get revenge.

I was practiced at reining in my emotions in work settings, but Matteo was part machine. If any fear or anger existed beneath that icy façade, it was too deep to detect.

"I'll need to inform her family, and you need to look into all possible avenues. You were awfully concerned about her lunch with Dante. Is there any chance he could be involved?"

The possibility made my stomach churn. "Her coworkers said she came back from lunch and acted normal, but I suppose anything's possible. I'll check with him and run by her place. Assuming he wasn't involved, he can help us search."

Matteo nodded. "Keep me informed."

I charged toward the street to flag down a cab on a mission to find my woman.

Lord have mercy on anyone in my path.

CHAPTER 25

Camilla

EIGHTEEN HOURS EARLIER

Being at the bank was so mentally exhausting that I was almost glad Filip was out of town. I could put on my comfiest pajamas and curl up in bed with my e-reader for the rest of the evening. No oppressive boss. No awkward lunches. Just me, myself, and I with a good book.

I melted back against the elevator wall, the promise of solace relaxing me as I coasted upward toward my apartment. Maybe I'd even soak in a bubble bath with a glass of wine. I wasn't sure what I had in the fridge, but it didn't matter. I'd eat moldy bread for dinner if it meant I didn't have to encounter another living soul until tomorrow.

Arriving on the twentieth floor, I walked to my door and let myself in. I moved to disarm the alarm only to find a green light glowing on the deactivated panel. How odd. I was religious about setting the alarm when I left the apartment. Work stress must have distracted me more than I'd realized. I deadbolted the door and turned on the lights, even more convinced I needed a night off to relax.

I walked from the entry around to the kitchen and froze. Dante stood propped against the counter, ankles crossed and posture relaxed as though he were at home in his own apartment.

"What the hell, Dante?" My hand clutched my chest where my heart had stopped from shock, then tumbled into a punishing rhythm as adrenaline surged in my veins.

Something was horribly wrong.

Dante had broken into my apartment. He didn't give off a threatening vibe. Even worse, he was eerily calm. The more I processed the situation, the more terrified I became. No matter his intention, this was unacceptable.

"You need to get out, *now*." The firm tone I sought was edged in fear despite my best efforts.

He smiled—a remorseful, treacherous twist of his mouth— then slowly pushed away from the counter. "You never would give me a chance. I suppose I should have expected your reaction to finding me here. Somehow, it still stings." He stepped closer, pondering his surprise.

I clutched my purse to my chest. "Dante, you broke into my apartment. I would be angry with anyone who did that."

"No." He shook his head. "I've been nothing but good to you. Listened when you talked and offered my protection, sent you flowers and checked on you when you were upset. I've warned you time and again and tried to show you that I was the better option, but when you walked into the Den together, the way you gazed up at him, I could see it was a lost cause. Something had changed. Something irrevocable."

My anxiety fermented into a paralyzing fear.

Something was wrong with Dante.

How had I not detected it before? Had he developed some kind of obsession with me? He'd been so casual about our friendship, aside from a couple of awkward instances. He claimed to have been campaigning for my affection but had never once been forthright about his intentions. I had known he didn't want me with Filip, but that was not the same as wanting me for himself. The knowledge cast a new light on all of our interactions from the first time I met him when he gave me his card and encouraged me to call him. I'd assumed he was being a concerned host. Did he not offer the same courtesy to every new member? Now, I wasn't so sure.

"I ... I had no idea. I thought you were being kind. I never realized ..." I stumbled over my words, trying to process it all.

His lips thinned in a sad smile as he stepped closer.

"Please don't hurt me." Helpless, frustrated tears began to well in my eyes.

"I have no intention of hurting you, Camilla." His voice was so reassuring, I almost believed him. "I do, however, need to take you with me. Things didn't go as I'd hoped, which only leaves me one alternative. I've waited too long to let this chance slip through my fingers."

Take me? Where? Why? The answers would undoubtedly mean bad things for me. Would Filip or my family be able to find me? Did Filip have any idea his friend was psychotic? There was no way I could overpower him, but would I ever be found if I left willingly? Would my family even figure out who was behind my abduction?

I had to get them a message. Leave a clue or find a way to tell them who had taken me. I couldn't grab my phone from my purse without him seeing and had nowhere to hide it beneath my clothes. How else could I get the message across?

The image of Dante's business card appeared in my mind.

After that first night at the club, I'd deposited it in the small zipper pocket on the outside of my purse when I transferred my wallet from the clutch I'd been using. I slowly lowered my hand so that my fingers hovered over the small, innocuous pocket. Relief washed over me when I discovered that I'd never zipped the pocket closed.

"Where are we going?" I asked, trying to engage him to keep him distracted.

"Somewhere safe. Somewhere you won't be needing *that*." He dropped his gaze to my purse.

It was now or never.

Heart pounding, I slipped the straps off my shoulder, turning the pocketed side toward me. With astonishing dexterity, considering the tremors now coursing through my body, I slid two fingers into the pocket and swiped the card from within, positioning it flat against my palm. I then set my purse on the counter, depositing the simple piece of cardstock beneath.

When I lifted my eyes back to Dante, he had a syringe in his hand. With his one swift movement, I felt a pricking sting in my neck, and the world went dark.

A FISSURE of pain lancing through my skull stirred me to consciousness. Cracking my eyes open only made the pain worse, but an unsettling sense of urgency refused to allow me the mercy of slipping back into the dark abyss.

Why did my head feel like it was splitting in two?

A peek through slitted lids revealed that I lay on an unfamiliar black leather sofa in an upscale apartment. Across from me sat an elegant glass coffee table, and beyond that, Dante peered at me from a red velour armchair. A flood of memories assaulted me.

Oh, God. He drugged me. Dante had drugged and kidnapped me.

My stomach rebelled. I pressed a hand over my mouth and fought back the urge to vomit.

"Here, have a sip of water. It'll help." Dante set a full bottle of water on the table before me, then sat back down and began scrolling through his phone as if he were looking after a sick friend rather than tending to his prisoner.

I pushed upright and took the plastic bottle with a shaky hand. Swallowing the room temperature water did help settle my rioting insides. My gaze swept the room—a luxury apartment somewhere in the city, the afternoon sun shining through large plate-glass windows. How long had I been out? Had Dante done anything to me while I was unconscious? I still wore my clothes, but the uncertainty made my skin crawl.

"Why are you doing this?" I rasped. My throat felt as though I'd been screaming for hours.

Vacuous black irises lifted to stare blankly at me. "They took everything from me—Filip's family. I've waited for the right opportunity to repay him. To hurt him. The man who had everything I should have had. I started to think it would never happen and had almost given up entirely. Killing Filip would have been too easy. I wanted to hurt him like they hurt me. But how could I do that when he didn't care about anything? No one I could easily use to hurt him. Then you arrived. When I saw the way he looked at you, I knew. You were the key."

"But you're his friend." I was too stunned to understand what he was telling me. I'd thought he had become obsessed with me, but now I wondered if I'd been nothing but a pawn. A means to an end.

A small callous smile lifted his mouth at either corner. "Keep your friends close and your enemies closer. Poor Camilla. Did no one ever teach you that?"

"You're going to hurt me to punish Filip?" The words were only a whisper. I was winded from the violent realization that I was in more trouble than I ever could have imagined. There was no rationalizing with hatred, and that was exactly what I was dealing with.

Dante hated Filip down to the marrow of his bones.

"It's unfortunate, isn't it?" he mused almost absently as if pondering one of life's great mysteries. "If you could have given me a chance and rejected Filip, I would have accepted that. Served him defeat by having you at my side and reveled in knowing he was denied the one woman he craved." When he peered back at me, his gaze was almost mournful. "I think I would have enjoyed that a great deal." He shrugged. "But that's not how it played out, so instead, we move on to plan B. And on that note, I need to get going. You've been out for over fifteen hours. I'll need to play my part if this is going to work." He stood and walked to a closed door, rapping twice against the wood. "It's time."

Someone else was in the apartment? Dante had an accomplice who knew he planned to hurt me? Or was this the person who would harm me while Dante was off pretending to be the loyal friend? How could I ever escape if I was being guarded?

Terror was a relentless python savagely constricting my throat.

I had to get away. I couldn't just let these monsters hurt me.

For the first time since I woke, my eyes darted around the room for something I could use as a makeshift weapon. The only thing in reach that would be heavy enough was a ceramic lamp, but that was probably too unwieldy to be of help. Maybe if I ran to another room. The kitchen was behind me, so I could grab a knife if I was fast enough. I started to peer in that direction but was distracted when Dante's accomplice stepped into view.

Righteous flames of fury scorched the blood thrumming in my veins.

"You *bitch*," I hissed, muscles coiling with the need to launch myself at the woman.

Liana, in all her redheaded glory, stood nonchalantly in the living room as though she hadn't just participated in a felony kidnapping plot.

She chuckled as if amused by my anger. "Looks like Little Miss Perfect won't be getting her man after all." She handed Dante something that looked like a white stick.

Not a stick. A zip tie.

Dante hauled me to my feet and forcefully secured my hands behind my back.

"Don't leave me here with her. This isn't you, Dante. *Please.*" I tried to reason with him with little hope of success.

He lowered me back to the couch and turned to Liana, ignoring me completely. "I don't know how long I'll be gone. You are not to harm her, you hear me?"

Liana rolled those perfect emerald eyes of hers. "I said I'd do what you asked. I don't give a shit about her so long as you get her out of the picture."

I detected a faint sneer from Dante. During our conversation weeks ago, I'd suspected that he wasn't a fan of Liana, and it appeared little had changed. Theirs was an arrangement of convenience. One which hinged on her not harming me. It was a small consolation, but enough to settle my nerves and give me time to escape.

My first course of action? Trick Liana into giving me information. Considering what I'd seen of her reckless tendencies so far, I could do the job in my sleep.

CHAPTER 26

Filip

Dante wouldn't be at the club for several hours, so I went in search of him at his apartment. I didn't tell him I was coming. I wanted to read his reactions in person to help me decide if he could have been responsible for Camilla's disappearance. I didn't want it to be true after knowing him for so long, but I wouldn't rule anything out.

He answered the door shirtless with specks of shaving cream still on his face. "Hey, man. What's up?"

"Camilla's gone missing." I stepped inside his place, studying him intently. I tried to discern the tiniest degree of derision that might signal he was complicit in her disappearance, but there was nothing. No guilty fidgeting or anxious glances. He appeared genuinely shocked at my announcement.

"Missing? Are you sure?"

"There was a murder at her office this morning. I tried to locate her, but her coworkers said she never showed up at work."

Dante stiffened, undoubtedly shocked. "A murder? What the fuck happened?"

I blew out a breath, both relieved and frustrated that Dante appeared innocent. I didn't want my longtime friend to betray me, but if he wasn't behind Camilla's disappearance, locating her would be far more difficult. The thought of her in the hands of the cartel made it hard to breathe.

"Her boss was somehow involved with the cartels, who have been trying to infiltrate the city. We've been looking for them but haven't had much luck flushing them out. I wanted to check with you since you had lunch with her yesterday. See if you had any ideas of where she might have gone or what might have happened."

"I don't, but let me throw on some clothes, and I'll help you look."

He hurried back to his bedroom, leaving me alone. I glanced around at the black-and-white-themed décor without truly seeing anything. My head was cycling through questions and information, trying to put together any tidbits that might reveal what had happened to Camilla. Nothing emerged from the darkness, like being in a waking nightmare where my eyes were opened, but I still couldn't see.

Dante returned in a few short minutes. "Where should we look first?"

"I want to check her place. Make sure she isn't there and see if the security footage shows anything." Hopefully, he wouldn't question why I hadn't gone there first.

He drove us to her building, the short trip rife with tension about what we'd find when we arrived. The elevator ride alone lasted three lifetimes. When we finally arrived at the door, it was locked without any signs of life inside when we knocked. I pulled out a credit card to try to jimmy the lock without any success. When that didn't work, I resorted to physical force. After two solid kicks, the door began to pull from its frame. I shouldered my way inside to a seemingly empty apartment.

I called her name. No response.

Everything appeared in order until I entered further and noticed her purse sitting on the counter. I'd seen her use a couple of different handbags, so it wasn't necessarily an ominous sign, but my pulse began to throb in my temples. My gut reaction was that Camilla was in terrible trouble.

I pulled open the black leather bag, finding her wallet and phone inside. "No wonder I couldn't locate her," I murmured. "The damn thing was turned off." I powered it back on but didn't have the passcode to access her information. "There's no way she left her apartment voluntarily without her phone and wallet. There are no signs of a struggle, so either she was caught completely by surprise or she was taken by someone she knew. Let's look around and see if we can find anything."

Every molecule of my being narrowed its focus to the task of finding Camilla. It was entirely possible that I'd lost her, and I'd never see her again. Fear and anger welled up in my chest until it hurt to breathe. I channeled the useless emotions into persistence and a burning conviction to do whatever it took to find her.

Dante searched the living room while I began to scour the kitchen, hoping that a junk drawer or discarded paper in the trash might give me a clue. When I came back around to where I'd started, a tiny white paper corner poking out from beneath her purse caught my eye. I reached over and slid the card out from beneath her purse, slipping it beneath my palm when I recognized the lion head emblem in the center.

The Lion's Den. It was Dante's business card.

She'd had lunch with him the day before, but why would she have placed her purse over the card? It wasn't like there was clutter on the counter, and the purse had simply been set atop haphazardly. Her place was spotless. She was intentional about everything in her life, and I had to believe that concealing his card beneath her purse was no less purposeful.

Could Dante have truly been behind her abduction?

I glanced over to where he stood, head down searching between the couch cushions. "See anything?" I asked, wishing I could beat the answers out of him.

"Not even crumbs." He rose and joined me in the kitchen. His left hand absently twisted the ring on his right pinky. His lion's head ring with the initials LD. Lion's Den. They always seemed backward to me, but I figured it was a part of the design the same as when an enlarged surname initial is placed between first and middle name initials.

What if the initials *were* in order? DL. Instead of Lion's Den, Dante... I considered my friend and his fondness for lions, and my conversation with Matteo came rushing back to me.

Killing Rocco Leone still seeps into my dreams.

Leone. Italian for lion.

The name of the family who had issued the hit on my father, inadvertently killing my mother. Dante's last name was Capello, but his parents had died when he was young, and he'd been adopted by another family. Had they given him their last name? Could he have been born a Leone?

I recalled the first time we fought back in high school. Dante went into a rage as if he'd truly wanted me dead. If I hadn't been such a proficient fighter, his fervor might have overtaken me. Back then, I wrote it off as teenage anger issues, but had it been more? When I took a mental step back and examined all the facts and history, my blood ran cold. I had no concrete evidence, but that innate sense we're all born with screamed that I'd unearthed the truth of the matter.

It took all my self-control to remain calm and act as if nothing had changed when inside, my thirst for violence was unrelenting. "Will you have a look at the bedrooms? I'd like to see about getting my hands on the security footage. She's definitely been here. Maybe we can see who else came to her place or when she left."

"Sounds good."

"I'll meet you down in the lobby." I walked away, unable to look at him a second longer. I called Matteo from the elevator.

"Find her?"

"No, but you were right about Dante," I growled, fingers twitching to crush the phone. "He's involved somehow. I think he's related to the Leone family."

"The kid. We killed both brothers involved in the plot to kill Dad. It was supposed to be just the men involved. The only reason one of their wives was killed was because she came at Dad with a gun. I'd heard one of them had a kid, but we never touched him. Couldn't have even if we'd wanted to, but he wasn't there when we tracked them down. Kids are never targets; it's the family way."

"I think this kid grew up with fantasies of revenge, and he's chosen me as his target."

"He know that you're onto him?"

"No. I'm about to check security footage at her place while he finishes searching her apartment. I'm going to play dumb and see if I can get him to lead me to her."

"Keep me posted. I'll update the others. We've got both families on the hunt."

The families were searching, but would she be alive when we found her? My throat tightened in a way I hadn't experienced since I was a kid. I couldn't respond.

"We'll get her back alive, Filip. On my word." With the slightest dip in his voice, Matteo went from boss to brother. His words were the perfect reminder to stay strong. I couldn't let doubts enter my mind. Camilla was alive, and I would get her back.

"Yeah." I nodded. "I'll be in touch."

The security footage had been scrubbed. Nothing was available for the past twenty-four hours, and the geriatric security guard I'd found napping at his desk had no idea how something like that could have happened.

I went back to the lobby and found Dante waiting.

"Get anything?" he asked.

Vile piece of shit. He knew there was nothing to find.

"It was erased. Someone knew what they were doing. What about you? Find anything in the apartment?"

"Nothing." He shook his head, lips pressed in a thin line as if he couldn't believe our bad luck.

"My brother's got a search started. I'm going to meet up with him."

"Is there anything I can do?"

"I'm not sure what the next move is, but I can let you know if we need help."

"Anytime, I want to do whatever I can. I'll take you to your brother. It's the least I can do."

"I'd appreciate that." I dug down deep and thought about Camilla before I extended my hand in a false show of gratitude. I'd rather choke him than shake his hand, but that wouldn't help. He couldn't give me answers if he was dead.

Dante dropped me at Matteo's building. I walked toward the lobby, but the second he pulled away, I ran for a cab. We were several cars back. Midmorning traffic flowed smoothly, and I started to think my plan might work. Then Dante stopped at a red light, waited until it would be impossible for us to follow, and gunned it across the intersection, disappearing from view.

CHAPTER 27

Camilla

"I f Filip had wanted to be with you, he would have claimed you already. You know that, right?" Screwing with Liana was giving me a sick sense of satisfaction. If I had to guess, I'd say no one had ever told little Miss Liana no in her entire life.

Did I just imagine it, or did her eyelid twitch?

"You've been with him for a hot minute, and you think you know anything about him? I've been a part of Filip's life for *years*."

"Exactly. Just a pretty knickknack on a shelf, taken down on occasion to be dusted off, used, and put back." I shrugged.

Liana attempted to intimidate me with a glare, but her attempt was laughable. "Our open arrangement was a mutual decision. I could have had him to myself if I wanted, which is exactly what will happen once you're gone. I'll be there to comfort him, support him, and give him what he needs."

"A rebound? Your endgame is to be his rebound fuck? Might want to reconsider; those never last."

Red blotches rose up the column of her neck, disappearing once they reached the thick layer of foundation below her jawline.

I ignored her anger and continued. "So, how did this partnership between you and Dante come about? I didn't get the feeling you two were besties."

Liana lifted her chin defiantly. "He approached me about a mutually beneficial arrangement. He needed a little help, and I was happy to see you disappear. It was a win-win."

"You think he needed you here to help? I'm pretty sure he could have tied me up instead of bringing in a guard. I'd say there was another reason. Otherwise, why risk anyone else knowing about his crime?" I was trying to get her thinking but stumped myself in the process. Why *did* Dante include Liana in his plan? The most obvious answer was to have a scapegoat on hand in case things went south. Did he plan on framing her for my disappearance?

"What are you getting at?"

"I just think it's odd, that's all." I glanced around the apartment. "This your place?"

Her eyes swept the room, her spine stiffening a fraction. "It is, but that doesn't mean anything. We needed someplace Filip wouldn't look for you, and my place made sense."

"I'll bet it did."

"Listen, this is Dante's show. I'm just lending a hand. It's his problem if the cops come calling."

I tsked, shaking my head slowly. "Right. Were you naïve enough to think my disappearance wouldn't make any waves? Or did Dante fail to tell you exactly who I am?"

There it was again—a tic in her right eyelid. Someone was more anxious than she let on. This was going to be even easier than I'd expected.

"You're nobody," she hissed. "A face on a milk carton and a distant memory."

The corners of my mouth drew back in a callous grin. "I'm the niece of the Lucciano family boss. That name ring a bell?"

The color bled from her face so drastically that I could even see it through her caked-on makeup.

"I see it does. Do you really believe the *mafia* will look the other way when I go missing? No, Liana. They'll dig. They'll find answers. They'll come for Dante and anyone else who was involved."

"Stop, just *stop*," she yelled, rushing into the kitchen. A drawer slammed before she reappeared with a roll of silver duct tape in her shaking hands.

"You can silence me, but there's no avoiding the truth," I pressed.

She used her teeth to rip off a piece of tape, then placed it over my mouth. I didn't fight her. I was already winning the mental battle. And besides, if she didn't change her mind about helping Dante, I preferred to make my escape attempt when she least expected it. When she was distracted, fretting over the dangerous situation she'd gotten herself into.

Hours went by.

With each ticking minute, Liana grew more fidgety. She turned on the television to distract herself, but her bouncing knee betrayed the storm brewing inside her. She checked her phone obsessively, glancing periodically toward the front door. Her nervous energy was at a boiling point, bubbling up closer and closer to spilling over.

When her gaze slid toward me twice in a matter of minutes, I knew I'd won.

"Look, I didn't have any idea who you were. None of this was my idea." She sounded like a petulant child, more upset about getting caught than remorseful about her actions.

I lifted a brow and stared at her. It was the only thing I could do with tape over my mouth.

Liana let out an exasperated sigh, then stomped over and removed the tape in a series of awkward tugs. It felt like the tape was taking my skin with it. I stretched my lips and jaw, easing the sting before looking back at her.

"The only chance you have of surviving this is to help me get out of here. I'll tell my father and my uncle you saved me. We can both get ourselves out of this." Anyone with two brain cells would know I was lying, but Liana was desperate enough to take the bait. To grasp at any hope that promised a way out.

Her chest heaved, and her pulse hammered at the base of her neck. "Dante would be furious. I'd never be allowed back in the club."

"Better to find a new club than to be dead or in prison." I kept my voice low and perfectly even to highlight the gravity of her situation.

I had her.

Liana's face crumpled in defeat just as the front door unlocked. Dante barged in, slamming the door behind him.

Dammit!

I'd been so freaking close. My fingertips had brushed over freedom before it was viciously snatched away, and I felt the loss like a kick to the gut. My shoulders rounded with the oppressive weight of frustration.

Dante was too agitated to notice my disappointment. He wasn't just upset, though; he was consumed. "Filip knows," he murmured, walking to the window. "I didn't give him enough credit." He stared out at the city with unseeing eyes, lost in his thoughts.

"Dante, tell me what this is all about. Maybe there's a way to work it out," I said softly, sensing his distress might be an opportunity to reason with him.

When his eyes clashed with mine, all hope vanished.

The venom in his stare was pure liquid rage. "This is about revenge. About showing the De Lucas that they can't get away with killing my entire family. There is no way of *working it out*."

His answer winded me.

Killing his entire family? Surely, they hadn't actually done that. "What? How?" I stammered.

"When I was only four, my uncle killed Filip's mother. It was a mistake. The families don't usually touch women and children, but there was a mixup, and his mother was killed instead of his father."

"I thought you weren't a part of the mafia."

"I'm not," he spat. "One organization killed my family. The other acted as though I'd never existed once my parents were dead. I want nothing to do with any of them." He turned his gaze back out the window. "My father was a member of the Morelli family, as was his brother. After Filip's mother was killed, the Gallos hunted down anyone involved. Filip's father lusted for blood, but he didn't just kill my uncle. Over a year, he eliminated my entire family. We went into hiding for months, but it wasn't enough. I had just turned five when my parents were gunned down in our home. De Luca never suspected I was there hiding in a cupboard, listening. I heard every scream. Every whimper. I flinched with each gunshot and cringed at the heavy thud of his boot pounding into my father's lifeless body. I relive that nightmare every time I close my eyes, knowing those monsters never paid for what they did."

What he described was appalling. My heart broke for that little boy cowering in a dark cabinet, terrified into silence. His emotional scars were horrific—discolored fissures marring his psyche. How did someone recover from something so life-altering? He'd been innocent. A victim in a war far beyond his grasp. Could I blame him for his hatred? Not entirely, but he was no less responsible for his own actions. People all over the world were unjustly injured and unfairly treated, but that didn't give them the right to ravage others. Filip had been just as innocent in what had happened as Dante. He'd lost his mother in the same dispute.

"Why try to hurt Filip? He was just a child like you were."

He exhaled a sardonic huff. "The system placed me with a cousin outside the life. They adopted me and changed my name, but I never forgot. When I was old enough, I dug for information to understand who had killed my parents and why. I learned about my roots and discovered the truth behind the De Luca family stealing everything from me. The moment I heard the name, I was stunned to realize the enemy had been right under my nose. I'd gone to school with Filip for years. I was sure it had to be fate. After that, I watched Filip prance around school with the cocky attitude of someone who could get away with anything. I had no doubt he'd been placed in my path for a reason —to avenge my parents' deaths."

"Or to unite the two families and start healing," I offered gently.

He shook his head. "I could never forgive them. Not when my mother's screams still haunt me."

"But you've done so well for yourself. You have a thriving business and a good life. Is revenge on Filip, who wasn't even involved, worth throwing it all away?"

His head whipped in my direction. "How could I ever live with myself if I didn't avenge them?" he yelled, thumping his fist against his chest. His agonized plea hung in the air.

My heart ached for him, but only for a moment.

Dante dropped his gaze and inhaled deeply. When he met my eyes again, he was in complete control of himself, as though he'd flipped a switch and shut off all human emotion. "I started over before; I can do it again."

His chilling resolve sent a shiver rippling down my spine.

Nothing I said would deter him. Dante was totally fixated on punishing Filip for his father's deeds, and I was his weapon of choice.

"I can't ... I won't be a part of this ... this ... whatever it is." Liana shook her head in stunned disbelief. She'd gaped at him, speechless throughout our entire exchange.

Dante shot her a glare that could have frozen over hell. "Your part in this is already fixed. There's no bowing out now."

"You take her and get out," she ordered him, a spark of anger giving her words strength. She crossed to where I sat and clenched my arm, dragging me to my feet.

Dante yanked me away from her, sending me flying back to the couch before his palm streaked across Liana's cheek. The slap resounded through the apartment. Liana gasped, clutching the side of her face.

"You think I give a fuck about what you want?"

Her shock wore off quickly, fury scrunching her face into a vicious sneer. "You've gotten yourself in deep with the fucking *mafia*, not me. I'll tell the authorities you just showed up at my place with an unconscious woman. I knew nothing about any of this. You're not dragging me down with you."

Dante's jaw clenched, and an eerie calm settled over him. His hand snaked behind him, where he extracted a gun from the back of his pants. He pointed the barrel at her chest and pulled the trigger.

No warning.

No second thoughts.

The blast vibrated through me. My shoulders clenched up around my ears in an innate defensive reflex. Liana flew backward, stumbling over the red velour chair and collapsing to the ground. Her body grew still aside from an expanding red stain blossoming across her chest.

I couldn't breathe.

It was as if my lungs had quit in solidarity for the dying woman before me. He'd shot her. Ended her life with cold-blooded indifference. She wasn't entirely innocent, and I didn't particularly like the woman, but she didn't deserve to die. Not even close.

I'd been resisting and pressuring this man as if I had any clue who he was. As if there were still some thread of friendship that connected us.

I'd been a fool.

The real Dante was a total stranger. Cold and broken.

"We're walking out of here, and you aren't going to make a sound." His voice was a jagged blade against my throat.

I followed his orders in a hazy fog, too terrified to argue.

CHAPTER 28
Filip

After Dante sped off in his car, I had the cab take me home to get some tools, then drove myself back to Dante's apartment. As expected, no one answered when I knocked. I made quick work of his lock, then disarmed his alarm with a specialized device. His security system was high-tech but not insurmountable. My entry and exit skills were just one of the reasons Matteo had found me useful over the years. I'd taught myself a number of shady life skills in my teens, the least of which was breaking and entering. Once I matured and had access to adult money, I added high-tech equipment to my arsenal. There were few places I couldn't get into.

The window shades inside his apartment allowed in a dusting of light, casting the room in a soft glow. I'd been in that same room countless times, but everything looked different now that I had a new perspective on my supposed friend. Now that I was certain he'd taken Camilla.

Above the fireplace hung a large grayscale painting of a lion's face, the only color its enormous golden eyes. I wanted to shred it to pieces, but that would have to wait. Finding Camilla was more important than my anger. I began to tear through his home, riffling through papers and emptying drawers. I searched the kitchen and his bedroom before moving to his office. His laptop was password-protected, but my tech guy could get me in. The question was, how long would it take. Time was something I couldn't afford.

There had to be some other way to figure out Dante's plan. I needed to know what he intended to do with Camilla and where he might have taken her. She wasn't at his place, and I would bet he didn't use the club either. Both locations were too obvious. Where else would he go?

I placed a quick call to the tech guy to let him know about the laptop and have him dig up all the properties owned by Dante under either of his last names.

I couldn't believe I'd had a treacherous enemy walking alongside me for so long. Such a prolonged subterfuge wasn't just a betrayal. It was insanity. I had to wonder if I'd ever known Dante at all. The prospect was unsettling at best, but with Camilla in his custody, it was absolutely terrifying. The danger was a complete unknown.

I had zero control over the situation.

A geyser of rage spewed up from deep inside me. I allowed a single outburst. A single violent eruption of emotion. I swept the contents of his office shelves onto the floor with a furious roar. I wished I could burn it all to the ground, but I had to channel that anger into something more useful. A focused state of mind that would help me find Camilla.

Taking several heaving breaths, I kicked aside the debris on my way to his desk and resumed my search. Dante didn't appear to bring much of his work home with him. A few receipts and bills were piled in a top drawer along with a filing cabinet full of his own personal financial documents, but that would take me hours to pore over, and I didn't have that kind of time or patience. I glanced once more through the contents of the top drawer, this time realizing a legal pad was at the bottom of the stack. The top page contained a collage of scribbled notes pertaining to the upcoming spring charity event the club held each year—lists of dates, themes, event planners, and party favor ideas. The following page contained a list of donors. I recognized most names on the list as regular contributors and was surprised to find Liana's name crossed off the list.

Liana came from money. She had more money than she knew what to do with and adored the prestige she garnered for being listed as a top-tier donor. Why wouldn't she be contributing to the event? Had the two fallen out? Dante was never a fan of Liana's, but he never turned away her money.

Something was off. It could have been totally unrelated, but I recalled Camilla telling me that Liana had shown up at the bank looking for her. Could Liana have been involved in her disappearance?

It was worth looking into. I had no better leads to follow, so I pulled out my phone and dialed Liana's number. The phone rang and rang. I wasn't in contact with her often outside the club, but she answered my calls every time I reached out. If I was being honest, I'd always known she wanted more from me. Her eagerness to accept my invitations. Glances sent my way when I chose a different partner for the night. But I'd convinced myself it wasn't an issue. A passing infatuation. She hadn't pressed the matter, so why create drama to reinforce the point?

Had her feelings for me run deeper than I'd realized?

The call clicked over to voicemail, an uneasy stirring upsetting my stomach. The evidence was totally circumstantial, but my instincts insisted I needed to follow the lead. I left a message then made a quick call to obtain her address. I made the twenty-minute drive in ten.

Her expansive apartment was the only unit on the thirty-fourth floor of a high-end building. The elevator landing outside her front door was swarming with cops. My heart plummeted in my chest like a lead weight. I took one lunging step forward only to be brought up short by a hand planted on my chest.

"This is an active crime scene. No one allowed through." A young cop smacked gum as he spoke, keeping me at bay with the same enthusiasm as a gas station clerk informing a customer that the bathrooms were closed for cleaning.

"I can see that," I gritted. "I'm a friend. What the hell happened?"

He shrugged, clearly getting off on the power trip. "It's an open investigation. I can't give you any more information than that."

Goddammit.

Was Camilla in there? Had she been hurt or killed? I had to find out what the fuck had happened before I went insane.

I could only see a small sliver of the apartment from the angle I was at, but as luck would have it, a familiar face passed across my line of sight. "Danny!" I hollered over the flurry of activity.

The cop we'd talked to outside the bank joined me near the elevator, relieving the rookie of his watchdog duties.

"Danny, what's going on in there? They wouldn't tell me anything."

"You know the woman who lived here?"

"Yeah, name's Liana Bisset."

His lips thinned. "She was shot in the chest. Didn't survive." He spoke under his breath, keeping our conversation private.

I suppressed the shock that threatened to paralyze my mind. If Dante was capable of murder, he'd have no problem hurting Camilla to get at me. A part of me had hoped this was all some misguided outburst—a man lashing out in a moment of pain who would come to his senses as time wore on—but that wasn't the case. Dante was committed to whatever madness consumed him.

"When did it happen?"

"Gunshot was reported about an hour ago. We arrived ten minutes later. No sign of the perpetrator."

Cops probably already had someone retrieving the security footage, not that it would reveal anything. If he scrubbed the film from Camilla's place, he would have taken care of the footage here as well.

"I know who did this," I confided quietly. I had no clue why Dante would have hurt Liana, but there was little chance this was a coincidence. "Is there any way you can get me inside to have a look? I might be able to figure out where he's hiding."

He propped his hands on his hips, and his eyes wandered up to the ceiling. "If I do this, you cannot touch anything, understand?"

"I want this guy caught as much as you do. I'm not about to fuck up your case, trust me."

His only response was to turn back to the apartment and escort me under the yellow caution tape. Liana lay on the ground in the living area, evidence markers scattered around her, eyes staring blankly up at the ceiling. Even in death, she was beautiful with her red hair fanned out around her. It was a horrible shame, yet I couldn't help but wonder how she'd ended up like this.

As my eyes wandered down her form, I noticed a small piece of duct tape stuck to her hand. It wasn't large enough to bind someone's wrists, but it would fit perfectly over a mouth. The tape could have been totally coincidental, but I doubted it.

Liana's left cheekbone was pink as though she'd been struck, but her pristine skin around her mouth showed no signs of having tape pulled from its surface. In my gut, I knew Camilla had been there. I'd have bet my life on it. I had no clue how Liana had gotten involved, but Camilla had been housed at Liana's apartment, which meant Camilla was still alive.

Relief coursed through me along with a sense of urgency.

"Thanks, Danny. I owe you."

"You said you knew who it was. You gonna tell me?"

I started toward the door and called over my shoulder. "I'll let you know as soon as I find him."

Danny would be annoyed, but he'd get over it. I had a psychopath to track down, and I didn't need the cops getting in the way.

On the way to my car, the tech guy called with information on several properties owned by Dante. I had him email me the details then read through them in the car. Aside from his apartment and the club, he had a place in Staten Island and a boat slip he leased from North Cove Marina.

I stared out my windshield and walked through what I'd learned. In theory, Dante could have taken Camilla anywhere, but realistically, his options were limited now that he was on the run. I doubted killing Liana was part of his plan, which meant he was having to improvise. He'd need to hide but stay flexible. Be on the move but avoid authorities until he came up with a new plan.

The boat was a perfect solution.

Once he launched onto the Hudson, he would be impossible to find. I turned on the car and peeled away from the curb, heading west to the marina, praying I got there in time.

CHAPTER 29
Camilla

"W" hy would you do that?" I whispered once we were in Dante's car, rubbing my wrists where the zip tie had been. "Why involve her if you were just going to kill her?" I was still terrified, but the fear had settled into a solid mass in the pit of my stomach.

I tried to make sense of what had happened, but my brain was a skipping record. I kept hearing the blast of his gun over and over in my head. Seeing Liana's body fall limp to the floor. Smelling the metallic tang of blood in the air. Despite the gruesome images that would haunt me forever, when I tried to process what had happened, my heart couldn't accept that Dante was evil. He'd been normal once, and I desperately hoped the person he'd been still existed somewhere deep inside him.

My questions lingered between us for several minutes before he spoke.

"She was supposed to take the blame and give me an alibi. I

never meant for her to die, but when everything went to hell so quickly, she became a liability."

"How would she take the blame? She would have told on you to exonerate herself." I tried to keep my tone curious and free from accusation. I wanted to understand without pushing him to anger.

"Her claims wouldn't have mattered when I had an alibi and evidence planted to implicate her. The authorities will find a file of information about you at her place. There's security footage of her approaching you at the bank. The browser history on her computer will show extensive searches on you along with sites describing how to successfully make a person disappear. All I needed was to avoid Filip's suspicion. If he took the bait and blamed Liana, I was in the clear, but the paranoid bastard scrutinized me from day one." Dante glanced over at me, his face a stoic shield of impassivity. "No matter. I had plans for all eventualities."

I took a shaky breath and watched as we drove farther west. "You didn't want Liana to hurt me, but I still don't know what your plan is for me. If Filip and the authorities know you have me, wouldn't it be best to let me go and run? They would move on eventually, and you could start over."

"*Never.*" His resolute response was the clang of prison bars around me. "As long as I have you, I have my revenge. That's all that matters."

Frustrated tears welled in my eyes, and my breathing caught. He wasn't ever going to let me go, and when he pulled into the parking lot of a marina, even my hopes of escape were dashed.

"You're taking me on a boat?"

He must have heard the panic in my voice because he speared me in place with a hostile glare. "We are going to walk to my boat just as quietly as we left Liana's apartment. You've seen how I handle problems. Unless you care for me to deal with you in a similar manner, I suggest you don't become a problem. Now stay put. I'll get your door." He gave me one last chilling stare before slipping from the car.

I had no idea what to do. The longer this insanity played out, the more worried I became that I might not return to the life I'd always known.

Hope and optimism run eternal. No matter how bad a situation, a small part of us—the survivalist part—croons, *it will get better from here*. Our own desire for improvement convinces us that the suffering will be short-lived.

But that voice grows weaker over time. Doubts set in and whisper nihilistic threats, submerging hope in the oily black residue of despair.

That was where I found myself as I sat in the passenger seat of Dante's car.

While he rounded to my side, I wondered how this could possibly end well for me. I didn't even know if Filip truly suspected Dante, or if Dante had simply been paranoid. Had Filip found the card I left? Did he know about Liana? Would Dante take me to another country, or was my final destination meant to be a frigid, watery grave?

My lungs burned as though miles of water already pressed down upon them.

"Let's go," he commanded quietly.

I did as he said, my knees wobbling with each step. The East Coast was still buried in winter though we'd slipped into the first days of March. The setting sun plunged the evening air down to arctic levels, keeping people indoors and the marina empty. I didn't see a single soul who might help me, even if I did have the courage to call out to them.

Dante led us to the second to last bay that housed a fifty-foot yacht. The magnificent vessel was constructed of immaculate white fiberglass with black-tinted windows. A work of art I would have been thrilled to explore under any other circumstances. However, being forced onboard at gunpoint made the boat feel like nothing but a cage.

He hoisted me up on deck, then began untying the ropes that held us moored to the dock. It only took a handful of seconds, so there was not enough time for me to hunt down a radio or phone. When he jumped aboard, he brought me with him through the main cabin to the indoor helm where he started the engine. The setup was similar to an RV where the driver's seat blended seamlessly into the interior living quarters. The finishes were all top of the line. A dining area sat directly behind the captain's chair, followed by a kitchenette and more seating.

Supplies were stacked on every available surface. He'd come prepared. We could be on the ocean for weeks. He might follow through with his promise and never let me go back home.

I watched helplessly through the large cabin windows as he guided us out of the small marina inlet and out into open water. Light from the setting sun glinted off the choppy Hudson Bay, creating heavy shadows in the valley of each wave. Birds glided and swooped in the air above.

The view was breathtaking. It felt like a betrayal.

How could the world look so serene in the midst of such chaos and turmoil?

I thought about my parents, sisters, and cousins that I might never see again. I couldn't even comprehend the possibility of such a travesty.

I pictured Filip's face staring intently into mine as our bodies became one and wondered if I'd ever see those mercurial eyes again.

A chasm opened up in my chest, ripping my heart in two.

I shot to my feet and walked toward the narrow stairs leading below deck. The tenuous fibers holding me together were snapping one by one, and I didn't want to come undone in front of Dante. My sorrow felt personal, and I wanted to grieve alone.

"Where are you going?" he barked at me without bothering to turn.

What did he think I was going to do? Hoist myself into the freezing ocean? I wanted to scream and rage, but it wouldn't do any good.

"I need to go to the bathroom," I snapped, then hurried down the stairs. My anger helped quell the rising heartache threatening to shred me.

I found a lavish bathroom in the belly of the boat, along with a single bedroom containing a queen-sized bed. Realization iced my scattered emotions. There was a possible intent behind Dante's actions that I'd been avoiding. It had danced around the back of my mind, but I'd refused to give it daylight. To put the unthinkable possibility into words. He had wanted me for himself, and now I was trapped on a boat with him.

It was too ghastly to entertain.

I closed the bedroom door, wanting to banish the thought from my mind. I went to the bathroom, my overstimulated mind slipping into a numb cocoon. When I returned upstairs, I took a seat at the dinette sofa diagonal from Dante. We were making headway into open waters, the city skyline growing more distant by the second.

I opened my mouth twice before I could get out the concern that had rocketed to the forefront of my mind. "I need to know what you plan to do with me." My voice was regrettably weak, but the fear that constricted my lungs wouldn't allow more volume.

"I'd planned to sell you—"

"You *what?*" The words were acid on my tongue. I wasn't sure I'd ever experienced such a tidal wave of emotion. I whiplashed from fear and despair to undiluted fury in an instant.

254 | JILL RAMSOWER

All self-pity was smothered beneath a heavy curtain of rage.

I'd worried he planned to force himself on me, but his true intent was even more vile than I could have imagined. I would rather have been thrown overboard than be auctioned off to the highest bidder, reduced to the husk of a human being existing solely to pleasure some depraved psychopath.

Hearing the sudden change in my voice, Dante glanced back at me.

He was too late.

I launched myself at him, wrapping my arm around his neck from behind and squeezing. I pinned him against his seat, the inside of my arm curved around his windpipe.

"You fucking *monster*," I hissed, grunting and spitting from the strain.

He'd been a friend—someone I'd even considered having a relationship with—and he wanted to sell me? Sentencing me to a life of unbearable misery for someone else's crimes? It was too coldhearted to comprehend.

Dante pulled at my arm, but I was a thing possessed. I pulled backward with all my weight. The ceiling was only about five feet off the floor at the front of the cabin, so I had to hunch in an awkward position. I didn't care. What he proposed was a fate worse than death, and I would have fought to my last breath before I let him hand me over to traffickers.

I had the upper hand until he slammed the engine into idle. The momentum change caused me to lurch forward and careen into the back of his seat, giving him the leverage he needed to break free of my hold. He leapt from the chair, reaching to contain my flailing arms as I scooted off the driving platform and worked my way down the main cabin.

"You can't do this," I wailed, tears burning at the back of my throat. His strength could easily overtake me, and it filled me with terror.

"Stop, Camilla. *Jesus*. I said I *planned* to, but you didn't let me finish. I changed my mind. Will you fucking *stop*?"

I stuttered in my defense momentarily, giving him an opportunity to grab my wrists. He whipped me around, holding me caged against his chest. I could feel his labored breaths against my back but was glad I couldn't see his face. I was so angry and hurt and confused. I couldn't bear to look into those mutinous black eyes of his.

"I don't understand," I cried softly. "You're not this man. You aren't the kind of man who could sell a woman." It was a statement and a fragile plea.

"Did you forget what I did to Liana?" he breathed close to my ear.

"No, but it doesn't change how I feel. You've been wronged, but that pain isn't who you are. You're better than this."

"I wish you were right." The words were hollow. The echo of a man who had already surrendered his future in a bid to rectify his past.

One arm came away from me, and I heard a drawer open behind me before his other arm released me completely. I walked two steps away before slowly turning to face him and the gun pointed at my head. Dante used his other hand to pull back the slide and cock the gun, making me flinch when the bullet clicked into its chamber.

Fear poured down my cheeks. "Please, Dante. Please don't do this." My chin quivered as I stepped backward, one tiny step at a time. I wanted to run, but there was nowhere to go.

How could this be happening? How could my life be over when it had only just begun?

I was swarmed with heartbreak and regret for myself. For Liana. Even for Dante, who had been fractured at such a young age. The injustice of it all was oppressive.

I lifted my eyes from the barrel of his pistol and finally peered deep into his bottomless gaze. I showed him my sorrow and heartache. My empathy and remorse. I allowed him to witness the depths of my faith in him.

The gun trembled in his hand.

"I desperately wanted to hate you when you rejected me. You complicated everything." His voice caught, and I felt it in the deepest parts of my soul. "It was supposed to be easy," he whispered.

"We can still fix this, Dante. I'll help you." My hand floated up to reach for him.

The crease between his brows furrowed deeper, and I was certain I'd broken through. That I'd found that kernel of light deep inside him where goodness still lived.

Then his shoulders tensed, and all emotion leached from his face. A blast of cold air flooded the room as the side door flew open near Dante.

"Put the gun down," Filip growled, his own gun in hand and trained on its mark.

My heart plummeted into my feet.

Where had Filip come from? With the engine still running and a fight ensuing, we hadn't heard another boat approach.

His appearance instantly erased the progress I'd made with Dante, who had fortified his tempered armor, shielding him from the world. Any access I had to him was violently severed with resolute finality. Even more unsettling was the deep-seated determination that smoothed his features.

I didn't understand what it meant. Something had changed, and my gut told me the result would be tragic.

"I said put it down, Dante. It's over," Filip barked.

Dante angled his aim a few inches to the side—movement Filip couldn't see from his vantage point. Everything suddenly became crystal clear in a heart-wrenching second when time ground to a halt. He lifted the veil from his eyes to reveal one final window into his soul.

Remorse. Agony. Sorrow.

Dante pled for my forgiveness.

The scene unfolded before me like a stretched rubber band shooting forward. All I could do was scream *no*, a worthless cry released onto the winds of the Atlantic night.

There was no way to stop him.

Dante fired his gun, the bullet going wide of me. Almost immediately after, Filip's gun echoed the first shot, but he had aimed to kill. Dante flew onto the sofa, his body slumping down onto the floor. My hands flew to my mouth, my feet anchored in shock. Filip's confused stare bounced between Dante and me as though he couldn't believe I was uninjured.

I collapsed onto the ground, sobs wracking my body.

Filip swept me into his arms and sat with me in his lap, holding me snugly against him. I wrapped my arms around his neck and released a torrent of emotions into his strong embrace. He rocked me gently, allowing me to purge my grief and fear and relief while he wrapped me in soft sounds of reassurance.

When my tears began to ebb, I sat motionless for several long minutes, simply feeling the boat rock against the waves.

"He killed Liana." It was the first words I'd uttered to Filip since he arrived.

"I know, sweet girl. I know." The sorrow in his voice mirrored my own desolation. It made me think that maybe he understood the complex battle of emotions raging inside me. I was relieved that someone who wanted to hurt me had been stopped, but that wasn't all. A part of me was heartbroken that Dante's madness had brought about his death. It was confusing. I'd watched him kill a woman without blinking. How could I feel sorrow for such inhumanity?

Filip seemed to grapple with the same conflict. He'd lost a friend too. What was worse, he'd been the one to pull the trigger.

I didn't blame him. He'd had no idea that Dante had been on the verge of surrender. Filip's dedication and bravery had been admirable. He'd hunted me down and saved me in record time, and I would always be grateful.

I only wished I'd been able to offer Dante the same salvation. He'd realized that with Filip on board, there was no escape for him. He was faced with one final opportunity to exact revenge by killing me on his way out, but he didn't do it. Something stopped him—some spark of conscience. If I'd had more time, could I have nurtured that spark and helped reform him?

The possibility gnawed at my ravaged heart.

Dante was a complicated creature, so there was no way to know what might have happened had Filip not shown up. He wasn't one to be manipulated or coerced. He didn't even let Filip take him alive. Dante died on his own terms, just as he'd lived.

"I think I'm ready to go home now."

Filip pulled back, drawing my gaze up to his own. He searched my face, scouring every detail with tender reverence. "I was terrified I wouldn't find you in time. And the possibility of you being hurt because of me, it was … it was unbearable." His voice was thick with emotion, laden with vulnerability. He clutched me tightly against him, his adoration a healing bandage wrapped around my wounded heart.

"None of this was your fault. Please don't blame yourself." So much harm had transpired in the name of heartbreak and pain. I didn't want the events of the day to perpetuate that negativity even further. "Dante was troubled, and the source of that was a traumatic event that occurred when you two were only children. You were both just innocent victims."

Filip pulled back again and searched my face as though he desperately wanted to believe me. Once the truth of my words settled over him, he lowered his lips and placed a delicate kiss on my forehead.

After helping me to my feet, Filip eased Dante onto his back and laid a blanket over him. We stood silently, each taking a moment to process the loss. I had to turn away before long, my chest buckling with grief.

Filip took the wheel and located the speed boat he'd procured to chase us down. I wasn't sure the methods he used had been totally legal, but I didn't care. He'd done what was needed to save me.

Once we had the other boat secured to the yacht, he called the authorities and navigated us back to shore. We were met with flashing lights and a huddle of officers. I gave a brief statement explaining exactly what had happened. We'd decided on the way back that the truth was better than a cover-up. Seeing my obvious distress, the detective allowed us to go home with strict instructions to go to the station the next day for a full interview. Reliving the details of that day would never be easy, but a shower and some sleep would go a long way toward easing the burden.

As we pulled away from the marina in Filip's car, my eyes lingered on Dante's lifeless vehicle left in the dark parking lot. He would never debark from his yacht and jump back in his car. He would never again entertain at the club he built and loved so much. Even if he had survived the day, he likely would have ended up in prison for Liana's death.

Such a tragic day in every respect.

His trauma had taken hold of him at a young age and stolen his life away. The most frightening part was how well it had hidden beneath kind eyes and practiced decorum. I had so many questions about how his thirst for vengeance had come about. Had his adoptive parents been good to him? If he'd not been present when his parents were killed, would he still have had the same thirst for revenge? Had he ever told anyone about witnessing their deaths?

As much as I wanted answers, nothing would change the past. Dante and Liana would still be dead. I couldn't undo what had happened.

I peered at Filip out of the corner of my eye and wondered how his mother's death had changed him. He was so incredibly strong, but he struggled with his own demons. I wanted to share that burden with him and was so glad I'd entrusted him with my past. Sometimes, that single thread of communication was all it took to start healing. Maybe a trust like ours was all it would have taken to start Dante on the road to recovery. Now, he'd never have that chance.

It was tragic, but the silver lining was that Filip and I still had one another.

I'd been terrified on that boat that I might never see him again, and now it was his hand clasped around mine. His strength and devotion made me feel capable of taking on the world. Even when my heart was heavy with loss, his presence alone calmed and comforted me. I wanted to be there for him in the same way. Show him understanding and acceptance. Be firm when needed, but always, *always* act out of love.

Life was too short to take a single word, deed, or person for granted.

I would never squander a single moment with him again. We'd been given the opportunity to continue our journey together, and that gift was priceless.

CHAPTER 30

Camilla

Filip took me to his place. Our relationship had evolved from such unusual circumstances that this was the first time I'd been to his home despite our deep connection. The apartment was surprisingly modest. It was spacious and had been totally remodeled, but the low ceilings remained, and the décor employed a sleek, minimalist feel that I found appealing. The furniture and fixtures were retro with clean lines and neutral colors. Adding to the simplicity, Filip appeared to be even more of a neat freak than I was. I found his home comfortable and inviting. Soothing, even. I was so particular about my own apartment that it was rare for me to feel equally at home anywhere else.

Filip insisted I ate before we called it a night. He threw together sandwiches for us and sliced an apple to share. It had been ages since I'd had food, but I hadn't been hungry in the midst of such fear and anxiety. Even after the fact, my stomach only permitted a few bites. Fortunately, he was satisfied with my efforts and finished my sandwich along with his own.

"Let's take a hot shower and head to bed." He placed a reassuring hand on my lower back and led me back to his bedroom.

We stripped down and filed into the large shower. Filip immediately pulled me against his solid chest and wrapped me in his arms.

"I told myself I wouldn't push you," he said over the pelting water, "but I need to hold you. Feel you in my arms."

The skin-to-skin contact was a balm to my soul, so I had no complaints.

We stood like that for long minutes before he finally released me. I washed my hair while he lathered my body, tending to me with careful precision. When we started to prune, we turned off the water and dried ourselves. Filip gave me one of his undershirts to wear to bed. An intoxicating aroma clung to the fabric—a faint trace of cologne and detergent that teased my senses. I put on my panties, lamenting that I hadn't had a fresh pair in two days but was too tired to do anything about it. Although, I wasn't so tired that I didn't ogle Filip's sculpted form from the corner of my eye as he slipped into a pair of briefs and crawled into bed. I would have had to have been dead not to notice him.

I followed him into bed, slipping beneath the covers on the same side and relaxing into his body when he pulled me snugly against him.

"I'd always known there was a competitive element to my relationship with Dante, but I never imagined it was grounded in something so ugly," Filip said as we lay in the dark. He had to be just as shocked as I'd been, and I was glad he felt comfortable talking it through with me.

"He told me your family had killed his parents after his uncle killed your mom." It was awkward to accuse his family of such an act, but the subject needed to be aired.

His chest rose and fell on a deep breath. "I wasn't old enough to witness what happened and draw my own conclusions. I just know what I was told. No one was innocent, and my father definitely had a lot of blood on his hands. Once the Commission was established a few years later, it created rules that govern the families. Retaliation killings are no longer enacted without grave consequences. Things are different now."

"I tried to talk to Dante about that—about letting go of the past—but he couldn't. He was there the night his parents were killed. A five-year-old boy hiding in a cabinet, listening to his parents being murdered."

Filip stiffened beneath me, then slowly relaxed. "Fuck, it's no wonder he was messed up."

We lay in silence for several minutes. I couldn't say what Filip was thinking, but I couldn't rid my mind of the image of little Dante, terrified and alone. I was relieved when Filip spoke and drew me from that dark, horrible place.

"Every year, my family gets together for my mother's birthday. It was just a couple of weeks ago, and this year, Matteo and I talked about what happened when she died. He mentioned that the Leone family had murdered her, but it never entered my mind that Dante could have been related to them. It wasn't until I found the card you'd hidden under your purse and saw the lion's head that things started to register."

"How did you even know I'd been taken?"

"I'm not sure how you'll feel about hearing this, but your boss was killed."

I shot up to my elbow and gaped down at him. "Donald? Donald's dead?"

He nodded. "Cartel killed him."

I sank back down in disbelief. "Holy crap," I breathed. "That explains why he'd been so upset lately. Some of our accounts were being audited by the FDIC, and he couldn't get access to them. He freaked."

"If he was laundering money for them and couldn't get their money back to them, that would have caused big problems for him," Filip confirmed.

I let the information sink in for a second. "So, how did that lead to you discovering I was gone?"

"Matteo and I were alerted to the murder and drove back to look into it. We've been monitoring cartel activity and wanted to verify it had been a hit. When I realized where the murder had occurred, I went looking for you to make sure you were all right but discovered you'd never shown up for work. I had no clue what had happened. At first, I thought the cartel might have taken you, but that card you left was the perfect clue."

"I'm glad you were able to find it," I whispered.

"Yeah, baby. You did good." He trailed his hand up and down my arm absently. "I tried to play it cool and trick Dante into leading me to you, but he lost me in traffic."

"That must be when he came to Liana's so upset. He told me later that he planned to frame her for my disappearance. I tried several times to talk him down from his ledge. I reminded him that you had nothing to do with his parents' deaths, but he'd fixated on you. You represented the enemy, so you were the person he wanted to punish."

Filip's heart rate thrummed faster. "I hate that you could have been hurt because of me. I know you say it isn't my fault, but who I am will always put you at risk."

I shifted myself on top of him, straddling his hips and bringing my face inches from his. "Who you are, Filip De Luca, is loyal, passionate, and devoted, and *I* decide whether the risk is worth it. Not you. I almost lost the chance to ever feel you against me again. I don't ever want to face that reality again.

You're it for me, Filip. You're mine." I flexed my hips, rubbing my now throbbing core against his rigid erection beneath me.

His hands gripped my hips, eyes scouring my face. "I love you *so damn much*." He rolled us in one swift motion, caging me beneath him, then slanting his lips over mine in a kiss that made me crazy with need. While his lips plundered my mouth, his hands slid my arms up and over my head. When he pulled away, he only left a wisp of air between us. "Say it, Camilla. I need to hear you say it," he breathed, his forehead lightly resting against mine.

"I love you, Filip. I live and breathe for you."

His body trembled, and his eyes drifted shut before he rose and stripped off my underwear. He didn't even take his briefs all the way off before lowering back down and aligning himself at my entrance.

I didn't know it was possible to connect with another person on such an elemental level. When his cock pressed deep inside me with our eyes locked on one another, I felt like two pieces of a whole finally coming together. I never considered my life lacking before, but Filip had changed me. He'd become a fundamental part of my being.

I was home in his arms. Safe and cherished.

We hadn't been in each other's lives for long, but whatever life threw our way, we could handle it if we were together.

EPILOGUE #1
Filip

"I never spent much time around Dante, but I never detected anything unusual when I was around him," Matteo mused as we exited the small private plane we'd taken to Virginia. The flight was the first opportunity I'd had in over a week to talk to him about Dante and our family's past.

"You and me both. I *was* around him, and I had no clue. It makes me wonder who else might be a wolf in sheep's clothing."

"In our business, you have to assume that about everyone, especially now that you're a capo. Power will paint a target on your back." A few days after the incident with Dante, Matteo held a meeting appointing me the newest capo in the Gallo family. Life had been extremely busy ever since.

"Yeah, but it's different when it comes from someone in my inner circle. It makes me question everyone around me."

"That's why it's so important to me that *you* become my underboss. The family oath may instill loyalty, but there is no substitute for blood."

"I guess it's good you've already started working on the next generation then."

Matteo gave me a sly look. "Now that you've got Camilla, you shouldn't be far behind."

I shook my head with a chuckle. "Not yet, but thanks for the vote of confidence. I actually have a sort of pet project I'd like to focus on—a business opportunity I wanted to discuss with you."

"What's that?"

I appreciated that he sounded curious rather than wary. In the past, that wouldn't have been the case.

"I spoke with Dante's lawyer and went through Dante's personal documents. As far as we can tell, he didn't leave a will. That would mean his ownership of the club would pass to his adoptive parents. I want to buy it from them. I'd hire someone to run the day-to-day operations, but I'd like to oversee the club and keep it running. I've seen the financials—it's a great investment—and I have my own personal interest in keeping the club alive."

"I don't see that being a problem. We can talk numbers when we get back home."

A rental car waited for us outside the airport hangar, per my instructions. Ever the leader, Matteo assumed the driver's seat while I automatically went for the passenger side. Some things would never change, no matter how high my rank in the business. I was surprisingly okay with that.

"Where to?" he asked.

I pulled out my phone and input the address into GPS. "Warehouse district not far from here."

Matteo guided us away from the airport in the twilight hours of a cool March evening. It would be a long night, but I couldn't think of a more worthy cause.

"When I asked if you'd accompany me, I expected more questions," I admitted between giving him navigational instructions.

"I read between the lines." His eyes cut briefly over to me. "This isn't the first time I've taken a trip of this nature."

I was stunned. Not that he'd gleaned the reason behind my trip, but that he'd conducted a similar mission before. Questions started to spring to mind but were squashed when an image of his wife came to mind. Her abrasive personality. Her quick anger and aloofness. She was unpredictable at best and terrifying at times. The walls around her were reinforced concrete trimmed in electric razor wire.

Why had it never occurred to me that she was like that for a reason?

Fuck.

If Matteo had wanted me to know what had happened, he would have already told me, so I didn't ask. Instead, we rode the rest of the way in silence.

Ten minutes later, we arrived at an industrial complex, weaving our way to the far back where the original occupants sat rusting and abandoned. A black SUV was parked out front of one of the warehouses. We parked nearby and made our way inside, a heavy duffel bag slung over my shoulder.

We locked the door behind us and wove our way through the offices to the main building where a man sat tied to a chair.

"Clarke?" I called out into the open space.

"Here." My old friend stood leaning against a wall in the shadows. "Took you long enough."

"I could say the same to you."

He smirked as he walked closer. "Hey, the bastard disappeared when he left New York years ago. You must not have been the only person our friendly principal pissed off."

"If he'd been easy to find, I would have done it myself." I reached out to shake his hand when he approached. "Good to see you, man. Kellan, this is my brother, Matteo. Matteo, meet Kellan Clarke. He specializes in acquisitions."

Matteo remained stoic, donning his mob boss face as he shook Kellan's hand. "Appreciate your help."

"Don't be too grateful. You haven't received my invoice yet." He flashed a shit-eating grin, then strolled to the door. "I'll be in touch."

Matteo's eyes cut over to me once we were alone. "Clarke?"

"I know. He's independent."

"The Irish are never independent. They're all fucking related to each other one way or another," he grumbled.

"We go back to grade school. He was my co-founder in that little boxing endeavor you were so fond of."

"That figures. Those guys bare-knuckle box before they're out of diapers."

I laughed, but it quickly died when my gaze landed on the subject of our trip, bound to his wooden chair. "Let's get to work. I hate to keep our friend waiting." I ambled over to where Hale sat slumped in his chair and set down my duffel. "Hey there, David. You can't know how glad I am to see you."

Hale didn't respond; he was gagged with a dirty rag.

I sniffed the air dramatically. "I see you've already pissed yourself. I wouldn't worry about it. It was bound to happen at some point in the process. Allow me to introduce myself. My name is Filip De Luca, and I believe you knew my girlfriend, Camilla Genovese."

The coward's eyes snapped shut, and his body began to shake with sobs.

I chuckled. "That's right. I see you remember. Camilla tells me you enjoy dishing out pain to children." I squatted down and unzipped my bag, widening the opening so that the contents could be seen. "I think it's time you practice what you preach."

Dripping sounded as urine cascaded off the chair onto the floor. He'd pissed himself again.

This was going to be fun.

EPILOGUE #2
Camilla

I 'd spent many long hours after Dante's death thinking about what had happened and how things could have been different. I thought about Filip losing his mother and my own struggles regarding the many ways Principal Hale had changed me. I desperately wished Dante had sought help and realized it was hypocritical that I hadn't done the same. Therapy didn't bear the same stigma that it used to, so why didn't more people see it as an option?

I had no answers, but I could be a part of the solution. Nearly a month after Dante's death, I met my new counselor for the first time and wrapped up our session with an overwhelming sense of relief.

"Thanks for meeting with me, Evie. I'm so glad Sofia gave me your name."

"Absolutely, and I can't believe you worked for Donald—such a small world."

"I know! I'm glad we were able to talk about that for a bit. I know I'm supposed to be the patient, but if you ever need to talk about him or anything, I'd be happy to listen. I can't even imagine how hard it would have been growing up with him."

I'd asked my sisters and cousins about finding a counselor, making an attempt to be more open with them. Mental health wasn't exactly something my family talked about, but I was hoping to change that. I was surprised when Sofia was quick to recommend a new friend of hers. I never imagined Evie and I would have been connected through her stepfather, Donald.

"I appreciate that." She smiled warmly. "I went through a lot of years working through those issues. At this point, my biggest concern is helping my mom. I'm glad she's free of him, but she isn't great at being alone."

"Well, good luck. You'll have to keep me posted."

"I will. I've got you set up for next week, so I'll see you then."

My chest swelled with a resounding optimism as I left Evie's office. Everything in my life was looking up. Donald's death led to a series of promotions to fill job vacancies, including my own advancement to junior vice president. I removed my resume from job sites and continued working with Trent, which was a tremendous relief. The climate inside the bank administrative offices had already seen a drastic shift from hostile to healthy.

Filip and I were quickly establishing a new normal at home— or at least, normal for us. I doubted my sisters would think we were normal if they knew what went on behind closed doors, but that was fine. Filip and I were perfectly suited for one another, and that was all that mattered. I didn't even balk at his hovering tendencies anymore, especially since the cartel issue had yet to be sorted.

When I told him I was going to counseling after work, he insisted on escorting me to and from my session. I exited the brownstone and found him waiting in his car outside. When he spotted me, he got out and met me at the passenger's side.

"Wait." He opened the door but stopped me from getting in the car. He slipped his hand from his pocket, dangling a black satin blindfold between two fingers. "First, we have to get this in place." He stepped behind me and gently tied the blindfold over my eyes.

"What on earth is this about?" I grinned, sudden giddiness bubbling up inside me.

"You'll see soon enough," he rumbled softly next to my ear, then helped me into the car.

The drive wasn't long, but it gave me plenty of time to whirl through the infinite number of possible destinations. Once we arrived, Filip guided me from the car and through the front door of a building. I hadn't realized before that the Den had a smell, but without my sight, I immediately honed in on a familiar combination of leather and oil.

A grin blossomed on my face as realization dawned.

Filip led me to the elevator and up to the second floor, where music pulsed from the main room as usual, but I couldn't hear any other sounds. It was a Thursday night, closing in on eight p.m.—somewhat early for the club but not too early for activity. Perhaps a performance had everyone's attention.

When Filip guided me into the main room rather than back to his private quarters, my excitement morphed into anxiety. What was he up to? Why were we still walking?

I strained my ears for any hint of what was happening around me but came up empty. By the time he encouraged me to step up onto what I recognized was the stage, my heart was hammering in my chest.

"Filip?" I questioned, squeezing his hand tightly.

"Shhh, it's okay. Here, look." He lifted the blindfold to reveal a completely empty room.

I scanned the area, stunned. "What's going on? Where is everyone?"

"The club is shut down for the next few days. Change in ownership."

My heart rate moderated back to a reasonable pace, and my brows drew together. "Then how did we get in?"

Filip grinned. "I bought the Den. Well, the family did, but I'm going to oversee its operations."

My eyes rounded and jaw dropped. "You *bought* it? How? Already?" It had been a month since Dante had died, but I knew the banking end of commercial transactions, and they never closed within thirty days.

Filip slid my jacket down my arms while he explained. "It's not a done deal yet, but the contract has been signed, and we'll be paying cash, which will make the process much faster than a mortgage transaction. Aside from a good financial investment, this place brought me the perfect woman. I wasn't ready to let it go." He eased my hair down from its messy bun then trailed his hands from the collar of my blouse down over my nipples, giving each a sensual squeeze. "We have the whole place to ourselves for the night, and I plan to take advantage." The seductive touch of his voice scraped across my skin, stoking a fire deep inside me.

"I'm starting to see the perks of ownership," I breathed.

Filip took two steps backward, his hungry eyes devouring me. "Strip," he commanded. Nothing was as sexy as bossy Filip in the bedroom or, in this case, in the club.

He picked up a small black square from the tufted ottoman. A remote. When he pressed a button, a set of leather cuffs suspended on a wire lowered from the ceiling.

My panties were instantly wet.

I removed my clothes until I was totally bare, never taking my eyes from his. Filip remained clothed. There was a power disparity to my nakedness, but that was a part of the thrill. A certain unknown element that was only enjoyable because of my total trust in the man before me. He would test my limits and take my body to extremes—rain down pleasure upon me until my mind shattered—and every touch would come from a place of love and respect.

Once he had my hands secured in the cuffs over my head, he slipped the blindfold back over my eyes. There was no one else in the building, but the cavernous room gave the feel of being watched. The mere environment was so erotic, my first release was bound to come barreling at me in no time.

The initial touch of Filip's hands on my sensitive skin made me gasp. He pressed himself close against my back, one palm slipping around to cup my sex, and whispered darkly, "Let's begin."

"I CAN'T BELIEVE my baby sister is eighteen. Where has the time gone?" I hugged Valentina the moment we arrived at my parents' house, but her eyes were glued to Filip.

"Well, I still can't believe you two had a secret fling going, and you didn't tell us!" She winked at Filip, who pulled her into a hug.

"It was none of your business, kid." He laughed when she gasped in mock outrage.

I'd told my family about Filip the first chance I had after Dante's death. My father had already been informed, but my sisters and cousins were mostly clueless. Some had suspicions, but none suspected how serious we'd become in such a short time.

"No calling me kid anymore." She waved her finger at him. "I'm officially an adult now."

"Sorry, Val," I cut in. "You'll always be our baby sister, no matter how old you get."

She rolled her eyes just as my parents joined us in the living room. Giada had already arrived with Javi and had been visiting with Val while Dad helped Mom finish up in the kitchen. We exchanged hugs and greetings, but Mom called our attention before we could filter into the dining room.

"Now that everyone's here, we have some news." She grinned broadly, but I detected a trace of watery eyes. My mom wasn't the emotional type, so whatever the news, it had her in an unusual state. "Your half brother was sent my information and given the option to initiate contact. It's been a month, so I began to doubt he would respond, but I received an email yesterday. Your brother's name is Connor Reid, and he wants to meet us." Her voice shook as she said his name, stirring up a swell of emotions of my own.

I had a brother. Connor.

What would he be like? Would we become friends? Would we see him at holidays or just exchange greeting cards like a distant relative? They were all questions no one could answer.

"That's wonderful, Ma. I'm so excited for you." Giada wrapped our mother in a warm hug. It was lovely to see because the two didn't get along until recently.

"Okay, okay. Let's go eat before the food gets cold. We can all take a guess at what he looks like." She sniffled, eyes now full of tears, and ushered us to the dining room.

We had one of the best family dinners I could remember in a long time. The addition of Giada's man and Filip helped diversify the conversation, and Mom was tipsy with excitement about meeting her son. I was pleased that my dad seemed genuinely happy for her. I could imagine it might be difficult to welcome an unexpected stepchild into your life. Dad might have known about the adoption, but meeting Connor was far different. There was the potential for tangible implications that no one could predict.

After we ate, my dad took the guys into his office to talk privately. Secrecy was nothing new in my house, so I didn't pay them any mind. Giada helped Mom get the dishes done, so Val and I moved into the living room. We'd just sat down when a knock sounded on the door.

"I'll get it." I jumped up and walked to the entry, knowing the guys wouldn't have heard the knock from Dad's office.

I opened the door to reveal a gorgeous young man on the other side. He wore a leather jacket with a silver chain peeking out from beneath his T-shirt collar. He had an edginess that contrasted with his good looks like a Rembrandt wrapped in barbed wire.

"Can I help you?"

"I need to speak with Valentina." He didn't smile or give the slightest hint at his purpose.

My little sister would have some explaining to do.

"Let me grab her." I closed the door without inviting him in and hurried around the corner to where Val scrolled on her phone. "Hey, get over here," I hissed. "There's some guy at the door for you. If Dad figures it out, you know he'll grill the guy, so make it quick." I hated for Dad to embarrass her on her birthday.

Val lurched to her feet, her face growing pale, and stumbled to the entry. I was too curious not to follow.

"Kane, what are you doing here?" Val asked, her voice strained.

"I think you know." He peered over her shoulder to where I lurked behind her. "I need to talk to Val alone."

I narrowed my eyes, not sure I liked what was happening.

Val turned back imploringly. "It's okay, Camilla, I promise. We'll just talk for a minute, and then I'll come back inside. Okay?"

My gut told me this guy was bad news, and considering how

Val had responded to his visit, I didn't like the idea of leaving her alone with him. But it was her birthday, and she was technically an adult. She wouldn't have sent me away if she was in danger, right?

I shot him a wary glance then retreated back toward the kitchen to join Giada and Mom. Seeing G made me recall the two of them huddled together and Val telling me she was dealing with a bully at school. Could that have been the same guy? He looked too gorgeous to be a bully, but Dante was a perfect example that pretty packaging didn't rule out rot on the inside.

Worry nipped and clawed at me.

Nope. I can't do it.

I wasn't in the kitchen for two minutes before I whirled back to the entry. Mr. Teen Vogue might have wanted privacy, but he was out of luck. I yanked open the door, a refusal poised on the tip of my tongue, but the front porch was empty. Val and Kane were gone.

Thank you so much for reading ABSOLUTE SILENCE!
The Five Families is a series of interconnected standalones, and the next book in the lineup is *Perfect Enemies.*

Perfect Enemies (*The Five Families*, book #6)
Valentina is the youngest of the Genovese girls, but she has learned strength and cunning from her older sisters and cousins. When a handsome new face at school threatens to blacken her senior year, she vows to make him pay. Kane Rivera may think he's tough, but he's never gone up against a Genovese.

Didn't catch the beginning of *The Five Families* Series?

Check out book 1, *Forever Lies,*
to learn about Alessia and the chance elevator encounter that
changed her life forever.

Flip a few more pages to read the first chapter!

A NOTE FROM JILL

Absolute Silence is the first book I've released since taking my books wide to all platforms. It was a scary change, but one I'm so glad I've made. I want to give a special thanks to my new readers on those platforms who took a chance on a new-to-them author and read my books. One day, hopefully, I'll look back on this time period and laugh about how anxious I'd been; but until then, each new sale and review warrants a mini-celebration!

If you enjoyed reading the book as much as I enjoyed writing it, please take a moment to leave a review. Leaving a review is the easiest way to say **Thank You** to an author. Reviews do not need to be long or involved, just a sentence or two that tells people what you liked about the book in order to help readers know why they might like it too.

ABOUT THE AUTHOR

Jill Ramsower is a life-long Texan—born in Houston, raised in Austin, and currently residing in West Texas. She attended Baylor University and subsequently Baylor Law School to obtain her BA and JD degrees. She spent the next fourteen years practicing law and raising her three children until one fateful day, she strayed from the well-trod path she had been walking and sat down to write a book. An addict with a pen, she set to writing like a woman possessed and discovered that telling stories is her passion in life.

Social Media & Website
Official Website: www.jillramsower.com
Jill's Facebook Page: www.facebook.com/jillramsowerauthor
Facebook Reader Group: Jill's Ravenous Readers
Instagram: @jillramsowerauthor
Twitter: @JRamsower

Interested in reading the book that kicked off The Five Families series? Check out the book readers are calling "one bombshell after another."

Forever Lies

By

Jill Ramsower

Here's a taste of Alessia and Luca's gripping tale …

CHAPTER 1

Alessia

It was fucking Monday all over again. Why did they have to suck so much? Mondays crept into the week far more frequently than any other day—at least twice as often as Friday—and they lasted three times as long as any halfway decent Saturday. Mondays are the first day of a diet and the last day before a paycheck, all rolled into one. They're starting your period while wearing white pants and getting a flat tire on the tail end of a road trip.

There is not a single redeeming quality about Mondays.

I shouldn't complain.

I was gainfully employed by the largest construction company in New York City. That's nothing to sneeze at. I was the Associate Director of Marketing with my eyes set on obtaining the coveted director's position. If only it wasn't already occupied by the smarmiest, most disgusting man in the city, my boss, Roger Coleman.

Even his name was sleazy.

He tainted each of my days, marring the work that I loved

with his presence like greasy food stains on a pristine wedding invitation. His lewd comments and presumptuous stares were the lingering aftertaste of rancid food, turning my stomach long after I'd had a taste of his vile brand of seduction. I did my best to keep our interactions professional, public, and as brief as possible, but that was difficult when we worked together regularly on important projects.

His advances had started out small—telling me how lovely I looked or commenting on my hair or eyes. In romance novels, having an older executive pursue the young professional may have sounded sexy and exciting, but when my fifty-five-year-old boss with a fake-and-bake tan and leathery skin started hitting on me, it was repulsive and unsettling. I'd done my best to discretely brush aside his advances and discourage his behavior in the hopes he would take the hint and move on, but after a year of working in the office, he had yet to cease his efforts.

Only once had his pursuit escalated to a physical level. Six months ago, at the company Christmas party he cornered me in a hallway and pressed me against a wall, his dick thrust against my stomach. He'd been drinking heavily, and I made the mistake of walking to a restroom alone. I'd been so repulsed and terrified, I didn't even hear the unquestionably revolting comment he made. I gave a stuttered excuse and tore from his grasp, leaving the party without another word.

The incident only lasted a matter of seconds but had been seared into my brain. He never acknowledged it, and neither did I. That's not to say I pretended it hadn't happened. The threat of his unwelcome attention was always in the back of my mind. I'd taken every effort to distance myself from the man, both professionally and physically. I made certain I pulled in coworkers to help on projects, so there was always an extra set of eyes working with us.

Our offices, along with several others in the suite, were

constructed with glass walls, which helped give me a certain degree of security—no hiding behind closed doors outside of the conference or break room. Another fortifying fact—Roger's advances weren't a daily affair, not even weekly. The problem wasn't their frequency; it was the uncertainty of not knowing when they might occur that was the most stressful.

Thus, the misery that was Monday.

Yet another week of wondering what lewd propositions I might have to fend off.

Unlike my sisters, I had made the choice early on to go into the family business. Had I known how complicated it would be, I might have pursued a job elsewhere. But now, I had put in a year of my time and was poised to move up the ladder—I wasn't going to entertain the option of quitting. I wouldn't let my scumbag boss make me walk away from what I'd dreamed about since I was a child—my family legacy.

Instead, I made sure the neckline of my blouse didn't hang too low and marched into work swathed in a protective shield of confidence. This week would be one of the better ones. My boss was only in for the day before he would leave on a week-long business trip to L.A.

I could survive one day with the devil.

Most of the morning passed uneventfully. I was left to my own devices, preparing for a full week of project meetings and impending deadlines. It wasn't until almost eleven when the intercom on my phone blared with Roger's voice.

"Alessia, can you come in here, please?"

A seemingly harmless request, but it stirred an overwhelming sense of dread in the pit of my stomach.

I didn't answer—there was no need. He could see me as I stood from my chair and made my way to his office next door. While I didn't so much as glance his direction, I had no doubt his beady eyes would follow my every step. Our offices lined the outer wall of windows—the glass walls allowing the rest of the employees to enjoy the soaring views from our building. It was a double-edged sword—no privacy was a good thing, but it also meant there was no escaping Roger's stare.

"Did you need something?" I stopped several feet from his small conference table where he'd laid out his presentation materials.

"You sure you can't come with me? You know the material as well as I do and would be an enormous help when I make the pitch. It's not too late to get you a ticket." He arched a brow, hands propped on his hips where he stood on the opposite side of the table.

"My sisters would kill me if I'm not there to help get ready for Mom's party this weekend. It's her fiftieth and—"

"I know, I know," he cut me off as I began to blather about my mother's pretend birthday. She'd turned fifty years ago, but the party had been the best excuse I'd come up with on the spot when Roger had initially asked me to accompany him on the trip. There was no way in hell I was traveling with the man. Fortunately, he hadn't bothered verifying my story, so I continued to uphold the ruse.

"You told me already. Well, get over here and let's run through everything one more time before I head to the airport." He waved me over with a frown, clearly disgruntled I hadn't caved to his pressure to accompany him.

The project was a relatively minor remodel proposal for a building in Brooklyn owned by a corporation headquartered on the opposite coast. I'd worked on the project along with a couple other people from our team. It was too small-scale for Roger to do the grunt work, but he was presenting our proposal because the contact was a friend of his. We had already given him all the pertinent information on multiple occasions, so I wasn't sure what I was supposed to say.

The chairs had been pulled around to clump on my side of the table with the various documents and exhibits spread out for viewing from the other side. His setup left little option except to come around to his side of the table, but I kept as much distance between us as was reasonably possible.

"It looks like everything is here," I offered as I perused the materials.

"What about the schedule of work?" he asked as he leaned forward to retrieve the document. "I noticed we listed a completion timeframe of six months, but I thought we had discussed moving that out to nine." His right hand snaked out to curl around my waist and pull me next to him while his other hand held out the document as if showing me its contents was the purpose behind his flagrant violation of my personal space.

Stunned by his action, I took the papers and stared at them dumbly. I didn't see the words on the page—I was entirely focused inside my head where my thoughts raced at a frenzied pace in an attempt to grasp my situation. My boss's hand lingered at my lower back, the insidious warmth seeping into my skin, before slowly dropping down to caress over the curve of my ass cheek.

I ceased breathing, and my ears began to ring.

His repulsive touch in such a private area made my skin crawl, but I couldn't seem to move a muscle.

I was frozen—horror battling with mortification.

The glass walls gave me a perfect view of the bustling office where a dozen employees scurried about their business. Never in a thousand years had I imagined he would make a move on me in plain sight of our coworkers, but he'd done a masterful job keeping his actions unseen. To all the world, we looked as though we were simply examining a document—his wandering hand only visible to the New York skyline out our tenth-floor windows.

"Um … we decided … to subcontract the welding work," I sputtered out. "Our guys will be busy on the Merchant project. Outsourcing will enable us to keep the six-month timeline the client requested." As I said the words, I frantically debated what to do. If I allowed him to continue touching me, it would no doubt encourage the asshole to take more liberties. If I confronted him or in any way made a scene, the entire office would know in seconds. Before I had a chance to decide, the intercom in his office crackled to life.

"Mr. Coleman, your flight leaves in two hours."

The instant his assistant, Beverly, began to speak, I pulled out of his grasp and fled the office. Bypassing my own office, I hurried to the restrooms and locked myself in a stall. Leaning against the door, head back and eyes closed, I tried to regulate my erratic heartrate.

Did that really just happen?

Could I have imagined the whole thing? Surely, my boss hadn't assaulted me in front of the entire office. As much as I wished it had been a nightmare, it wasn't. Each agonizing second had played out in living color, and I had stood immobile like a squirrel starring down an approaching car. What was wrong with me? Why hadn't I pulled away instantly? Why hadn't I turned in his balding ass months ago to HR? I'd had my reasons, but they seemed less and less valid with each new day. My conflict and self-doubt brought on a barrage of guilt and blame that bowed my shoulders with their oppressive weight.

I needed to get out of the building.

I exited the stall and went through the motions of washing my hands before walking to my office with my eyes lowered to the geometric patterns of the grey commercial carpeting. Grabbing my phone, I texted my cousin to move up our lunch date, then snagged my purse and scurried out of my office. Normally, I would inform a coworker if I was leaving early, but I couldn't do it. I felt exposed—like anyone who looked at me would know what I had allowed to happen. I couldn't force myself to take that chance—to let them see the shame in my eyes. Instead, I kept my head down and hurried out the closest exit.

I couldn't allow my boss's behavior to continue.

The realization was daunting.

I had a number of options on how to handle the situation but wasn't sure which would be best. My one saving grace—he would be gone for the rest of the week, so I didn't have to face the issue immediately. I wasn't normally the type to procrastinate, but in this case, I would put off dealing with him as long as I could. I shoved the incident into a dark corner of my mind—somewhere next to the misery of my first period and getting lost as a child in the subway.

Aside from my boss, I loved my job. Marketing in and of itself was enjoyable, but marketing on behalf of my father's company gave the job added meaning. Call me a goody-two-shoes, but I'd always been the parent-pleasing child who desperately wanted to make Mom and Dad proud. More specifically, it was my dad I endeavored to impress.

He was a tough nut to crack.

If I came home with a ninety-nine on my report card as a child, he would tell me 'good job' but always ask why it wasn't a one-hundred. Vicenzo Genovese expected nothing less than the best, which is why I started at the bottom of the totem pole and had been working my way up. He wasn't the type to plant his daughter in a vice president's position straight out of school. He made it clear from day one when I expressed an interest in working for Triton Construction that I would have to earn my job.

You can't know how to lead if you never learned how to follow.

Those were some of his favorite words.

Words I had taken to heart.

As I stepped into the elevator and turned back to face the lobby, my chest swelled with pride for the organization I would someday help run. Triton was tangible for me—not only could I point to the buildings we created all over the city, but we provided the income that supported our employees and donated millions of our profits to charitable causes. I viewed the company as a living thing and wanted nothing more than to foster its growth.

Whatever trials I had to surmount to call Triton my own were worth the effort. The thought brought a small smile to my face as I exited the elevator onto the second floor. The building was designed with a grand lobby on the first floor, flanked by two elegantly curved escalators on either side. The main elevators traveled to the first floor, but I preferred to exit on the second floor and ride the escalators down to the lobby so I could peruse the bustling activity on my way down.

My eyes danced from one person to the next as I scanned the occupants of the lofty room. A woman sporting sneakers with her high-powered suit stepped onto the opposite escalator going up. I wondered if she was health conscientious or merely late when she powered up the escalator, swiftly climbing each step in quick succession.

A heavyset man paced in the center of the room, phone held to his ear, arm waving animatedly in the air as he broadcasted his conversation for the world to hear. Living in the city, many residents learn to ignore the constant presence of others and carry on as if they were in a room by themselves. My parents ingrained a sense of propriety in us girls that made it impossible for me to forget the myriad of people around me. This man clearly had no such inhibitions.

As my eyes wandered toward the front of the lobby, they were instantly drawn to a man in a deep blue suit, striding purposefully away from the security post. At first, I glanced around half expecting a movie crew to be filming him. He was masculine beauty personified—dark hair, perfectly styled back, closely cropped on the sides, a dusting of dark hair on his angular jaw, and deep-set eyes that didn't stray from his intended destination across the lobby.

The man's suit fit his form without any extra length in the legs or sagging in the shoulders—it had to have been tailor-made. The fabric had a hint of a sheen, giving the suit an expensive look even from a good distance away. He didn't wear a tie, just a white dress shirt with the top button undone. His gait was deliberate but not hurried, easy confidence wafting from him like steam from a rain-soaked summer street.

I had never seen the man before. I'd come to recognize many of the building's occupants, but there was no chance I would have forgotten this man. My eyes were glued to him as he strode a dozen paces between the escalators and passed the man on the phone. I was so enthralled in his sight, I didn't notice the end of my ride and stumbled forward as my foot hit the solid floor at the end of the escalator. I would have been mortified if he had noticed, so I didn't dare look back. Instead, I lifted my chin and continued on, hoping to exude the same sense of poise and control I had just witnessed in him.

Once I was out on the sidewalk, I shook my head, unable to stifle a laugh at my own expense. I might as well have been a child gawking at the toys on display in the window of an FAO Schwarz. I hadn't been that captivated by a man in … I wasn't sure I'd ever been so entranced by a man. It was a shame, too. So many eligible options in the city, and so few were of interest.

I walked the block over to where I had plans with my cousin, Giada, for lunch. She'd been my best friend for as long as I could remember. Our mothers were sisters-in-law, and we were born one month apart. Where she was the oldest of three girls, I was the middle, but our personalities had always been perfectly suited.

It was as if we were born to be close friends—soul sisters.

We ate lunch together at least once a week, often at the same deli where I was currently headed. It was close to my office and had the best Kaiser rolls around. I reached the place first after moving up our lunch so unexpectedly. Grabbing one of the four tiny tables inside, I played a game on my phone while I waited.

I'd never been big on social media. My parents didn't let us girls get on Myspace or Facebook when we were younger, and now that I was on my own, it had never felt all that necessary. Outside of Giada, I didn't have a ton of friends, which was fine with me. I had two sisters and three female cousins—that was plenty of girl drama in my life.

"Hey cuz, what's going on? Hope you didn't have to wait long. I got here as quickly as I could." Giada plopped down in the seat across from me, impeccably dressed, as always, long auburn hair falling in thick waves down her back.

"Hey G! Not long at all. Sorry to spring the time change on you."

"Not a problem. I hope everything's okay."

"Yes and no. Let's grab our sandwiches, and I'll tell you about it over lunch."

"Please tell me it's not your dickhead of a boss again."

I rolled my eyes and grabbed her hand. "Food first, then talk."

We ordered and took our food back to the table as the deli slowly began to fill with people on their lunch hour. I quietly relayed the events of the morning, attempting to keep the conversation just between us in a restaurant the size of a shoebox.

Giada was fuming by the time I finished. She was the only person I had told about my lascivious boss and knew about each of his disgusting antics. "Al, I know you want to be respected at work, but you can't let that man keep doing this shit."

"I know. I realize it's not going to stop if I don't do something about it. You know how hard I've worked to make a name for myself at Triton. Even then, there are still people who whisper that I've gotten where I am because I'm the boss's daughter. I wanted to handle the situation on my own and not have to raise a stink, but I'm out of options."

"You don't have to raise a stink, just tell your dad. He'll fire that guy's ass in a heartbeat—no one has to know why." In theory, her suggestion seemed like the easy answer; however, life was rarely so simple.

"You remember in high school when Mindy Jenkins kept trying to fight me and bullied me every chance she could get?"

"That bitch made your life hell—of course, I remember!"

"Then you should remember that not long after it started, I tried to get my dad to help me. There was a planning meeting after school for an upcoming dance, and I tried to avoid going so I could stay away from Mindy. Not only did my dad refuse to help, he insisted I go to the meeting. He told me there were always going to be hard situations in life, and if he went around fixing things for me, I'd never learn how to handle them on my own. I know he'd want me to deal with Roger myself, so that's what I've been trying to do. Clearly, not effectively, but I was trying. Plus, if I run to daddy for help, everyone in the office will see me as a spoiled kid."

"What does it matter what those people think?"

"It matters because they'll never respect me if they think I didn't earn my job."

"They don't have to respect you." Her bright red lips lifted in a smirk. "They just have to work for you."

"Says the woman who's never worked a day in her life," I

smiled back teasingly, knowing the comment wouldn't bother her in the slightest.

"You should be so lucky … oh, wait—you are! You have plenty of money; you don't need to deal with this bullshit."

"What am I supposed to do, go shopping and host parties all my life? I'm not my mother, that's not enough for me."

"Too bad," she mused. "I'll have to find someone else to accompany me on my shopping runs and spa treatments."

"Whatever. That's not you either, and you know it." I narrowed my eyes and tossed one of my chips at her.

She laughed, her vibrant green eyes shining. "I know no such thing. What I *do* know is if you don't do something about that boss of yours, I'm going to come up there and raise holy hell. Got it?"

"I get it," I smiled at my best friend. "And I promise I'll file a complaint with HR. In the meantime, he's gone for the rest of the week!"

"Fabulous! We should take a long lunch break and hit Saks later this week."

"You're incorrigible."

"So, is that a yes?"

I threw my head back and laughed. "Yes, I think that could be arranged."

"Boom! Now, get your ass back to work and file that damn complaint," she ordered with every ounce of moxie in her five-foot frame.

"Yes, sir, Colonel, sir." I saluted her as I stood, then hugged my amazing friend. Not every girl was lucky enough to have a Giada in their life. I thanked my lucky stars on a daily basis that I'd somehow managed to score the best cousin ever.

I walked back into work feeling optimistic and empowered. I would file the dreaded HR complaint and finally get Roger out of my life. There would be interviews and an inter-office investigation, but it would be worth it in the long run. Inappropriate comments were one thing, openly assaulting me was an entirely different can of worms. Not to say the comments were acceptable, but they hadn't seemed nearly as threatening when his assaults were purely verbal.

When I rounded the corner toward our offices, my eyes found Roger's assistant, Beverly. She was a middle-aged woman who was pleasant enough, but I'd never spent all that much time talking to her. Roger preferred to work directly with me, of course, and Beverly mostly kept to herself. She peered up at me from her desk and gave me a tight smile that was laden with pity.

She knew.

It was there, etched in each of her features, leaving no room for question. She had called into the office as a distraction, knowing exactly what Roger had been doing.

A blur of emotions turned the lunch in my stomach into a heavy lump—gratitude to the older woman for helping me and excruciating embarrassment. We both knew I wasn't to blame, but that didn't stop the waves of shame from bringing a heated glow to my skin as I scurried into my office.

CPSIA information can be obtained
at www.ICGtesting.com
Printed in the USA
LVHW111453100123
736854LV00021B/209